"DON'T TOUCH ANYTHING!"

Sheriff Mercer spoke sternly before peering at a pile of papers on a nicked, cigarette-scarred kitchen table. He slipped on his bifocals and took a close-up look at the top sheet without touching it.

"What is it?" I asked, trying to see over his shoulder.

"Looks like business forms. Everything's labeled Sea Scatterer. He's got letterhead, receipts, billing forms, business cards—the usual."

I started to reach for the papers when the sheriff grabbed my wrist.

"Uh-uh. I've got to get a search warrant. Nothing I find here is admissible without one."

I made a face, but I knew he was right. With a last glance around the dingy, unkempt room, I followed him out the door on rubber legs.

As I shut the door and turned to face the sheriff, I sucked in my breath. He stood facing me, his index finger turned up, as if he were signing "up" or "wait a minute." Then I noticed his fingertip—there was a dark red dot. Blood? I followed his glance to the waist-high railing of the deck that had caught my fall, and peered over the side.

Something that looked like a melon bobbed just below the murky surface of the water. But waving about in the peaceful motion of the lake, I could make out the gentle sway of human hair. . . .

A QUIET UNDERTAKING

A CONNOR WESTPHAL MYSTERY

PENNY WARNER

BANTAM BOOKS

New York Toronto London Sydney Auckland

A QUIET UNDERTAKING

A Bantam Crime Line Book / January 2000

CRIME LINE and the portrayal of a boxed "cl" are trademarks of
Bantam Books, a division of Random House, Inc.

ISBN 0-553-57965-7

Published simultaneously in the United States and Canada

Bantam Books are published by Bantam Books, a division of Random
House, Inc. Its trademark, consisting of the words "Bantam Books" and
the portrayal of a rooster, is Registered in U.S. Patent and Trademark
Office and in other countries. Marca Registrada. Bantam Books, 1540
Broadway, New York, New York 10036.

PRINTED IN THE UNITED STATES OF AMERICA

OPM   10   9   8   7   6   5   4   3   2   1

To Tom, Matt, and Rebecca

ACKNOWLEDGMENTS

Many thanks to the following people, who helped me with the details of the mystery:

Bob Durkin, funeral director
Susan C. Eggers, Hardy Boys expert
Robert Evans, police officer and criminology instructor
Althea Katz, shooting instructor
Paige Morgan, Hardy Boys expert
Keith Melton, California Highway Patrolman
Maureen Meyer, school library media generalist
Bob Nelson, Hardy Boys expert
Joseph Paglino, homicide detective

Thanks to everyone who read the manuscript: Jonnie Jacobs, Peggy Lucke, Lynn MacDonald, Camille Minichino, Constance Pike, Edward Pike, Michelle Smythe, Susan Stadelhofer, Vicki Stadelhofer, and Diana Todd.

And a special thanks to Amy Kossow, Stephanie Kip, and Cassie Goddard.

ACKNOWLEDGMENT

Many thanks again to those wonderful people who provided research materials:

Neil Gordon, Sword Master
Susan M. Zioge, history bibliophile
Robert Conte, police officer and amateur historian
Michael N. Brennan, attorney
Diane L. Cronin, Navy nurse
Gail McCoy, Children's Cancer Foundation
Joanne Montour, archival information
Keith White, Military Intelligence
Irene Fangher, medical literature

And thanks to my computer support people:
Richard Lapp Sr., Frank M. LaDue, and Carolyn
Matthews, Connecting Point, Red Bank, Michael
Barnes, Sprint Co., Joseph Yost, and the Scott's Corner
staff.

And special thanks to Mary Ann Berner, Grace Morcand,
and Diane Coddish.

"... my eye was caught with
the glimpse of something shining
in the bottom of the ditch ...
It made my heart thump,
for I was certain it was gold."
—JAMES MARSHALL

"I wanted the gold and I found it;
    Came out with a fortune last fall.
But somehow it's not all I hoped for;
    Somehow the Gold isn't all."
—ROBERT SERVICE

A QUIET UNDERTAKING

How did I get myself into this?

I wiped a clump of damp bangs from my sweaty forehead with the back of my hand. Hunkered down beside a jagged volcanic rock, I cocked my gun, then low-crawled among the manzanita and Sierra thistle toward the safety of a cluster of trees.

I squatted, waiting; my eyes scanned the underbrush. Nothing moved except a river of perspiration down my chest.

Fear has a way of pushing the senses into overdrive. Suddenly I could see every blade of field grass quake. Feel the relentless pressure of the warm breeze against my overheated body. Smell my floral lotion fighting pungent sweat. Even my saliva tasted different—sticky, salty, sour.

In spite of the density of the blue oaks and needle pines, and the camouflage of the rugged terrain, it was difficult to stay out of the line of fire. And I had lost track of the man who was stalking me with a loaded gun in his hand.

Before I could find new cover, I saw something fly past my head, narrowly missing my ear. Ducking flat, I felt my black T-shirt stick to my sweaty skin like a giant Band-Aid.

Damn! How had he spotted me? I'd been careful not to

make any noise as I crept through the tangle of shrubs and soft pine needles. Not that I could be certain I hadn't made any sound, being deaf. But it felt like I was quiet. I scanned the overgrown grass, oak trees, and jutting rocks for movement. He was out there. With a gun. Determined to shoot me.

A flicker. I became aware of movement next to one of the big oaks. My heart beat double time as I tried to leap behind a large, spiky bush, praying he didn't see me. The dive onto the rough ground cost me a scraped elbow and knee. My skin burned under my clothes. I rose halfway, panicked, searching for someplace to hide.

Too late.

A sharp sting pierced the back of my thigh as the impact of the shot knocked me back to the ground. I rolled over in the weeds and dirt, then pushed myself up, my leg searing from the pain. Twisting around, I checked the wound and winced at the sight of a bright red starburst.

"Shit! I'm hit! I'm hit!" I screamed, as I forced myself to stand. I plugged the neon orange barrel into the nose of the gun and waved it back and forth, high in the air.

"And no one told me it was going to hurt this much!"

I rubbed the back of my leg where I'd been struck, trying to soothe the smarting skin, but I only managed to spread the sticky crimson color over my hands and my black jeans. Frustrated, I started toward the base, but before I could move more than a few steps, another shot hit me in the back. This one didn't hurt as much, but it pissed me off even more.

"I said I'm hit, you idiot! Knock it off!"

A man wearing camouflage fatigues and a fluorescent red armband waved an apology from the safety of his tree. I couldn't make out who it was, since a mask and eye protectors covered half his face, but I'd remember him. He had two blue circles on the front of his shirt from a previous battle, and I promised myself I'd hunt him down and kill him if it took the rest of the day.

"Did they get you?" Jeff Pike, the teenaged referee standing on the sidelines, waved me in. He and his younger brother hosted the paint ball events every weekend. They both wore holey camouflage T-shirts and baggy cargo pants, along with the orange vest that was de rigeur for all the paint ball refs. The Day-Glo vests set them apart from the battling teams so they wouldn't be shot inadvertently. I could read Jeff's lips, since he only wore safety goggles, unlike the other players, who sported face masks.

When I reached the base, I removed my face and eye protection. Jeff threw me a towel to wipe off the sweat.

"He shot me in the *back*!" I said, using the towel to dab at the red paint on my pants. "*After* I'd already been killed. Is that fair?"

"It was probably an accident. Maybe he didn't know you were shot."

"I waved! I yelled! I stood out in plain view. The guy's an idiot."

Jeff grinned, revealing a wad of chaw and a pierced tongue. He probably got complaints like this all the time from sore losers like me who were shot early in the game. But I was determined to capture that damn flag sometime today—if I had to take out every last member of the opposing team myself.

While the rest of the troops continued without me, I sat on top of a picnic table that overlooked the battleground. As large as a football field, and surrounded by trees, bushes, and rocks, the area had been a popular spot for paint ball games for the last several years. Simmering in the hot California sun, I pushed up my long sleeves and poured water from my plastic bottle on my skinned elbow, then took a few swallows.

Scanning the field, I spotted my teammate and more-than-a-friend, Dan Smith, hiding behind a tree not far from the other team's flag. Although I couldn't see those clear blue eyes and salt-and-pepper beard behind his mask, I recognized his large muscular arms. I'd know those arms anywhere. Gun in hand, he looked ready to make a run for it at the first opportunity.

Sheriff Mercer of Flat Skunk was also clearly visible from my vantage point, crouched on one knee behind a small rock. I couldn't find his deputy, Marca Clemens, or my office assistant and the sheriff's son, Jeremiah Mercer, but I knew they were somewhere out there, darting around the playing field as they attempted to kill our opponents and bring back our flag.

It didn't look good. We'd already lost two games, and the Flat Skunk Stinkers' star player—that would be me—was out before the battle really began. We had to beat the team from Whiskey Slide or, as I understood it, we'd be buying the brew. I wanted to sign a warning to Dan. He'd learned quite a few signs, although it wasn't second nature to him the way it was for Jeremiah, or Miah for short. But any form of communication from the sidelines was against the rules. "Dead men tell no tales," the ref had cautioned.

Sheriff Mercer stood up suddenly, looking a bit disoriented. He was about to be attacked by a sniper. It was all I could do to keep from yelling, "Look out—behind you!"

But it would have been too late anyway. A splotch of red had already appeared on his camouflage vest.

Sheriff Mercer waved his plugged gun in the air with one hand while he fumbled with something in the other. His cell phone. So much for wartime authenticity.

He lumbered up the grade, removed his mask, and joined me at the picnic table, puffing from lack of regular exercise and sweating from the heat. The sheriff had definitely been off his game. He'd seemed distracted for most of the morning. Even took out one of our own teammates accidentally, at one point.

I'd been worried about the sheriff these past couple of weeks. He'd been off his game at work as well, making small errors, and I wondered if something was up. Then again, maybe it was normal. The man was pushing sixty, ate way too many pizzas, and the most exercise I'd seen him get was on the playing field today.

As soon as he'd quenched his considerable thirst, he returned to his cell phone, turning his head for better reception. I'd seen other cell phone users do the same thing, and wondered what exactly the problem was. Could they not hear anything when the phone was pointed in certain directions? After turning full circle, he slid off the picnic table and headed over to the base trailer, where the young refs kept the rentable guns, goggles, paint refills, and CO_2. I'd once heard a rumor that Jeff and his pals were members of a local paramilitary group. If so, they were naturals for running the paint ball games.

Curious, I watched the sheriff shamble out of sight behind the building. I returned my attention to the game and noticed Dan headed in my direction, his chest sporting a red splatter of paint. He joined me at the table.

"What happened? I missed your death," I said, offering him a last drop from my water bottle.

He said something I couldn't make out, since he still had his mask on. I pulled it off and asked him to repeat what he'd just said.

"Some moron sneaked up behind me. I never heard it coming."

I glanced at him. "That's no excuse. I never hear it coming."

He grinned sheepishly. "Frankly, without being able to hear, I don't know how you lasted as long as you did. Do you have super X-ray vision or something? ESP? A sixth sense I'm not aware of?"

"All deaf people do," I teased. "We know what you're thinking, what you're feeling, and what you want at all times."

"Oh yeah? What do I want right now?"

"You want to have sex on this picnic table."

He laughed, but he didn't deny it. He did, however, squirt me with his bottle of water.

After a brief arm wrestle for the bottle, which almost turned into the previously mentioned sex on the picnic table, we called a truce and returned our attention to the Flat Skunk Stinkers. The Whiskey Slide Wolves seemed to be gaining the upper hand, as Deputy Clemens—sporting two paint blotches—waved her gun in surrender. Still, I had hope. Maybe we were wearing out our opponents, and Miah was still in the game. Then again, maybe we'd just go home hot, tired, sore, and humiliated.

"You didn't tell me those shots would hurt," I said to Dan, rubbing my throbbing leg again.

"What a baby," he teased.

"Am not."

"Are too."

"Am—" I spotted the sheriff heading toward us, still puffing, but now looking grim in addition to tired.

"Sheriff. You don't look so well. Are you all right?"

He ignored me, but that wasn't unusual. Folding the phone, he stood there frowning, then withdrew his notepad and scribbled a few words. Flipping the pad closed, he glanced at me as if he hadn't known I was there.

"Sheriff . . . ?" I repeated.

"Sorry, C.W. Did you say something?" He tucked the notepad in his back pocket and checked his watch.

I rephrased it. "Yes, Sheriff, I asked you what was wrong. Are you sick or something?"

"I'm fine. Just got a lot on my mind."

"Was that bad news?" I nodded toward the phone.

"What?"

Maybe I was mumbling, or my speech was deteriorating. "I said, did your caller say something unpleasant? You looked upset after that call."

"It was Sheriff Locke, over at Angels Camp."

"What's up?" I hadn't met Peyton Locke, the gold country's first female sheriff, but I could sense Sheriff Mercer had received an important bulletin. Getting information from him, however, was sometimes like pulling gold from a miner's tooth.

"I don't know exactly. She was called out to one of those storage places that people rent when they don't have enough space in their garages to keep all their crap. The woman who rents the compartments found something strange in one of them. Peyton wants me to meet her out there."

"Why does she want you? Isn't that her territory?"

"The renter of the storage unit lives on a houseboat on Miwok Lake. That's halfway between Flat Skunk and Angels Camp, so we sort of share the jurisdiction."

"What did she find?" I knew I had only a fifty-fifty chance of getting an answer, depending on the sheriff's mood.

"A bunch of boxes. Cardboard boxes, stacked to the ceiling. The compartment is apparently filled with them."

"What's inside the boxes? Stolen goods? Drugs? Mama Cody's leftover meatloaf?"

He shrugged. "Ants."

At least that's what I thought he said, having no context in which to place the lip-read word. When I repeated it back to him, he shook his head.

"No, not ants. *Ash-es,*" he said, overenunciating. His lips stuck out like a monkey's. "Boxes and boxes of ashes."

"How odd. Why would someone store boxes of ashes?"

The sheriff looked at me, frowning. "Sheriff Locke thinks they're cremains."

"Cremains?" Dan repeated.

"Human remains," I said.

And in spite of the sweltering spring day, I shivered.

A frenzy of activity on the battlefield distracted the three of us from the news about a room full of cremated bodies.

"I got the flag! I got the flag!"

I couldn't actually make out the words, but I knew what Miah was shouting. The sheriff's twenty-two-year-old son jumped up and down as he screamed. In his hand he held the opponent's flag, a square of red that featured a grinning wolf. At the same time, Andrew Montez, my friend Del Rey's son, who was home from college, waved our team flag—a cartoon skunk—to show we still had it. Our teammates leaped around Miah, slapping his hand or back or butt.

"I don't believe it! We won! We finally won," I said to Dan, joining in the excitement as I watched the paint-splattered soldiers rejoice at their triumph. The sheriff, Dan, and I headed down the gentle slope to help our team celebrate the victory. Apparently the sheriff's recent news wasn't so urgent he couldn't take time out to congratulate his son. The other team, sporting blue armbands and dark scowls, began to gather nearby.

One by one the Wolves fell into a circle around the

Stinkers, arms crossed, jaws set, including a man in a wide-tread motorized wheelchair who'd surprised me earlier by joining in the game. At that point the victory party became a little too lively for my taste. As the Wolves closed in, the slapping turned to punching, then pounding, then all-out battering.

"Sheriff!" I screamed, but he was already in the midst of the melee.

I still couldn't make out the words being shouted back and forth between the teams, but the body language was clear. This was no longer a victory dance, not with those fists flying. This was a real battle.

In a few minutes Sheriff Mercer and Dan had the group under control, but it had taken some aggressive posturing and a little strong-arming. The sheriff and Dan had wrestled two men to the ground, and now sat straddling them. I recognized one dirt-encrusted face from our team: Del Rey's son Andrew. He had been hanging around Miah since he'd returned to Flat Skunk a couple of weeks ago. Now the sheriff had Andrew on his stomach, the young man's arms pulled tight behind his back.

I didn't recognize the other man, but his lean physique was no match for Dan's brawny strength. Dressed in full military fatigues, with a few fake bushes strapped to his waist and helmet, the man lay sputtering on the ground. He spat words of anger into the dirt as he tried to wriggle free. Smeared camouflage makeup streaked his face.

I moved in closer as Sheriff Mercer released Andrew, who had calmed down considerably. His mask had been knocked to the ground, and he sported a red mark under one eye—not paint. His brown Chico State T-shirt had a rip up the back, revealing a scraped and sweaty torso.

The other guy still lay facedown on the ground, his wrists locked in Dan's tight grasp. I couldn't make out anything the flattened captive said. But I could read Sheriff Mercer clearly when he yelled, "What the hell is going on here!" The sheriff scanned the dusty, haggard crowd as they picked up their masks and goggles and brushed themselves off.

Andrew sat up and spoke first. He was easy to read,

with a mouth shaped just like his mother's. "This jerk said Miah cheated! He's a liar. He's just pissed off 'cause we won the game."

Miah said something, but his back was turned to me so I missed the details. Although Miah signs, he must not have felt like interpreting the conversation for me under these circumstances.

"Well, for Christ's sake," Sheriff Mercer said. "You guys are old enough to play a fair game without it turning into a schoolyard fight, so knock it off. Dan, let him up." The sheriff gestured toward the man still lying on the ground under Dan.

Dan slowly pulled himself off the prone player and stood. His victim sat up, brushed himself off, and spat again in the dirt as he rose. He mumbled something to Dan that looked menacing, but Dan stared him down and the guy shifted his eyes to the sheriff, who was shouting at him. I caught the sheriff's words in midrant.

". . . like you, Berkeley! Now get your guys and move out or there'll be no more games for the Whiskey Slide Wolves, you hear?"

The military-garbed man—Berkeley—and his grumbling teammates sauntered off, after making a few familiar gestures in our team's direction. In a moment of petty one-upmanship, I signed something rude back in American Sign Language, then felt a pair of eyes staring at me. I turned to see the man in the wheelchair watching me intently. He lingered a moment, as if he might say something, then pushed the steering knob to the side, spun around in the dirt, and rolled away.

I guessed we wouldn't be getting any free beer from the other team.

"What an asshole!" Andrew repeated, gently touching the reddened splotch beneath his eye. For a moment I thought he meant the man in the wheelchair, then realized he was referring to the man who'd attacked him.

Sheriff Mercer examined Andrew's eye. "That's going to be a shiner. Your mom's going to kill you. Go put some ice on it. Miah, take him back to the base."

Andrew and Miah made a Mutt-and-Jeff pair as they

shuffled off toward the game trailer. Andrew had the body of a football player, while Miah could have been a basketball star. Andrew wore his hair long, in a ponytail; Miah always sported the latest punk style—today a dip-dyed shock of blond with dark roots. The remaining Flat Skunk Stinkers gathered their gear and headed up the grade en route to their trucks, cars, and cycles.

"What was all that about?" I asked the sheriff. I knew I must have missed something, not being able to lip-read everyone during the fracas.

"Huh?" Sheriff Mercer replied.

I repeated the question.

"Oh, just one team calling the other team cheaters 'cause they lost. That guy, Berkeley, he's a real nuisance. Don't know why he even comes out here to play. Never seems like he has any fun. He takes the game way too serious. Did you see that military getup?"

"Who is he?" Dan asked. "Some escapee from the NRA?"

"Name's Berkeley Mondshane."

"I know that name from somewhere," I said. "Is he an attorney or something? I've seen a sign with his name on it."

"Should have been a lawyer, since he loves to argue so much. But in his line of work, his clients can't talk back to him. That's probably why he likes his job so much."

"What does he do?"

"He's a mortician, like Del Rey."

"Oh, yes! I've heard Del Rey talk about him, and not too kindly, either," I said.

"Yeah, he owns the Mondshane Mortuary over in Angels Camp. Makes caskets and sells them all over the country, when he's not playing war games, that is. Shit, which reminds me. I gotta go see a woman about some ashes. Almost forgot about it." With that, the sheriff lumbered toward the parking lot.

In the midst of the excitement, I'd also forgotten about the sheriff's disturbing phone call from Sheriff Locke. I suddenly had a vision of human remains leaking from a storage compartment. The image made me shudder.

"Sounds like a story to me," I said to Dan before bolting for the parking lot. I caught up with the sheriff just as he was opening the door to his patrol car.

"Sheriff!"

The sheriff turned around and faced me. "I don't think this calls for reporters quite yet, C.W. I'll let you know if it's anything."

"Yeah, sure you will. Sorry, but I'm coming, so don't bother trying to talk me out of it. It's been a slow news week, and I need the copy. If it's anything interesting, my readers have a right to know. It's a matter of the Constitution's—"

I'd lost the sheriff's attention. He'd turned to see a commotion a few cars over. Andrew and the camouflaged mortician were at it again, only this time the fight was strictly verbal. With Berkeley Mondshane facing away from me, I could only make out half the conversation, and with difficulty at this distance. All I caught was Andrew saying something like, "You leave my mother out of this!" before he and Miah jumped into Andrew's VW and drove away.

Grandma's Attic Self-Storage Company stood out against the rolling green hills of the Mother Lode country like military barracks, only not half as interesting. Apparently the local historical society hadn't yet demanded a more aesthetically pleasing facade. The three rows of aluminum-sided buildings, painted a disturbing turquoise blue, looked abandoned. The roll-up door of one unit, situated in the middle of a long block of connecting compartments, stood open. Aside from the two patrol cars parked in front—one from Flat Skunk, one from Angels Camp—the business seemed deserted.

Dan and I pulled up behind Sheriff Mercer, who'd dropped his deputy at the Flat Skunk office and picked up his uniform jacket and gunbelt. We got out of my Chevy, me with my notebook, Dan with a camera I'd asked him to carry in case I needed pictures for the newspaper. Sheriff Peyton Locke must have heard us arrive. She appeared from inside the shadowy storage room, hands on her gunbelt.

"Hey, Peyton." Sheriff Mercer greeted her with a similar stance, as did Dan, an ex–New York cop sans belt. Must be a police thing, standing that way. I tried it, hoping it would give me more of a feeling of authority, but I just felt stupid. Instead, I gripped my notebook and tried to look alert.

"Hi, Elvis. What's with the blood? Did you shoot someone?" Sheriff Locke pointed to Sheriff Mercer's shirt, barely covered by his uniform jacket.

Sheriff Mercer flushed slightly after glancing down at his clothes.

"Oh, it's just paint." Was that a grin he was trying to conceal?

"You've been playing those war games again? It looks like you lost."

Peyton Locke appeared to be in her early forties, with an athletic build under her uniform. She'd tucked her dark hair into a twist at the back of her head—regulation, I assumed. No fake nails or polish, no jewelry, and no makeup except for a little mascara. I could see why Sheriff Mercer was trying to stifle that smile. He was attracted to her. No wonder. She was naturally pretty, physically fit, and seemed available—no ring.

I glanced at the sheriff and nodded at the storage unit, reminding him why we were here. After rearranging his belt and making brief introductions, he said to Sheriff Locke, "What'cha got here?" and moved in the direction of the compartment.

The two sheriffs entered the place and Sheriff Locke flicked on the light. Dan and I stood just outside and scanned the room, which I estimated to be about ten feet wide by fifteen feet deep. The heavy scent of dust tickled my nose as it wafted out into the sunlight. I took in the bizarre collection of boxes, stunned by the sheer number of them. Hundreds, the size of shoeboxes, were stacked to the ceiling, filling the entire room.

There were so many tightly packed boxes, the walls bulged on either side of the compartment. The air grew denser as I moved inside, the smoky aroma reminiscent of the smell in my family's fireplace after the flames had burned out. As a kid, I'd loved playing in the ashes, making designs, feeling the soft texture as the feathered layers dissolved in my fingers. I was fascinated with their tenuous beauty.

I wondered if cremated ashes felt the same as fireplace ashes. I had no plans to find out.

"Jesus!" Sheriff Mercer said, moving forward to examine one of the boxes. Most were intact, but a few at the bottom were squished and yellowed, and seemed to be losing their contents. I caught a glimpse of swirling particles in a ray of sunlight and worried about inhaling something—or someone?

Each box was labeled with a Dymo Labelmaker strip. I took a tentative step in and scanned some of the embossed letters. They were names, some I recognized as former residents of Flat Skunk, now supposedly residing in the Pacific Ocean. I shivered when I read the name "Sparkle Bodie," one of Flat Skunk's more memorable residents.

I glanced at Dan, who had also moved into the compartment for a better look. He stopped suddenly and spun around, as did both sheriffs. I turned to see what had attracted their attention and found myself facing a short, wiry woman wearing a black Harley Davidson T-shirt.

"What's goin' on?" I think the woman said. The cigarette dangling in her thin lips made her hard to read. It looked to be a longtime habit, given her golden teeth, parchment skin, and dark-stained fingertips.

Sheriff Locke spoke up. "Elvis, this is Crystal Tannacito, owner of the storage company. She's the one who found the boxes."

Crystal Tannacito inhaled deeply, blew a line of smoke sideways from her mouth, then flicked the butt to the ground and stomped it out with her red lizard-skin cowboy boots. Her Dale Evans hair tried to convey her age as mid-thirties, but her face screamed forties, even fifties. She was as thin as a model, but the clothes were Salvation Army, not Saks, not even Sears.

"Who are you?" she said, squinting at me, then Dan.

"I'm the publisher of the *Eureka!* newspaper. This is my . . . photographer."

Dan gave me a look. The sheriff glared at me. Crystal shrugged. "That throwaway paper? It's full of ads. Never read it."

I forced a smile, controlling the urge to ask her what was new in the *Enquirer*.

Sheriff Mercer pulled out his small notepad. "Can you tell us how you happened to find these boxes, Ms. Tannacito?"

I stood poised with my own pen and pad, while Dan went back to reading the names on the boxes. The sheriff shot him a don't-touch-anything glance, and Dan tucked his hands into his denim pockets. Being a former cop, he knew the drill.

"Lookit, I mind my own goddamn business, you know. These storage units are supposed to be private property for the renters. Unless, acourse, I suspect there's something illegal goin' on. And then, goddamn it—"

"Did you suspect something?" Sheriff Mercer asked.

"Nope. Seemed like everything was fine to me. So like I said, I was mindin' my own, when one of the other storage renters—Cleatus MacMath—he has the unit next door to this one. Anyways, he come by the office with a complaint."

I watched the sheriff jot down the name, wondering how he spelled Cleatus. He wasn't the best speller in the world. I knew that from reading his words over my TTY.

"What did he complain about?" Sheriff Mercer asked.

"He said his goddamn walls were caving in."

"His walls were caving in?"

"Yep, and that there was dust all over his stuffed animals."

"He collects stuffed animals?" I interrupted, envisioning a giant pile of teddy bears and plush bunnies.

"Yep. You know, deer heads, foxes, rabbits. Stuffed. Had a bunch of them. Cleatus is a hunter, you know. Belongs to one of them gun clubs or something. Anyway, there was this goddamn grayish dust all over everything. I could see why he was p.o.'d."

"What did you do?" asked Sheriff Mercer.

"I got my master key and told him I'd take a look. When I rolled up the door, this smokelike cloud came puffing out. I thought for a moment the place might be on fire, but it wasn't. Then I seen all these goddamn boxes."

Crystal pulled her cigarette pack from her yellow windbreaker pocket and lit up another smoke. When she inhaled, her cheeks sank in so far I could see the impressions of her teeth.

"You opened the boxes?" asked Sheriff Locke.

"Yep. I was curious about what all he had in 'em, 'specially since all of 'em had names on 'em and everything. I even recognized a couple of the names. But when I opened one of the boxes, it took me a minute to realize what they was. Ashes, for crissake!"

"Ashes," the sheriff repeated.

"And not just regular ashes. Goddamn human remains. This room is full of dead people!" She took a long, nervous puff, then seemed to relax as she let it out.

"How do you know they're human ashes?" Sheriff Mercer asked.

"Cause of the names on the boxes. My uncle Eugene. Right over there." She pointed into the shadows with the cigarette.

"Ms. Tannacito, who rented this storage unit?"

"That's how else I knew they was human ashes. 'Cause of who rented the space. It all makes sense now, sorta. I got the name and address right here."

She pulled a folded index card from her jeans pocket and handed it to Sheriff Mercer. He scanned the name, then glanced up at her. I read his lips as he spoke: "Jasper Coyne." The name was not familiar to me.

"Do you know him?" he asked Crystal.

"Not really. Keeps to himself. But I know he ain't sposed to be storin' ashes. He's sposed to be scatterin' 'em at sea."

Sheriff Locke nodded. "I know him. He's a fisherman, lives over on Miwok Lake, on a houseboat. Gets drunk now and then and causes a commotion, disturbs his neighbors. He's spent a few nights in the drunk tank, but nothing more than that. Seems like a loner."

Sheriff Mercer nodded, and jotted down the information from the card into his notepad.

"Have you seen him lately?" he asked Crystal Tannacito.

She shook her head, then picked a fleck of tobacco from her tongue.

"Well, I'm going to take a look inside, then I guess I'd better pay a visit to Mr. Jasper Coyne and find out what's been going on."

Dan emerged from the storage unit into the late afternoon sunlight and joined our small circle. "Sheriff, you might be interested in something over here." Dan shot me a look I couldn't read.

"What is it?" Sheriff Mercer said, following Dan inside.

"These boxes. There's a rubber stamp imprint on some of them."

The sheriff bent over, pulled out his reading glasses, and read the printed information. I could make out his response clearly—it was a word he used often when things weren't going well. "Shit."

"What?" I asked. Sheriff Mercer shot me the same look that Dan had given me. Something was up. As far as I knew, I didn't have any relatives who had been cremated. My Cornish great-grandparents, Sierra and Jackson Westphal, lay safely in Pioneer Cemetery in Flat Skunk. I hoped.

"What is it?" I demanded again.

Both men glanced back at the box they had just been examining. I peered closely at the words stamped on the outside.

My heart skipped a beat. The boxes had come from the Memorial Kingdom Mortuary in Flat Skunk. The owner of that mortuary was one of my closest friends—Del Rey Montez.

Why on earth were Memorial Kingdom's ashes stacked to the ceiling in this unit—when they should have been floating in the ocean?

While the two sheriffs questioned Crystal Tannacito in more detail, I took the camera from Dan. I figured it was a good time to sneak into the storage area, check out the boxes, and take a few pictures for the *Eureka!* before they started talking about search warrants. It wasn't officially a crime scene. Yet.

Of course, I wasn't putting anything over on Sheriff Mercer. He knew I wasn't past breaking a few rules to get a story. He gave me a stern look as I stepped inside. But I knew what he wanted to say: Don't touch anything. I didn't plan to. Unless it was absolutely necessary.

Keeping my distance while snapping a few shots, I captured a wide view of the room and some close-ups. Satisfied with the initial sample, I studied the boxes in front of me. They were stacked ten to twelve high, ten across, and about twenty deep. That was a lot of ashes.

I glanced over at Crystal Tannacito, who was talking nonstop and accenting her words with her cigarette. No wonder deaf people don't smoke much—it's not easy smoking and signing at the same time. I didn't know what the smoke signals meant, but I could read her red outlined lips against her thin face—as long as that cigarette wasn't in her mouth.

"Like I said, I got a complaint from Cleatus, the renter next door, saying his goddamn wall was bulging, so I tried calling this Coyne guy but never got an answer. Not even a goddamn machine. Anyways, I opened it up to check and see if everything was okay—it's my legal right, you know. Says so on the contract. If I suspect there's anything shady going on, I—"

She turned her head and I lost the rest of her words. I figured it wasn't anything new. She seemed to be enjoying the attention she was getting and relishing telling her story over and over. I made a mental note to talk with her when the sheriffs were finished. It was a long shot, but she might have a newsbite for the *Eureka!*

Someone tapped me on the shoulder and I jumped, startled.

"Find anything?" Dan asked, nodding toward the boxes.

"Nothing special, except I recognize a few names. You?"

He pressed his lips together, then said, "Boone's here."

My face dropped. "Oh, no!"

Boone was Dan's older brother by ten years. He'd died recently and was supposed to be floating with the fishes, his ashes sprinkled over the Pacific Ocean.

I remembered Dan had wanted to oversee the ceremony, but the ash distributor didn't allow it. I'd learned a lot about the process from an article I'd written for the *Eureka!* on the Memory Kingdom Memorial Park. According to California law, ash distribution at sea must be done by a professional. Accompaniment by relatives is at the discretion of the distributors, and even then they need special permission. Alternatives are available—family members can rent a space for the ashes at a columbarium, sprinkle the remains at designated memorial parks, or keep the urns at home on the mantel. But they can't just sprinkle their loved ones anywhere they like. That's called littering.

I was at a loss for words. What do you say to someone who has just discovered his brother's ashes are stacked in a warehouse?

After a moment, Dan said, "I sure would like to know

what was going on with this guy, Jasper Coyne. Was it some kind of scam, or what?"

I shook my head. This act of deception seemed especially cruel. What kind of a person would stuff Loved Ones in a warehouse instead of following their wishes? And why?

From the corner of my eye, I noticed Sheriff Mercer making a parting gesture to Sheriff Locke and heading my way. I scooted out of the building before he could arrest me for trespassing. He gave me another one of his looks as he pulled the louvered storage compartment door closed.

"This is off limits until I can get a warrant," he said, then he headed for his patrol car.

"Where are you going?" I asked, as he shut the car door. I leaned down to see his face better through the open window.

"None of your business, C.W."

So he was going to play hard to get. Not a problem. I knew him too well.

"You know, Sheriff, I'm going to want some new head shots of you to go with this story. Now that you've lost all that weight, you don't even look like that old picture I usually use. Can you come by later for a photo shoot?"

"I suppose," he said, firming his jaw and cocking his head. I had a feeling he was practicing his pose. Newspaper stardom was Sheriff Mercer's Achilles' heel.

"Going to Miwok Lake?" I segued flawlessly.

He turned on the ignition. "Maybe."

"Going to meet Jasper Coyne, huh?"

"I thought I might take a look at his houseboat. See if he's there and what he has to say. Hope you got your pictures, C.W., cause Peyton's going to seal the compartment. So you stay outta her way, you hear?"

I shook my head. "Don't you know by now that I don't, Sheriff? I lost my hearing when I was four. Meningitis. Remember?"

"You know what I mean, C.W." He flushed in spite of himself.

"Well, I wasn't planning on hanging around here anyway. In fact, I thought I might follow you."

The sheriff made a face, but before he could argue, Dan appeared. He looked even more unhappy; I had a feeling he was having trouble dealing with the discovery of his brother's ashes.

"Connor, I've got to get back to the office. There's something I have to do." He frowned. "You coming?"

I glanced back at the sheriff. My facial expression said it all. Sheriff Mercer shrugged and nodded toward the door. I tossed Dan the keys to my Chevy. I don't usually trust anyone to drive my car, but Dan treats my '57 Bel Air better than he treats me, so I know it's in good hands. If only he'd caress me the way he does that shiny red steering wheel.

I jumped into the shotgun side of the patrol car before the sheriff could rethink his decision. He didn't often let me tag along, but he knew I'd follow him anyway. He was learning to cut out the middleman.

Miwok Lake is located about halfway between Angels Camp and Flat Skunk. It would take about twenty minutes to get there. Plenty of time to find out what the sheriff had learned from Crystal Tannacito.

"What else did the storage woman have to say?" I asked as we pulled out of the parking lot, twisting around in the seat so I could read Sheriff Mercer's lips.

"Huh?"

I asked him again.

"Well, you heard most of it—I mean . . . you know what I mean."

He flushed at his faux pas, the second one in the last ten minutes. Many hearing people are embarrassed when they use "hearing" terms, but it doesn't bother those of us who are deaf. We're used to it.

"Does she know Jasper Coyne very well?"

"What?"

I stared at him a moment. Sheriff Mercer seemed to read my mind. "The car's noisy. You need to speak up, C.W."

I repeated the question.

"She says he seemed like a nice enough guy, quiet, didn't talk much. Unlike her. God, that woman doesn't shut up. Anyway, she said Coyne mostly minded his own business. Came and went on a regular basis, driving his truck, hauling boxes. That's about it."

"She never noticed anything unusual then?"

The sheriff shook his head.

"What about Sheriff Locke?"

Sheriff Mercer glanced at me. I noticed his neck was flushed with color.

"What about her?"

"Did she say anything about this Coyne guy? She seems to know him."

"Oh," Sheriff Mercer said, looking a little sheepish. "Uh, no. Just that she's taken him in a couple of times for D and D."

The sheriff loved to abbreviate whenever he could. I guessed this one meant drunk and disorderly.

"Caught him shooting his gun into the water a few times," he continued. "More frequently these past few months. She said she thought he was harmless, though."

I was tempted to pursue the sheriff's curious reaction to the mention of Sheriff Locke. Obviously he had a crush on her. I wanted to tease him about it, but if I made him mad now, he might not let me go with him to the houseboat. I'd save the fun for later.

My next question was interrupted by a call on the sheriff's cell phone. I couldn't make out his lips, since they were obscured by the receiver, so I watched the rolling gold country landscape of tumbleweeds, jagged volcanic rock, and holstein cows, as I thought about Del Rey. Did she know anything about this warehouse full of ashes? I shook that thought away. The Del Rey I knew was honest to a fault, especially when it came to critiquing my wardrobe and hair. And she truly cared about her clients. She would never knowingly be a part of something less than—what?

Sheriff Mercer hung up just as we took the Miwok Lake turnoff.

"More trouble?" I asked, always searching for the next headline.

The sheriff looked disgusted. "That was Principal Krumboltz. He caught a bunch of kids shooting up the school. Luckily it's Sunday and school isn't in session. Jesus, what is it with kids and guns today?"

They had certainly been making the headlines lately, in papers other than the *Eureka!* So far, we'd only had a few minor incidents in the Mother Lode, mostly vandalism. But the rising violence among kids was a concern even in these sleepy western towns.

"Where do the kids get the guns?" I asked.

"From their parents, most often. But lately it's been getting worse. Not all the guns we've been seeing are from the family attic."

I thought about our community's so-called progress as we drove down Poker Flat Road to the parking lot, where recreational vehicles of all sizes and shapes filled multiple spaces. Kids today seemed to begin adult behavior earlier than previous generations. Drinking, drugs, sex, and now violence with deadly weapons were all more common, and began at a younger age, than when I was a kid.

Miah and Andrew had escaped the gun and gang lure, but both had had trouble with drugs and alcohol in high school. It had been a bone of contention between Miah and his father, the upstanding Flat Skunk sheriff. Del Rey and Andrew seemed to have worked through it more smoothly, although Del Rey's nineteen-year-old daughter, Courtney—now calling herself Freedom—currently seemed to be at risk.

After circling the area, Sheriff Mercer headed down the lake's frontage road where the houseboats were moored. Most of the residences looked as if they'd been built by hand, an eclectic collection of flattops, A-frames, and boxy shacks floating incongruously on the water. Each houseboat was connected to a short rickety pier, each entrance blocked by a variety of chains, ropes, or cords. Several sported Keep Out signs instead of the more common welcome mats, and a few looked eminently sinkable. Wouldn't catch me living on shaky footing like that. Being deaf, I like the solid earth under my toes to give me a sense of stability and connectedness. Besides, due to my hearing loss, I have a touch of vertigo. I get seasick if I look at an aquarium too long.

Sheriff Mercer checked his notes, then located the sign he'd been searching for. Instead of numbered addresses, the houseboats were identified by colorful names. We'd passed *Rock-a-Bye Baby, Miwok Mooring, Drifting Off, Ahab's Tale,* and *Gone With the Waves,* before arriving at *Sea*

Scatterer. It didn't take a big leap to figure this was Jasper Coyne's place.

"Looks deserted," I said, getting out of the sheriff's car.

"They all do," Sheriff Mercer replied, glancing up and down the dock. There didn't seem to be much going on at this low-income part of Miwok Lake. The houseboats on either side of Coyne's floated some distance away, the windows dark, the decks empty except for a few lounge chairs. These people either valued their privacy and kept to themselves— or the floating houses were abandoned.

Jasper Coyne's home on the water had seen better days. At least, I hoped it had. Weatherbeaten wood planks, which looked to be held together with moss, formed the squared-off living quarters. Fishing gear lay propped against one side of the house, and colorful lures and flies mixed with fishhooks hung from the eaves of the flat roof. Several empty bottles of Jack Daniel's spilled out of a torn paper bag that rested near the tie-up, along with a broken deck chair and old copies of *Field and Stream* and *Guns and Ammo* magazines. No telling how long any of that stuff had been sitting there.

The sheriff turned toward me just before setting foot on the boat. "Wait here." He held out a hand to reinforce his command. "I don't know what to expect, but I'm not taking any chances. So just stay put."

I nodded, giving the sheriff a false sense of security. He cautiously approached the distressed front door, one hand on his gunbelt, the other reaching for the doorknob. The knob seemed to turn easily, and the door swung wide. His mouth opened at the same time; he was probably calling out in case there was someone inside, then he moved in slowly and disappeared from my view.

Craning my neck, I stepped from the short pier onto the deck of the boat, trying to catch a glimpse of the sheriff. Inching my way forward, I passed the cloudy windows that obscured the view of the interior. I was about to reach for the door when it jerked open, and I jumped a foot. If it hadn't been for the waist-high steel cord around the perimeter of the boat, I would have fallen overboard.

"Shit! You scared me!"

The sheriff shook his head. "I told you to stay there! When are you going to listen—" he cut himself off.

"As soon as I get that next operation."

"Stop it, C.W. You know what I mean."

"Is he there?" I regained my composure and tried to peer inside, around the sheriff's bulk.

"Nope. Nobody home. Looks like he hasn't been there for a few days, but it's hard to tell. Some guys live like this— dishes in the sink, empty bottles on the counter, clothes all over the place."

"I thought all guys lived that way. Can I peek?"

"Got a warrant?"

"No, but neither did you, and you went inside."

"Door was open . . . I . . . thought I heard him say 'Come in.' Just wanted to make sure everything was all right." The sheriff couldn't look me in the eye as he told this whopper. I grinned and nodded.

"I think I hear him calling me, too," I said, reaching for the doorknob. Before the sheriff could say, "It's a miracle— she can hear!" I was inside.

"What a dump." I waved an invisible cigarette around à la Bette Davis. The sheriff had been observant in his brief scan of the room. Crusty, critter-ridden dishes were piled in the sink. A half bottle of Jack Daniel's stood on the counter—no glass nearby. Filthy overalls and T-shirts were strewn about the cramped quarters. I could hardly take a step without walking on something. The place smelled like week-old lasagna made from sweaty socks and soaked in alcohol. A wave of nausea swept over me like rolling surf.

"Don't touch anything!" Sheriff Mercer spoke sternly, before peering at a pile of papers on a nicked, cigarette-scarred kitchen table. He slipped on his bifocals and took a close-up look at the top sheet, without touching it, of course.

"What is it?" I asked, trying to see over his shoulder.

"Looks like business forms. Everything's labeled *Sea Scatterer*. He's got letterhead, receipts, billing forms, business cards—the usual business paperwork. Seems he hired himself out to a number of mortuaries in the Northern California area, not just Del Rey's."

That was a relief, although I wasn't quite sure why. Maybe because it meant if he was doing something illegal, he was duping the mortuaries instead of working with them on some kind of scam.

"What do you make of it, Sheriff?" I wished he'd pick up a few of the papers so I could see if there was anything underneath the stack. Like some incriminating evidence.

"I can't be sure, but my guess is Jasper Coyne is pocketing the money from the mortuaries, and storing the ashes in the rental compartment instead of distributing them at sea."

"But why—" I started to reach for the papers when the sheriff grabbed my wrist.

"Unh-uh. I've got to get a warrant. Nothing I find here is admissible without one. He may be back any minute and then we'd be in real trouble. Let's get on out of here before we're accused of illegal trespass."

I made a face, but I knew he was right. With a last glance around the dingy, unkempt room, I followed him out the door on rubber legs. The last thing that caught my eye before leaving was something glinting in the dim light along the far wall. I thought for a moment it might be a weapon— a gun or a knife? I moved in for a closer look. It turned out to be a half dozen tarnished silver and gold trophies for some kind of sports achievement, on a small shelf screwed into the wall. Was our man once a star athlete? Perhaps not—the name on the trophies read "Levi Coyne."

I didn't have time to think it through. As I shut the door, I turned to face the sheriff. He stood with his index finger pointed skyward, as if he were signing "up" or "wait a minute." Then I noticed his fingertip. There was a dark red dot on it. Blood? I followed his glance to the waist-high railing that had caught my fall earlier, and peered over the side.

Something that looked like a melon bobbed just below the murky surface of the water. But waving about in the peaceful motion of the lake, I could make out the gentle sway of human hair.

As Jeremiah would say, I hurled.

Right there, over the side of the houseboat, I spewed on what might have been a crime scene. Automatic response. Couldn't stop myself. Must have been the combination of rocking boat and rolling waves, not to mention the rotting corpse beneath the surface of the water. Sheriff Mercer looked at me in surprise as I wiped my mouth with the back of my hand.

"Hey! Cut it out! You're contaminating the crime scene! I thought you had nerves of steel."

"I do have nerves of steel. But my stomach lining is very sensitive. I always toss when I see a dead—"

I looked down. I couldn't finish my sentence. The matted hair still floated like a mutant jellyfish just under the surface. I didn't need to remind myself it was human hair. My stomach took care of that.

Sheriff Mercer pulled out his cell phone and said something I didn't bother to lip-read. I had a feeling I knew who he was calling. The paramedics. I wanted to tell him it was too late, but he knew that. I'd only recently learned it's routine to call the EMTs. Like in court, where a person is not considered guilty until proven so, a person is not considered dead until officially pronounced so.

I pulled myself away from the seasickening view and sat on my haunches, trying to put my stomach back where it belonged. It took some concentrated breathing and forced relaxation, but by the time the sheriff got off the phone, I had my sea legs.

"Is it Jasper Coyne?" I said to the sheriff, resisting the compulsion to sneak another glance into the water. Sheriff Mercer leaned over, trying to get a good look at the floater.

"Prob'ly. After they hoist him up, we'll make an official ID."

"Do you think he . . . drowned himself?"

The sheriff held up the finger still stained with blood and rubbed it with his thumb. "Hard to say. Could have. Or maybe he slipped and hit his head on the railing here. Look at this rope."

He indicated a thick length of knotted cable secured to the side of the boat. The other end reached into the water alongside the submerged body. It appeared to dip straight down into the murky water, disappearing into the darkness.

"Think it's the anchor?"

Sheriff Mercer nodded. "If you look close, you can see how it's tangled around his legs. He must have got caught up in it somehow."

Another wave of nausea rocked my boat and I had to glance away again. After several slow, deep breaths, I thought I had enough control over the rest of my breakfast to speak. "God!"

"Kinda ironic. It looks like he drowned just inches under the surface of the water."

I stared again into the cloudy lake and tried to imagine how such a thing could happen. The sway of his hair, swishing back and forth in the water, was hypnotizing. And then nauseating.

"I gotta take a walk." My head was spinning. The sheriff nodded and I returned to the pier to steady myself and catch my breath. When I felt the latest wave subside, I returned, with more questions. Sheriff Mercer was on his cell phone again, so I made a detour and slipped back into the living quarters.

The sheriff had come to trust me over time, knowing I wouldn't deliberately contaminate a crime scene or interfere with his investigation. But if I pushed it too far, he got territorial and I had to back off. I tread a fine line between digging out information for my newspaper and staying on the good side of Sheriff Mercer. We'd grown close over the past year or so, and I'd come to care about him as a sort of curmudgeonly uncle. Sometimes I thought he felt the same way; other times I had a feeling he just put up with me. Maybe because I'd hired his son to help me out at the newspaper office, which kept him out of trouble. Or maybe it was only so he could get his mug in the *Eureka!*

With the sheriff occupied, I had a chance to snoop around a little, out from under his watchful by-the-book eye. I was looking for some clue as to what Jasper Coyne might have been doing before he drowned, and my glance fell on a pen with the words "Memory Kingdom Memorial Park" on it. Del Rey's pen. I guessed it wouldn't be unusual for an ash scatterer to have a mortuary pen.

Using the pen, I moved the pile of papers on Jasper's desk so I could read them. Most of them bore the letterhead from Del Rey's mortuary. The rest of the paperwork consisted of receipts, check stubs, and monthly bills.

Still using the pen as an extension of my hand, I pulled open a couple of drawers and shuffled through the miscellaneous junk. One drawer held a deck of cards, bent, worn, and slightly stuck together, a bunch of combination locks, screws, and bolts, and a variety of spent bullets. I remembered Sheriff Locke saying Jasper liked to shoot his gun into the water when he was drunk.

Another drawer held more scraps of paper, receipts, business cards, and other notes. I pushed the pile around with the pen, gently lifting layers, until I noticed some familiar handwriting.

The paper featured no letterhead or other printed information. The note was brief. It read: "Jasper, there will be no more money coming in. Leave me the hell alone or I'll contact the sheriff." It was unsigned. But I knew that curlicue script. The note was written by Del Rey.

Del Rey Montez and I had become friends when our dogs became acquainted at the Memory Kingdom Memorial

Park. Del Rey's predecessor, French McCluskey, had made an effort to turn the grounds into a family gathering place, complete with picnic tables, flowers, rolling lawns, and a playground. While my Siberian husky, Casper, and her malamute, Frosty, chased each other's tails, Del Rey and I talked over bag lunches. When she told me she had a sister who was blind, and how it had affected her family, I felt a kinship I hadn't known for a long time. We discovered we had a lot in common, and for the first time I was able to share my frustration at how often disabled people were ignored, underestimated, and discriminated against. She really seemed to understand.

"—are you doing? I told you not to touch anything."

I managed to catch the sheriff in midadmonition as he reentered the main room of the houseboat.

"Nothing. And I didn't touch anything." I held up the pen.

"What's that?"

"A pen. I used it to look through some of the papers, like they do on TV."

Sheriff Mercer shook his head and snatched the pen out of my hand. "Did this come from here?"

I nodded.

"Did you touch it?"

Duh. I nodded.

"Goddamn it, C.W."

I thought about distracting him with my latest find. But I hesitated. If Del Rey were somehow involved, I didn't want to bring it to the sheriff's attention. He'd find out eventually, but it would be better if I had a chance to talk to Del Rey first. Now all I could do was open and shut my mouth like a floundering fish. That was a dead giveaway to the sheriff. He knew when I was speechless, I had something important to say. He glanced at the drawer.

"What did you find, C.W.?"

Lifting each sheet of paper by a corner, Sheriff Mercer sifted through them until he found the one that had concerned me. He shot me a look, then removed the note from the bottom of the pile. He carefully folded it and tucked the paper inside his notebook.

"Arthurlene Jackson is on her way. You better wait outside until she gets here."

Before I could make my exit, the door swung open. Sheriff Peyton Locke stood in the doorway, looking official in her uniformed stance. I could almost feel the glow from Sheriff Mercer's reddening face. The guy had it bad.

"What's she doing here?" I think Sheriff Locke said. I can't be certain, because I was on my way out. I left Sheriff Mercer to do the explaining, while I waited on the dock for the coroner, worrying about Del Rey's connection to Jasper Coyne.

Arthurlene Jackson, the medical examiner for Calaveras County, arrived fifteen minutes later, just about the time I was feeling I could take on some soda crackers and a flat Coke. She'd done something different with her hair, cinching the tiny black curls into a puffball at the top of her head and tying it back with a colorful scarf. The white lab coat fell loosely from her slim shoulders, allowing her African motif shirt and black slacks to peek through. A large wooden choker of carved wild animals hung from her elegantly long neck.

"Hi, Connor." She greeted me cautiously as I stood up. "You again?"

"I had nothing to do with it," I said and flipped my palms up in a premature gesture of surrender. "I'm a reporter. I'm here for the story, doing my job, just like you."

"Awfully defensive, aren't you?" she said, raising an eyebrow. Without giving me a chance to respond, she moved past me toward the houseboat. I turned to see both sheriffs standing outside the door. I thought about following her, but a moment later the paramedics arrived. They shoved me out of the way in their haste to reach the victim.

From a distance I watched the uniformed man-and-woman team use ropes and a hook to hoist the body from the water. It took the help of both sheriffs, but they managed to haul the victim to the surface. It was not a pretty sight. The white, bloated body lay on its back, shrouded in dark, twisted clothing. I inched closer and regretted it, as my stomach began to churn.

The body didn't seem to have a face.

Feeling the need for another walk, I headed back to the

pier and sat down with my head between my knees. When my breathing returned to normal, I opened the door to Sheriff Mercer's car and pulled out my camera. After all, I was a reporter, and I knew I should take some pictures for evidence. Interesting thing about the camera. Often when I get behind the lens, I can take pictures of anything, from mutilated body parts to vivid roadkill—even Mama Cody's meatloaf, a famously ugly Flat Skunk sight. The lens somehow helps me keep my distance. It's when I look directly at something horrific that I lose it.

I snapped some close-ups using a telephoto lens, took a few slow breaths to keep my equilibrium, then snapped a few more of the houseboat for context. Got a nice picture of Sheriff Mercer looking official. He'd like that one. I was about to take a shot of Sheriff Locke when I read her lips through the telephoto lens.

"—yes, I think she's involved. And I think we need to talk with her. She had to have known about the ashes—" Sheriff Locke turned away and I lost the rest. But I knew who she was talking about. Del Rey.

I moved onto the deck, avoiding eye contact with the wet blob that lay at their feet—not that eye contact was a possibility for him.

"Sheriff Locke," I spoke up. "You can't mean you suspect Del Rey Montez of anything. Del Rey is an honest businesswoman who cares about her clients. She can't have known anything about those ashes."

I turned to Sheriff Mercer for confirmation. He said nothing, only frowned and looked away. "Sheriff!"

He finally faced me, opening the notebook he'd been holding and glancing at the sheet of paper tucked inside.

"It doesn't look good, C.W."

"What are you talking about? All you found in there were some old letterheads and receipts!"

He snapped the notebook closed. "And that note."

"But it's unsigned!" I was almost pleading.

"It won't take long to prove who wrote it." And like me, he already knew.

"Sheriff! You can't—"

He cut me off. "Calm down, C.W., calm down."

Sheriff Locke turned toward me, overenunciating her

words. Sheriff Mercer must have told her I was deaf, and now she thought exaggeration was the best way to communicate. Unfortunately, it just made it harder to read her.

"Ms. Westphal, Sheriff Mercer and I found some other papers hidden inside that we can't discuss at this time."

I looked at Sheriff Mercer. He shrugged. "It looks like Del Rey might have been paying Jasper Coyne large amounts of money for some time."

I waited for him to go on. When he didn't, I said, "For his services, I'm sure. She hired him to distribute her clients' ashes and then paid him—"

Sheriff Mercer began shaking his head. "These were much larger payments than what might be expected for sea-scattering services."

"What do you mean?"

"I can't go into it—"

"Why not?"

Sheriff Mercer frowned. "Look, C.W., I'm sure we'll be able to clear all this up once we have a talk with Del Rey. There are some . . . discrepancies . . . and I need to find out what's behind them. Especially now that Jasper Coyne appears to have drowned."

I glanced back at the body, where Dr. Arthurlene Jackson was poking and prodding with gloved hands. When she stood up, she signaled the paramedics to take him away. They moved into action, zipping the body into a clear plastic bag and lifting it onto a gurney that had been collapsed to the floor. As they raised it and wheeled it off the deck to the waiting ambulance, Sheriff Mercer pointed toward the deck railing, explaining something to Sheriff Locke.

That's when I remembered the blood on his fingertip. Was Jasper Coyne already injured when he went over the side?

As Sheriff Mercer pulled into the small parking lot adjacent to his office in Flat Skunk, I gathered my backpack and camera. He said something about having to make a few calls before taking the next step—interviewing Del Rey. I knew I didn't have much time if I wanted to beat him there and prepare her.

After dropping my camera at the *Eureka!*, I checked to see if Dan was in his office just down the hall. An ex-cop, he'd been doing some carpentry and maintenance for Del Rey, but she had finally found someone permanent. He wasn't around now, and I wondered if he was working on a little investigation of his own. I knew the location of his deceased brother was really bothering him.

Fortunately, I'd left my bike at the office, and I rode the short distance to Memory Kingdom Memorial Park at high speed. The lawn area out front was sparsely populated—only two young mothers and their toddlers occupied the benches and swings. I spotted someone driving a golf cart along the edge of the grounds, and assumed it was Sluice Jackson, the old caretaker and former prospector, until the cart made a turn and I could see the profile of the man. It wasn't Sluice. Must be the new handyman, I thought, won-

dering if Sluice had retired completely now. He hadn't been
the same since he'd fallen into an open grave a few months
back. Del Rey only kept him on because she had a soft heart
and knew he had nowhere else to go.

Parking my bike, I headed up the path to the Dis-
neyesque memorial home, another creation of the former
mortician. French McCluskey had owned a chain of ceme-
teries and mortuaries throughout the Mother Lode, but after a scandal at Memorial Kingdom, he'd moved to the gold
country town of Jackson to run Café Max, a combination
coffee shop, bakery, and gift boutique. He'd sold off indi-
vidual locations to people looking for a solid business in-
vestment in this retirement mecca.

Del Rey had worked for French as an embalmer for
years, and had saved enough money to put a down payment
on the Flat Skunk location. Under her creative expertise, the
mortuary business had boomed—not because of an increase in dead bodies, but because of the occasional rental
of the funeral home for E. Clampus Vitus meetings, Hal-
loween parties, and Over-the-Hill Birthday bashes. She'd
been able to send both her kids to college without anyone's
help—her husband had been killed in a car accident years
before—and had enough left over to mail supplement
checks to her sister, who lived in an assisted-care facility for
the blind.

I found Del Rey leafing through a copy of *Mortuary
Management,* admiring the latest in cremation urns and de-
signer coffins.

"Hi, Del Rey."

She looked up, flipped the magazine closed, and greeted
me with a cheery smile.

"Connor! What are you doing here? Aren't you supposed to be out covering the latest sex scandals in the gold
country? What's new on the newspaper grapevine?"

I pressed my lips together, trying to figure out what to
say. I wanted her to know what was going on before Sheriff
Mercer—or Sheriff Locke—made an official visit. They might
call it tampering with an investigation, but I preferred to see
it as helping an innocent bystander.

"Not much in the way of sex scandals around here
lately, unless you count the love affair we all know is going

on between Mama Cody and Sluice Jackson. And I don't
think my readers want to know the steamy details of that
relationship, do you?"

Del Rey laughed. "So that's where my old handyman's
been going every afternoon. I thought he was taking a nap.
Well, I guess he *was* going to bed, all right. Hoo!" The
thought seemed to make her shiver.

"Speaking of handymen, looks like you got a new one."

Del Rey nodded. "Thank God. Not that Dan wasn't
wonderful, but I really needed someone full-time, and I
know Dan doesn't want to be a handyman the rest of his
life."

"So the new guy is working out?"

"So far. It's only been a little while." She paused. "Is something on your mind, Connor? You seem a little distracted."

"No, everything's fine. I was just wondering how things
are going." The perfect opportunity to speak up and I'd lost
my nerve. I sat down on one of the brocade love seats that
lined the walls of the front parlor. The Victorian decor was
probably meant to be homey, but it came off looking like a
scene from *Great Expectations*.

"How about a soda?" Del Rey ducked behind the
greeter's desk and pulled out a couple of diet Shastas. She
handed me my usual—grape—and kept the black cherry for
herself. Always on a diet, Del Rey nonetheless retained an
insulating layer that made her appear soft and comfortable.
If I skinned my knee, she'd be the first one I'd run to for
pampering.

"Truthfully," she said suddenly, "I'm going nuts. That's
how things are going."

I tensed. "What do you mean?"

She laughed. "How would you like it if two surly post-
adolescents moved back in with you after a few years away
at college? I love 'em dearly, but they're driving me crazy."

I let out the chestful of air I'd been holding. "Yeah, I
saw Andrew earlier this afternoon at the paint pellet game.
When did he get home?"

"A week ago. He's job hunting, but it's not going well.
With a bachelor's in math and a minor in computer science,
you'd think he'd be snapped up by some big corporation. But
all he can get is busboy at the Nugget. He's talking about

opening up his own microbrewery in town. Guess he got a degree in beer at Chico State, too."

"And why is Courtney home?" I took a sip of the grape soda and licked the residue from my upper lip. I had a feeling the purple mustache would clash with my outfit.

"Courtney? You mean 'Freedom'?"

"Oh yes. I forgot." I smiled.

"Yep, changed her name—again. Said 'Courtney' was too girly. Said she wanted something 'gender-free.' I have to call her 'Freedom' from now on."

My smile turned to laughter, in spite of myself. I knew Del Rey wasn't pleased, but I was sure the situation was temporary. When I was thirteen, I had wanted to change my name to Marcel, after Marcel Marceau. It lasted a week.

"She says she's not going back to Chico. She was on academic probation, and has decided she's had enough formal education. After trying three roommates, four boyfriends, and five majors—the last being philosophy—she's decided to come home and become a bass player for a punk-ska band, whatever that is. At least she has a job in the meantime. She's working part-time at the body-piercing and tattoo boutique in Sonora. God help me."

Behind the complaints about her kids, I could tell Del Rey was proud of them, and glad they were back home. I hated to complicate things further, but I knew the sheriff would be there any moment. I couldn't stall any longer.

"Del Rey, something's happened."

Her Betty Boop eyebrows peaked. "I knew it! What? Is it something about the kids?"

I shook my head. "It's nothing like that. Sheriff Mercer got a call to inspect a storage warehouse over near Angels Camp. Seems someone complained about a bulging storage compartment. When he took a look, he found . . . well, ashes."

Del Rey blinked. The thickly mascaraed lashes framed her eyes like little flowers. "Ashes? What kind of ashes?"

"Human ashes. Cremains. Boxes and boxes of them. And some of them are labeled 'Memory Kingdom.' "

"I . . . I don't understand. What do you mean, they're labeled Memory Kingdom?"

I said nothing.

"You don't mean . . . they're *my* ashes? But they can't be! My ashes are handled by a man who scatters them at sea. I've been working with him for years—"

"Jasper Coyne?"

She stared at me, openmouthed. "Yes, how did you know?"

"He was the one who rented the storage compartment."

"Oh, God—"

Before she could say another word, Sheriff Mercer entered the room. He didn't look bereaved, so I knew he was here on business. In fact, he looked downright peeved.

"C.W., what are you doing here?"

"Just sharing a drink with my friend."

He shot me a look, then said, "Well, would you please excuse us? I have something to discuss with Del Rey."

"No!" Del Rey burst out, rising to her feet. "I want her here. What is it, Sheriff? Connor's told me about the ashes. What's going on?"

The sheriff shot me another look. If looks could kill, I'd at least be in the right place for a really terrific embalming.

Sheriff Mercer repeated the story I had just told Del Rey. Then he took it a step further.

"Del Rey, what is your connection with Jasper Coyne?"

"I have a . . . business relationship with him, that's all. I've been hiring him to scatter client ashes at sea for years. He has a boat, and my clients seem to prefer—"

"When was the last time you saw him?"

"I . . . I don't know. Uh, maybe a couple of days ago, when I paid him for his latest services."

"You didn't mail him a check?"

"No, I paid him in person."

"You went to his boat?"

"No, he came by in his truck and picked it up. Why?"

"Well, there's some indication that he hasn't been fulfilling his services. Perhaps not for several years now."

Del Rey melted into the overstuffed velvet chair. "Oh, my God." She looked at the carpet, as if trying to get her bearings. She appeared to be genuinely stunned.

The sheriff broke into her thoughts. "Del Rey, did you know anything about this?"

Del Rey seemed to be somewhere else. It took her a moment to respond. "No, no, of course not, Sheriff. I had no idea . . ."

"We found some uncashed checks on Coyne's houseboat. Made out to Coyne. Signed by you."

"Yes . . . I'm sure they were payments I made for the sea scattering services. . . . I—"

"A couple of the checks were for very large sums of money."

Del Rey blinked again.

"Del Rey?" Sheriff Mercer was watching her face intently.

She took a deep breath, as if composing her thoughts while regulating her breathing. After another calming breath, she continued.

"I did give him a couple of large checks. And yes, it was for more than the scattering services. He . . . he needed the money. It was a loan. I was just trying to help him out a little. He'd been having some hard times."

I stared at Del Rey, puzzled. "But why, Del Rey? Were you and this Jasper Coyne good friends?"

Del Rey pressed her lips together, then spoke. "Look, you're sure to find this out eventually, and I'd rather it come from me. I . . . I don't want this to get out—I need to protect my family—but . . ."

She paused. "Jasper Coyne . . . was my first husband."

Before I could think it through, a shadow passed behind Del Rey, catching my eye. Andrew stood motionless in the doorway, his eyes dark, his brows knitted. Del Rey had been too busy gazing at her feet to notice, but when she looked up and saw me staring over her shoulder, she turned around.

Andrew was gone.

"Who's there?" Del Rey stood, calling into the shadows behind the heavy draperies. The alcove led to a hallway that offered access to the rest of the funeral home. Andrew had disappeared inside.

But before I could tell Del Rey that her son might have overheard our conversation, a figure slowly stepped forward into the light of the parlor. I held my breath, expecting to see Andrew again. A stranger stood in his place.

"Chunker! What are you doing sneaking around? I thought you were moving those new caskets—" That's all I caught of Del Rey's tirade before she turned her head.

I watched the middle-aged man rub his three-day beard growth nervously, then pull his Forty-Niners cap over his eyes. As he reached up, his jacket sleeve slid down, offering a glimpse of his exposed forearm. It was covered with multicolored tattoos. I made out half a vulture and a thorny rose before he stuffed his hand down into his jacket pocket.

I glanced back at Del Rey, who looked flushed as she faced Sheriff Mercer. Had I missed something? She returned her attention to the scruffy handyman in overalls and plaid jacket. "Go on back to your work now, Chunker. I've got business to discuss."

The man nodded slightly and backed out of the room, a ripple of drapery accenting his exit. When Del Rey turned back to us, the sheriff and I were both staring at her.

"What?" she said, taking her seat again. She began picking at the nonexistent lint on her cream-colored stirrup pants.

"Is that your new handyman? I thought I saw him riding on Sluice's cart when I got here."

"Yes," Del Rey said, and it seemed like she was forcing herself to meet my eyes. The gaze was so intense, I felt as if she were trying to read something more into my comment. I waited for her to continue. When she didn't, I groped for something else to say.

"Is that his real name—Chunker?" I thought I had misunderstood.

"That's what we—I mean, that's what he calls himself. Chunker Lansky."

The sheriff added, "What do you know about him? I could do a background check—"

Del Rey looked irritated. "That's not necessary, Sheriff. As I told Connor, Sluice is getting on. He can't handle all the work anymore. When this guy came looking for a job, I hired him. End of story. Is there something else you wanted to talk to me about?"

I glanced at the sheriff. He stood frowning at the empty doorway. Neither of us mentioned Andrew's earlier presence.

"Sheriff?" Del Rey said.

The sheriff seemed a little slow on the uptake today. Eventually he said, "All right, Del Rey. Why don't you tell me everything you can about Jasper Coyne. I need help clearing up a few things."

"Like what?"

"Like, when did you first begin doing business with Mr. Coyne?"

The sheriff pulled out his notepad and sat down on a nearby chair. I followed suit, without the notepad. Del Rey gave me a quick glance; I smiled, giving her a nod. She turned to the sheriff.

"I met Jasper Coyne several years ago—"

"When, exactly?" Sheriff Mercer interrupted.

Del Rey sighed. "Twenty-three years ago, to be exact. We . . . met in mortuary science college in Sacramento. I got into the field because my grandfather was a mortician. That's how most of us get into mortuary science. We have relatives in the business. Anyway, I grew up fascinated with the caskets and makeup and all that mysterious stuff you find in mortuaries."

"And Coyne?" Sheriff Mercer prodded.

Del Rey shrugged. "I think he went into the business as a form of rebellion. His father wanted him to be a fisherman, like he was. Jasper didn't think that sounded too exciting. He was eighteen, just out of high school, partying all the time. Fishing wasn't how he wanted to spend the rest of his life. He thought he wouldn't have to work too hard if he became a mortician. The income is pretty much guaranteed, 'cause people die all the time. And he figured he'd have plenty of leftover hours to get drunk and go shooting. We got married right about that time. But it didn't last long. Only a few months."

I wanted to ask why it ended, but I kept quiet. I also wanted to know why she'd never told me any of this before.

Del Rey eyed her manicured fingernails. "Eventually he ran out of tuition money. His dad wouldn't pay it, his mom had run off years ago, so he had to earn the fees himself. He did odd jobs around the college—modeling for the students who had to practice making up the bodies, cleaning out the ashes and packaging them for distribution—that kind of thing. But it wasn't enough."

"So he dropped out," the sheriff said.

Del Rey began to fidget with the antimacassar on the chair wings, twisting it around her arm like a lace bandage. She couldn't keep her hands still as she talked.

"Yeah. And that was it for us. He finally gave into his dad and went into the fishing business. But Jasper had the last laugh. He ended up combining fishing with the mortuary business by hiring out as a cremains distributor on the side. Really pissed off his dad. After his father died, maybe ten years later, Jasper and his brother Levi inherited the fishing boat and their dad's houseboat. Jasper bought out his brother, and went into the ash distribution business full-time."

"So you hired him to distribute your ashes, and paid him for his services. And then you gave him extra money cause he was broke. Do I have this right?" the sheriff asked, reviewing his notes.

"It's true, I . . . I didn't just hire him for scattering the ashes. To be honest, I . . . I wanted to keep in touch with him over the years."

"Even though you got divorced?"

She pressed her lips tight.

"There was no animosity between the two of you?"

Del Rey said nothing.

"I just don't get why you'd keep giving him money after all these years. Especially since the marriage didn't last but a couple of months." Sheriff Mercer stuck his finger in his ear and gave it a whirl, as if to stir up his thoughts. "Did you owe him something, after all these years?"

"No, nothing like that."

"Come on, Del Rey. Why did you keep paying him so much money?" The sheriff leaned toward her. "Was he blackmailing you?"

Del Rey pulled back, furious. "No! Of course not! Jasper would never blackmail me. I . . . I told you. I just felt sorry for him, that's all. Once his father died, he never seemed to make ends meet. So I sent him a little extra cash now and then, when he needed it. Is that against the law?"

"A lot extra, by the looks of it," said the sheriff, ignoring her challenge.

Del Rey squirmed. "If you check the stubs, you'll see it was only recently. When he came to me, asking for a loan, he seemed desperate. He wasn't himself lately, that's for sure. I figured he really needed it, so I gave it to him."

"Cause you're such a soft touch," I said gently. She was. Everyone in town knew it. Del Rey was the first person to call when a cause needed a donation, a kid needed a part-time job, or a transient needed a handout.

"I can't help it. You know that, Connor."

I did. But I was beginning to wonder if there were other major things I didn't know about Del Rey.

"Well, I'm going to have to take a look at your books, Del Rey. There's something here that just doesn't add up, now that—" He cut himself off.

"Now that what?" Del Rey asked. She looked back and forth between the sheriff and me.

"Did you know about his drinking?" Sheriff Mercer asked abruptly.

"Yes. He and Jack Daniel's had a bond that couldn't be broken, not even by . . ." She stopped herself.

"He was a drunk, Del Rey," the sheriff said harshly. "He was a lousy husband. He cheated you out of your money by not distributing the ashes. And now, for some reason, he's got you wrapped around his little finger. You've got a real codependency problem, if you ask me."

Since the breakup of his own marriage last year, Sheriff Mercer had been reading way too many self-help books.

"I know what I am, Sheriff, thank you very much. But you don't know a thing about my personal life. So I'd suggest—"

He cut her off. "All right then. Tell me, Del Rey, so I'll understand. 'Cause this situation with Jasper Coyne isn't just about scamming the mortuary for a few dollars."

"What do you mean?"

The sheriff glanced at me, then straightened up to deliver his bombshell.

"Jasper Coyne was pulled out of Miwok Lake this morning. He apparently drowned."

Del Rey's usually pink cheeks and flushed face lost all color. Her wide round eyes filled with tears as the news of her first husband's death took hold. I'd never seen Del Rey cry before.

"Oh, God, no!"

I instinctively put an arm around Del Rey, while Sheriff Mercer studied her response. I knew it was his job, but it irritated me to see him so detached. I'd never make a good cop if that's what it took.

"We . . . we hadn't been . . . getting along lately . . ."

The crying began full force. As Del Rey sobbed into her hands, I grew concerned about her overreaction to the death of a man she hardly knew anymore. Did she still love him after all these years?

Through her tears, she choked out a few words that were not easy to read with her face distorted and her lips stretched taut. "I just saw him . . . had a fight . . . never thought . . . all I wanted . . . now it's too late . . ." She bent over her hands again, still mumbling.

"Del Rey, what is it? Why has this upset you so much?" I asked, hugging her, smoothing her hair like my mother used to do to comfort me.

Del Rey looked up at me with wet eyes, as if pleading for me to understand. "Don't you see?" she said between gasps. "Now he'll never be there for us . . . I always hoped someday . . . but now . . ."

"What are you talking about, Del Rey?" I glanced at the sheriff to see if he understood any of this, but he looked even more confused than I felt.

Del Rey took a long, deep breath and let it out slowly. "Andrew . . . Andrew is Jasper Coyne's son."

I was stunned. I had always assumed that Mario, the husband who'd been killed in a car crash, was Andrew's father. And as close as I'd thought I was with Del Rey, she'd never hinted at anything different. As for Courtney, I never really thought about who her father was. But I sure never would have suspected Chunker! I glanced at the sheriff to see how he was taking this, but at that moment, both he and Del Rey jumped and turned toward the doorway. I turned to see what had startled them.

Andrew stood there again. At his feet was a pile of broken glass.

Del Rey rushed to her son as he stood staring down at the amber shards. Beer bottles. There must have been half a dozen. Luckily they were empty. Had Andrew drunk all that beer?

". . . Andrew!" was about all I caught, forced to watch her body language instead of her obscured lips.

Andrew remained stiff and still, while Del Rey bent down to pick up the broken glass. After a momentary pause, Andrew knelt down to help her. I could see them conversing but had no idea what was being said. I looked at the sheriff for an explanation but he shook his head. It must not have been the appropriate time for an interpretation.

Mother and son stood up again, their hands gingerly filled with the larger pieces of the broken bottles. Del Rey turned to me and mumbled something like, ". . . his beer bottle collection . . ." before hurrying off to find a depository for the glass. Del Rey had told me Andrew was saving bottles for his start-up brewery. He must have been adding these to his collection. The sheriff, Andrew, and I remained where we were for an awkward moment, until Del Rey returned with a broom, breaking the tension.

"Well, I'd better head off," Sheriff Mercer said, as Del Rey began sweeping up the rest of the shattered glass.

She nodded without looking up.

"Come on, C.W. Let them have some privacy. I'll talk to you later, Del Rey. Bye, Andrew."

I gave Del Rey a gentle hug, patted Andrew's back, then followed Sheriff Mercer out of the Memorial Kingdom Mortuary and into the fading daylight. It felt refreshing to escape the artificial glow of the mortuary lighting. The late afternoon sun beat down on the shimmering lawn of the cemetery park, and my skin prickled in the California heat.

"I've got some things to do, C.W. I'll see you later."

"Sheriff." I wasn't ready to let him go. "What exactly do you think is Del Rey's involvement in this?"

"Well, it's logical that she used Jasper's services. Whether there's more to it than that, we'll have to see."

"But what about her explanation for lending him the money? Of course she would want to help out Andrew's biological father. And she seemed to take Coyne's death pretty hard."

"Like I said, we'll see. In the meantime, you keep out of it. I'll let you know if there's anything to report for your newspaper."

"Where are you going?" I asked boldly as he turned to go.

"Huh?" he said, turning back around.

"I said, where are you off to?" Briefly I wondered if the sheriff might be having some kind of health problem. He didn't look sick. No flushed face, shortness of breath, or open wounds. More like something was on his mind. Something important enough to distract him from the matters at hand? I'd never seen him this . . . detached.

"I'm going to see a man about a home."

I blinked. "Why? Are you moving?"

"Not a house. A funeral home." With that, he drove off in his patrol car.

I started across the lawn, taking a shortcut through the cemetery to the street, where I'd left my bike. I caught sight of the handyman who'd interrupted us inside the mortuary. What had Del Rey called him? Clunker? No, Chunker.

I was prepared to give him a nod if he spotted me, but he didn't look in my direction. In fact, he seemed very intent on something in the distance. I strained to see what he was staring at, curious about this stranger who had come to work for Del Rey so suddenly. I followed his line of vision and spotted what looked like a baggy-clothed teenager practicing skateboard tricks in the mortuary parking lot.

When the skater stopped moving and turned around, I caught a glimpse of her face. It was Del Rey's daughter, Courtney-Freedom. Why was Chunker watching her so closely? Granted, she was pretty good on that skateboard, but his fascination seemed to go beyond mild interest in her skating stunts.

Glancing to the side, he caught me staring at him. He grabbed his rake and ducked out of sight.

A chill enveloped me that the heat could not touch. This guy was up to something.

Back at the *Eureka!*, I found Miah at his computer, working on an article I'd assigned him about the rise in violence among children. Flat Skunk had been lucky. But in neighboring Whiskey Slide, bullets had been fired at the middle school, luckily when it wasn't in session. And there were other incidents: an accidental shooting in Murphys when a nine-year-old boy was injured by his twelve-year-old brother while playing with their father's shotgun. A fifteen-year-old girl had been caught brandishing a handgun at a high school in Jackson. A cache of illegal weapons was found at the home of a nineteen-year-old drug dealer in Bogus Thunder.

I glanced over Miah's shoulder. His notes surprised me: "The U.S. has the highest rate of gun deaths—murders, suicides, and accidents—in the world. Guns are now considered a public health hazard. . . ."

"Wow, that's amazing," I said, interrupting Miah's typing.

He swung around to face me and signed, "That's just the tip of the iceberg. According to the Internet, thirty-five thousand people die from gunshot wounds every year. And ninety-seven percent of weapons used in this country are illegal."

"Good stats. But just because a gun is legally purchased doesn't mean it's safe."

"Yeah, but it's a step in the right direction. My dad got me a rifle when I was in high school. He taught me how to use it, though. And he keeps it locked up."

I sat down at my own desk, realizing the not-in-my-backyard belief was disappearing quickly. Pushing the depressing news aside, I had Miah phone Del Rey. She'd been promising to buy a TTY but hadn't gotten around to it yet. There was no answer, so I asked him to leave a message on her machine about her handyman's unusual interest in her daughter. I hated being a busybody, but I'd hate myself more if anything should happen to Courtney. I just wanted Del Rey to be aware.

After finishing up an overdue article on the Clampers' Shootin' Spree Roundup the following weekend in Murphys, I decided to take an early evening beer break at the Nugget Café. I found Dan in his next-door office on my way out, and he agreed to join me after I mentioned I might split a patty melt with him. Mama Cody's were always loaded with grilled onions and bell peppers—the best in Flat Skunk.

"What have you been working on?" I asked, after sliding into a red leatherette booth at the café. Before Dan could answer, Jilda stopped by to take our orders. The ingredients for my do-it-yourself mocha appeared before we could resume our conversation. I poured the chocolate milk into the coffee and took a sip.

"Been doing some checking. Trying to follow up on how my brother's ashes ended up in that warehouse. So far I've traced his body from the Rio Vista morgue to the Memorial Kingdom Mortuary, where he was supposed to be cremated."

I frowned. Even Dan seemed to have doubts about what happened at Del Rey's mortuary.

Dan caught my look. "I'm not doubting Del Rey. I'm just telling you what I've found out so far. According to her records, his ashes were boxed and sent over to the *Sea*

Scatterer. But the sheriff won't let me see Coyne's records until after the investigation."

"What are you going to do next?"

Dan shrugged, then sat back as Jilda brought our plates of food. I ate my sandwich hungrily, but Dan only picked at his.

"Is there anything I can do?" I asked, after insensitively taking in a mouthful of sandwich. He couldn't understand my garbled speech, so I signed, "Me, help you?" Dan had been studying sign language, and although he hadn't picked it up as quickly as Miah, he had the basics.

He shook his head while I tried to swallow the lump in my mouth.

"I'm going to try the back door. See how someone gets a permit to distribute ashes, who he has to report to, where he's allowed to dump. I might find out something coming at it from a different angle."

"How is that going to help? You know they ended up at the storage warehouse. He probably just did it cause it's easier than taking the boat out to the ocean and scattering the ashes, and he makes a bigger profit by just storing them."

"I don't think it's that simple. It's important to me to find out the truth about what happened to Boone."

Suddenly my sandwich lost its flavor. I pushed it back and took a sip of my cooling mocha.

He reached over and touched my hand. "I'm going to take off. How about dinner tomorrow night? I'll probably be in a better mood, and maybe I'll have some information by then."

"Sure. How about my diner, sevenish. Ever had Hangtown Fry?"

Dan made a face. "So far I've managed to escape that particular gold country delicacy. I'm not too fond of oysters, even if they're disguised with bacon and eggs."

"Oh, but you haven't had Connor style. It has a definite San Francisco twist."

According to California legend, the unique dish called Hangtown Fry was created during the gold rush of 1849. When a dirt-covered miner from Shirttail Bend arrived at the Cary House in Hangtown (now Placerville) with a handful of gold nuggets, he demanded the most expensive meal on the menu. When told it would be either oysters or eggs, he asked the cook to mix them together and serve up the dish. It's been a popular request at the cafés and diners along the California Mother Lode's gold chain for nearly a hundred and fifty years, but I prefer it slightly altered. Instead of bacon, I use prosciutto, and instead of oysters, I use crab or shrimp. Makes all the difference.

I walked Dan back to the office. It was late, and Miah had gone home. At the *Eureka!* I thumbed through the telephone directory for an address in the Miwok Lake area. While Dan had his backdoor technique for gathering information, I'd try my straightforward approach and see where it got me. The sheriff didn't say I couldn't ask a few questions. He just said I had to stay off Jasper Coyne's boat.

The directory listed one other Coyne in the vicinity: Levi Coyne. The name I'd read on the trophies at Jasper's place. This was going to be a piece of cake. It was too late in the day to pursue my plan, so I packed up and headed home. Tomorrow was another day.

I awoke early the next morning, eager to get started on my investigation. Rather than use the California Relay System to interpret for me on the phone—a slow and cumbersome way to communicate—I decided to head over to Levi Coyne's place in person and have a face-to-face. If nothing came of it, I'd only have lost a couple of gallons of gas. And if he was in, I wanted to see his reaction firsthand. When it comes to body language, I don't need to hear. The body speaks volumes. Knowing that, I slipped into a pair of khaki pants, a red top, and a tan blazer, then checked the mirror to see if I looked like a reporter for a change. Lois Lane had nothing on me.

After walking Casper, I left him with a fresh bowl of dog food, a vat of water, and a new chew toy in the shape of a rubber newspaper. Then I hopped in my Chevy and headed toward Lake Miwok.

Pulling up to the address I'd jotted on my notepad, I

double-checked it for accuracy. The place was not what I expected. A large sign over the front door read: "Mystery Mansion."

I parked the Chevy in the small lot reserved for inn guests, grabbed my backpack, and mentally created a reason for my visit—an article for gold country tourists featuring this unusual inn. I stepped up the ramp to the front porch, taking in the building's facade. Mystery Mansion wasn't exactly a mansion, more like a big Victorian house with a wraparound picket fence. Some of the upstairs rooms overlooked a portion of Lake Miwok, and probably cost more because of the view. The front door mat didn't greet me with the usual welcome. It read: "Do You Have a Warrant?"

I reached for the doorknocker, which was shaped like a raven that "pecked" at the door when I pushed its tail. Cute. While I waited, I glanced at the peephole in the door. Was I was being watched? Then I noticed a second peephole, placed considerably lower than the one at eye level.

No answer. I did some more rapping and tapping with the black bird, then stepped back and peered into the lacy curtains to the right. Someone was sitting in a chair facing the window, peering at me.

I pulled back, embarrassed at being caught trying to see inside. The shadow moved away from the window. Tapping my foot, I tried to wait patiently for the host to appear while rehearsing my speech for gaining entrance. I was hopeful an article in the *Eureka!*—in essence, free publicity—was an opportunity no businessperson could refuse.

It was several minutes before one of the double doors finally swung open. With my notebook in hand, I stood ready with my practiced pitch.

In front of me sat the man in the wheelchair I'd seen at the paint ball games.

Yes?" he said.

Completely caught off guard, I forgot my whole spiel and blurted out, "I . . . I was looking for . . . are you, by any chance, related to Jasper Coyne?"

He nodded tightly. "I'm his brother. But I'm afraid he's not . . . available." He glanced at the notebook in my hand. "And if you're from the press, I have nothing to say." He started to close the door. I kept it open with one hand.

"Wait! I'm . . ." What could I say? That I wasn't from the press? I had to think fast. "My name is Connor West-phal. I do own the *Eureka!*, but I'm not here to do a story on . . . what happened."

"I'm sorry, I'm not talking to any reporters." Again he tried to shut the door.

"Please. I'm not here for the paper. I'm here for my friend, Del Rey Montez. Do you know her?"

The man shook his head. "Not . . . really. I know she owns a mortuary in Flat Skunk—"

"May I come in, just for a moment? Del Rey is in trouble, and I think you might be able to help her. Please."

Pleading isn't my strong suit, but if Del Rey was some-how involved in Jasper Coyne's ash-scattering scam, Jasper's brother might be able to tell me something that could help clear up her involvement.

The man in the wheelchair appraised me thoughtfully. "I know you, don't I?"

I smiled, hoping his recognition of me would soften him. "Yes, I saw you at the paint ball games yesterday. I'm surprised you remember me."

"There weren't many women there. You stood out."

I avoided the obvious retort: that he stood out too. Instead, I said, "I'm sorry your team lost. But it was a good game, at least until the end."

"Idiots. Getting into a brawl over nothing. Bunch of wanna-be militiamen, thinking they're really fighting a war."

"You don't take the game seriously then, like your teammates do?"

"God, no. Like you said, it's just a game. Why, do you get really into it?"

I shook my head. "That was the first time I ever played. Actually, I was terrified out there, being stalked by some guy in full camouflage. Sometimes it didn't feel like a game."

He nodded, scrutinizing me, then pulled the door wide and ushered me in with a wave of his hand. I entered the foyer, a small square space flanked by a sitting room on the right and a dining room on the left. The man gestured toward the sitting room and I found myself in a cozy blue and yellow parlor, surrounded by oak bookshelves, overstuffed chintz chairs and sofas, and ornately framed portraits of some familiar faces.

"Welcome to Mystery Mansion," he said, wheeling to the center of the room and spinning around to face me. I took a seat in one of the chairs near the window so I could lip-read him more easily. "The owner's a bit of a mystery nut, as you can probably tell. I'm Levi Coyne, by the way." He leaned over to shake my hand. I stood up and met him halfway.

Settling back into the chair, I glanced around the room. The three small end tables held miniature stained-glass lamps, each accompanied by an antiquarian book and a weapon: a jeweled knife, an antique pistol, and a bottle labeled with a skull and crossbones. From the middle of the ceiling hung a brass and crystal chandelier, suspended by a thick rope wound in the shape of a hangman's noose. A brass candlestick sat on one end of the mantel, a lead pipe on the other.

I felt like I was standing in a three-dimensional game of Clue.

"This is a great place! It would make a wonderful feature story for the *Eureka!*"

"Yeah, I suppose. See that bookcase over there?" He made a sweeping gesture with his arm.

I studied the case briefly, then nodded.

"Secret door," he said.

"You're kidding!"

"It leads to the kitchen. Portia—she's the owner—thought it would be fun to include a few secret passages, so she had them built in. Personally, I think she read one too many Nancy Drews when she was a kid."

"You can never read too many Nancy Drews," I said, smiling.

"Oh yeah? Take a look at the carpet."

At first glance it appeared to be a standard floral pattern, but as I stared, letters emerged that began to form words, not unlike those 3-D Magic Eye pictures.

"It's some kind of puzzle! I can't quite read it, though. What does it say?"

He smiled mysteriously. "Portia would kill me if I told you. You'll have to figure it out for yourself. I'm sure you've noticed the portraits on the walls. As you can see, they're not exactly our ancestors."

I grinned at the familiar faces in the gallery. A man in a deerstalker cap smoking a pipe. An elderly woman, her hair done up in a gray knot, knitting, a cat lying on her lap. Aside from Holmes and Miss Marple, I also recognized Nancy Drew, Sam Spade, Charlie Chan, and even Jessica Fletcher.

When I looked back at Levi to continue reading his lips, he seemed to be waiting for my attention before going on. "It's all Portia's idea. I just live here."

"You don't help her manage the place?"

"Well, I've got my own projects. But Portia was kind

enough to let me live here when I had no place else to go, so in return, I try to help out with some of the chores. I manage the books, take calls, things like that."

I studied Levi Coyne as he continued talking about the bed-and-breakfast. I wanted to know more about the brother of the mysterious Jasper Coyne. He appeared to be in his forties, physically fit—at least from the waist up—and not unattractive, despite the two-day-old stubble and a few scars on his face. His hands were nicked around the knuckles and the nails lined in black, like my auto mechanic's hands.

When I realized he'd stopped talking, I tried to cover. I hadn't been lip-reading his last few words.

"I . . . I'm sorry about your brother," I said, changing the subject. It was time to get to the point. His face remained expressionless, but his hands visibly tightened around the arms of his chair.

"It was going to happen sooner or later. He drank too much. And he was careless. When the sheriff told me he fell off his boat and drowned, I wasn't surprised."

Levi didn't seem overly distraught either, I thought.

"Were you close to him?"

"I haven't been for a long time. I used to live with him, on the boat. Back before my accident. But afterwards . . . well, living on the boat wasn't so easy in a wheelchair. So Portia took me in. Guess she still sees me as a brother-in-law."

Brother-in-law? "You mean, Portia was married to Jasper?"

He nodded. "Didn't work out, though. None of his marriages lasted very long. She left him after a few months and bought this place. Fixed it up from nothing. She's done well for herself."

"When was she married to your brother?"

"About twelve years ago. She was his second wife."

And Del Rey was his first.

"You said you didn't really know Del Rey, your brother's first wife."

"No, I didn't see my brother much at the time he met her. Like I said, though, it didn't last long between them either."

"When did Jasper get the houseboat?"

Levi shifted in his chair. "Let's see. After the divorce from Del Rey, he moved in with my dad, who was living on a houseboat on Miwok Lake. Our mom was never around. I was in college, on a scholarship. Jasper helped my dad with his fishing business, until Dad died about ten years later. Then Jasper took over the boat and the business, married Portia, got divorced again. He really started to change after that."

"How?"

"He kept to himself. Began drinking more. Started tossing ashes out at sea full-time, instead of fishing. Bizarre, if you ask me."

I nodded. "What do you know about his sea-scattering business?"

Levi tensed for a moment. "You know, you're asking a lot of questions. What's all this have to do with Del Rey?"

"As I said, she's a friend of mine and I'd like to help her out. There's some question about your brother's ash distribution business." Well, I couldn't tell him everything.

"Like what?"

"I don't know exactly. The sheriff found some of the ashes Jasper was supposed to have scattered in a warehouse. Since some of the ashes were from Del Rey's mortuary, the sheriff thinks there may be a connection to his . . . uh, untimely death. Do you have any idea why your brother might have stored those remains?"

He shrugged. "Mind if I ask you a question for a change?"

"Okay."

"How long have you been deaf?"

This was the second time he'd caught me off guard. Most people don't ask me directly about my hearing loss. I couldn't decide if the question was rude or if I appreciated his straightforwardness.

"Since I was four."

"You speak very well."

"But you still knew I was deaf."

"I've met a few deaf people. When you're disabled, you become a little more sensitive to other people's disabilities. Are you bitter about it?"

"No. I can't remember what hearing is like. Deafness is

all I've really known. It's a little inconvenient at times in a hearing world, but I don't have to worry about noise pollution, barking dogs at night, or rap music."

He laughed. "Good point. Do you ever get asked any stupid questions?"

"All the time," I said. "When one woman found out I was deaf, she asked if I knew braille."

Levi laughed and shook his head.

"Another woman asked me why there was a sign for the word 'noise' when deaf people couldn't hear it anyway."

"Unbelievable."

"How about you? Do you get strange questions?"

"Oh, yeah. Mostly from kids, who don't know any better. They're just curious, especially about my chair. They always want to know how fast it goes. But more than once an adult has asked me if I can still have sex."

"Oh, my God! How rude!"

I swear I couldn't help myself, but I glanced at his lap. It was almost Pavlovian. I met his eyes and could feel myself blush.

He smiled. "I can, by the way. I still have some feeling there."

"I . . . didn't mean to . . ." For the first time in a long time, I was completely flustered.

"It's okay. Really. I think you understand more than most people."

I nodded, still embarrassed by my reflex. It was time to get back to the subject before I made any more blunders. But I found I had one more question to ask. "Do you ever feel bitter?"

"About what happened? Naw, I'm over it. It was a long time ago."

"Do you mind if I ask what happened to you?"

He wheeled his chair to an antique desk and pulled out a bottle of Jack Daniel's. The brothers apparently drank the same whiskey. He held up the bottle as an offer but I declined. Too early in the day for a beer, never mind the hard stuff. After filling his glass, he wheeled around and faced me once again. He took a long swallow, then began.

"It happened about five years ago. I got in a fight. Jasper and I were at this bar, playing pool. We'd been drinking a little. A lot, really. This guy, well, he was a friend of Jasper's then, started shooting off his mouth about Jasper's ex."

"Portia?"

"No, Del Rey. I don't know exactly what happened, but somebody took a swing and then all hell broke loose. This guy hit me with a beer bottle, knocked me unconscious, and I fell backwards down some stairs. When I woke up, my brother was carrying me to his truck. That's about all I remember. I woke up the next day and couldn't feel my legs." He shifted in his seat.

"Jasper didn't take you to the hospital?"

Levi shook his head. "Not at first. He thought I was all right, that I just needed to sleep it off. My God, we were both so drunk. And I think he was worried about being arrested. So he just drove me home and put me in bed. He felt real bad when he realized what had happened, but it wasn't his fault. I was paralyzed the moment I hit the bottom of those stairs in that bar."

"I'm sorry."

Levi shrugged. "The guy who hit me went to prison for five years for attempted manslaughter. And I've gotten active in the rights for the disabled. Built my own customized wheelchair—all-terrain. I can still play most sports. I just can't slide into home."

I was impressed. I'd been deaf for so long, I didn't know what I was missing when it came to sound. But according to the trophies I'd seen on Jasper's mantel, Levi Coyne had once been a champion athlete. It must have been devastating to lose that, and yet, here he was, playing paint ball games, designing state-of-the-art wheelchairs, and working to change things.

"Well, Levi. I appreciate your time." I rose to leave. "And I'm sorry once again for the loss of your brother."

He nodded. "You still thinking about doing an article on the Mystery Mansion? Portia would love that. She's real proud of this place. She should be back soon."

"I'll interview her when this other situation is cleared up."

As I stepped away from the place, I turned back to give it a last look. Tucked off to the side sat a pair of motorcycles and a shiny black classic English taxicab with the name

"Mystery Mansion" printed on the side. If one of the cycles belonged to Portia, I wondered who the other one was for. Her lover?

It wasn't until I was on the road again that I realized Levi had never answered my question about why his brother might have stored those ashes.

Since I was halfway to Angels Camp, I stopped by Sheriff Locke's office before heading back to my own. I wondered if she'd found out anything more about the ashes, and thought it might be a nice chance to get acquainted. I didn't expect her to be as accommodating as Sheriff Mercer, but it was worth a try.

Angels Camp is a quiet town, when the annual frog-jumping festival isn't hopping. The Angels Camp sheriff's office is about the size of a trailer. That's because it is a trailer. Sheriff Locke has no dispatcher or deputy, and works the office alone. When she needs backup, she calls one of the local cops or another county sheriff to help out.

I found her sitting at her small metal desk reading my newspaper when I entered. Without glancing up from her paper, she asked, "Can I help you?" Then she set it down and met my eyes. "Oh, it's you."

"Hello, Sheriff Locke. Reading anything interesting?"

She folded the *Eureka!* and placed it on top of some paperwork. I caught a glimpse of two names before they were obscured by my newspaper: Del Rey Montez and Portia Bryson. How many Portias could there be around here? I figured Sheriff Locke must have made a connection between Jasper's exes.

"Pretty good police blotter. But still too many ads."

I wanted to return the compliment by saying, "Pretty good sheriff's department, but still too many criminals." Instead, I pulled up a chair opposite her so I could read her lips better.

"Miah's doing a piece on kids with guns for the next issue. Got any thoughts on the subject?"

"My views aren't particularly popular in the department, but I don't have a problem with kids who are taught how to use guns properly. I was raised in this area and my dad taught me how to shoot when I was nine. We always had guns in the house, but we knew to respect them."

"What about these kids who are going around shooting up everything? Think their parents are responsible?"

She shrugged. "Personally, I don't think those kids are getting the weapons from their parents."

"Where, then?"

"Guns are like drugs today. Kids just seem to know where to buy them. And the parents don't know a thing about it."

"You think there's some kind of illegal gun dealer around here?"

"Yeah, I do."

"Mind if I have Miah interview you about this, for the article? Sounds like you could contribute some valuable information."

"I don't have anything concrete to offer, but I'm happy to talk about what I do know."

I nodded. "How's the investigation into Coyne's death going?"

She shrugged. "Nothing much yet. At least, nothing I can report to a journalist. Sorry."

"Just thought I'd ask. ME's report come in yet?"

"Not yet."

"I . . . stopped by Angels Camp and met Levi Coyne, Jasper's younger brother. Have you talked with him yet?"

Sheriff Locke nodded. "I went by last night to notify him of his brother's death."

"How did he take it?"

"I don't think there was much love lost between the two of them. Did he say anything to you?"

I thought for a moment and realized he'd said very little about his brother. I summarized the conversation for the sheriff, ending with a mention of the fight.

Sheriff Locke nodded. "God, I'd almost forgotten. It was so long ago—five or six years, wasn't it?"

"Did you know Jasper didn't take his brother to the hospital that night, after he was knocked unconscious and fell down a flight of stairs?"

Sheriff Locke blinked. "I don't recall. Like I said, it's been a few years."

"Did you know the woman he's been living with, Portia Bryson, was once married to Jasper?"

Sheriff Locke's eyes widened. "You found out quite a bit from your little talk. I only just learned that this morning, after doing a little checking."

"Doesn't it seem odd that Levi's been living with his ex-sister-in-law for the past five years?"

She shrugged. "Not really. People around here seem to form all kinds of strange relationships. Gets pretty complicated when you try to figure it all out."

"Speaking of relationships, do you mind if I ask you a personal question?"

"I don't know. Try it and find out."

"You know Sheriff Mercer is recently divorced."

"Yes." Was there a faint blush under those creamy cheeks? "Well, I was wondering if you might want to come to dinner some night at my place. I thought I'd invite the sheriff, too." God, where did that come from? Now I was playing matchmaker? What next? An invitation to a Tupperware party?

"I'd love to. Thank you. What can I bring?"

And she cooks, too. The sheriff was going to love me for this.

I came away from Sheriff Locke's office feeling I had wasted not only the last half hour, but the hour before that, with

Levi Coyne. Had I really learned anything from either of those visits, except that Levi had overcome his disability and Sheriff Locke returned Sheriff Mercer's crush?

Levi had said that Portia would be back soon. Perhaps it was time to pay another visit to the Mystery Mansion.

One of the motorcycles was missing when I arrived. Damn! I'd probably missed her again, I thought, as the raven pecked the front door. I waited a few minutes, then stepped down from the porch trying to force myself not to peek in the curtains.

The door opened and a woman, maybe forty to forty-five, dressed in a "Murder, She Wrote" T-shirt and long floral skirt, stood at the door, eyes wide. Her hair was cut short and dyed jet black—obviously a home job.

"Welcome to Mystery Mansion. I'm Portia Bryson. Do you have a reservation?" Although she forced a smile, her eyes were red-rimmed. Had she been crying?

I stepped forward and offered my hand. "No, actually . . . I'm Connor Westphal. I . . . publish the *Eureka!* newspaper and thought I might do an article on your delightful inn. I was here earlier and I talked to Levi, but he said you were the one that really ran the business, so I wonder if you have a few minutes?" I waited, hoping Levi hadn't told her about our conversation. If he had, she would know I was completely making this up.

Luck was with me. The woman's face brightened slightly. I felt bad about misrepresenting myself, and promised to make good on my offer to do a story on the place. Later.

"Sure. Come on in." Brushing her full skirt back, she opened the door, allowing me to pass. She gave me a ten-minute tour of the downstairs, starting with the rolltop reception desk that Holmes might have used, except this one hid all the modern accoutrements: fax, message machine, computer. Along the wall behind it dangled a row of room keys, each attached to a miniature weapon, except for one connected to a foam floater. I feigned surprise as she pointed out the secret passageways, coded messages, and whimsical portraits.

"It's a wonderful inn, Ms. Bryson. You did all this yourself?" I glanced around for any sign of Levi, but he didn't seem to be around. So far, so good.

"Please, call me Portia. Yes, pretty much. Levi lives with me, and he's been a big help. But the concept was mine, and I did all the finishing touches. I love mysteries, so I thought I'd pour my love of the genre into my inn and make a business out of it."

I asked a few more questions about the place, then tried to figure out how to segue into the more interesting topic of her ex-husband's recent death. She hadn't said a word about him the entire time I'd been there.

"You know, since you're a mystery buff, I wonder what your take is on that collection of ashes they found over in that storage warehouse. I was thinking of writing an article about that, too, but I can't get a handle on it. Any thoughts?"

Portia visibly stiffened, but she said nothing.

I went on, thinking my rambling might stimulate a response from her. "You have heard about it, haven't you? A bunch of cremated remains were hidden there, stacked to the ceiling in boxes. They never would have found them except that the ashes were starting to drift over—"

Portia turned her head, then stood up, as if she heard something in another part of the house. A phone? Or Levi?

"Excuse me a moment, will you?"

I wondered if Levi had overheard us and called her into the other room to blow my cover. While I sat staring into the carpet, I finally figured out the secret code embedded in the pattern. It said, "Redrum." She must have liked Stephen King. I remembered the quote from his book, *The Shining*.

"Did you figure it out?" she said, after reentering the room carrying two glasses of iced tea. I hate iced tea, but I took the proffered glass and set it down on a nearby end table, next to a jeweled dagger. I scanned her for telltale signs that she'd spoken to Levi.

"Redrum. Murder, spelled backwards. Very clever."

She smiled. "Sorry about my disappearance. The telephone—it never stops ringing. Now, where were we? Oh, yes. You were asking about the inn."

Actually, I hadn't been. Nice try, though. "Oh, look, I'm sorry for rambling on about the ashes. It didn't occur to me you might have a relative who'd been cremated . . ."

She waved me off. "No, no. I . . ." She took a sip of her drink. I took a pretend sip of mine. "The ashes. Curious, isn't it?"

I nodded. What did she know about her ex-husband's secret stash? I had to pursue it. "You know, they found the guy who had rented the storage compartment. He lived on a houseboat on Lake Miwok and apparently drowned yesterday. Guess we may never know why he stored those ashes instead of distributing them at sea, like he was supposed to."

She nodded and sipped more tea. "You know, this room has—"

"I believe his name was Jasper Coyne." I watched Portia as I spoke the words. She fastened her gaze on some distant point.

"Portia, you didn't happen to know Jasper Coyne, did you?"

Portia's head jerked to face me. "I thought you came here to do an article on my inn. But you're really here for a story on Jasper, aren't you?"

"Actually, I'm working on both stories—"

"I'm sorry, but I think you should leave." She stood up.

I followed suit. "You were married to him at one time, weren't you? I—"

"Listen, I don't know how you found out about that, but I haven't seen Jasper Coyne for, what, four or five years now."

"But you were married to him. And you took in his brother. Surely you must have—"

She cut me off again. "Listen, Ms. Weston. I only have this to say about Jasper Coyne. I was married to the man a long time ago. It didn't last more than a couple of months. I got rid of his name and took my maiden name back, and I really haven't seen him much since. Now if you'll excuse me, I think we're done here."

I'd blown it. I wasn't going to get anything more from Portia Bryson. "I'm sorry about his death, Ms. Bryson. If there's anything I can do—"

Portia started to respond, then her eyes shifted from mine to a spot behind me. I turned to see what she was staring at. Levi Coyne sat in his wheelchair in the doorway, frowning. I had known it was only a matter of time before he showed up and blew the whistle on my little game. Briefly I wondered where he'd been that he hadn't heard us earlier.

"Levi! You must remember Ms. West—" She turned to me for help.

Levi Coyne wheeled into the room and headed for the concealed bar. Portia winced almost imperceptibly as he removed a bottle of Jack Daniel's from the secret compartment. After pouring a glass, he turned to face us both.

"Of course I do, Connor."

I felt like a kid caught with a handful of stolen candy. I hadn't really done anything wrong, except maybe lying to the bereaved to get information.

"Yes, I . . . I'm sorry. I just wanted to see if . . . I guess I'd better be going—"

I pressed my lips together, fearing I might say something really stupid and make everything even worse, if that was possible. Slinking toward the door, I headed out to my car. I knew the two of them were standing at the window, watching my every move. I didn't even glance back to see if the second motorcycle had returned.

I felt really rotten about misrepresenting myself to the degree I had. I hadn't out-and-out lied, but I had gone there with a purpose than I'd led them to believe.

The car started to chug.

Shit! With all the driving I'd been doing, the Chevy was nearly out of gas. I lucked out. The "Eat Here and Get Gas" station was only a few yards away. I pulled in and began filling the tank with unleaded. The Chevy was a gas guzzler—one of the problems with owning a classic car—and she drank down the liquid like a dry miner at a roaring stream.

I'd just replaced the cap beneath the license plate, when a motorcycle whizzed by. Although the driver was helmeted and covered by a leather jacket, I recognized the colorful skirt peeking out.

I wondered where Portia Bryson was headed. I had to hurry if I wanted to find out.

Thrusting the cash at the attendant, I snatched the change from his hand and hopped into the car. In a matter of minutes I had Portia Bryson in sight. I kept my distance in case she recognized the car in her rearview mirror. Driving around in a red-and-white '57 Chevy Bel Air had its disadvantages when it came to surveillance.

Portia turned the cycle onto the Miwok Lake exit and followed the road to her destination. I pulled in slowly, just keeping her in view, then parked some distance away behind a large scrub brush. I watched as she swung her leg off the cycle and righted the kickstand.

Tugging at her helmet, she set her black hair free, and gave the wild strands a few pulls in an effort to arrange the style. She hung her helmet over one handlebar and glanced briefly from side to side. A second later she ducked under the police line and moved onto the boat's deck.

I got out of the Chevy and followed on foot. It was obvious she was involved in this mess in some way, or she wouldn't have driven out here in such a big hurry. But what was her connection—aside from being Jasper's ex-wife?

Getting out of the car and standing behind the bush, I watched Portia fumble in the purse slung around her shoulder. Apparently she found what she'd been searching for; she pulled it out and jammed it into the front door of the houseboat.

The key attached to the styrofoam floater—Jasper must have given it to Portia.

More curious than cautious, I stepped up to the boat as she disappeared inside. I waited a moment to see if she might come right back out, then I ducked under the police line and onto the deck. Crouching down, I waddled up to the window and, wishing I had a periscope, inched my head up until I could see inside.

I needn't have worried about being seen through the porthole. The glass was coated in so much filth, it no longer served as a window. I had two choices: confront her, and take the chance I'd get knocked off the boat, or wait until she left and try to figure out what she'd been looking for.

With an imaginary flap of my wings, I took the chicken's way out and waited, picking up one of the whiskey bottles that still lay on the deck.

I didn't have to wait long. In less than five minutes, Portia came out the door. She was empty-handed—I guessed she hadn't found what she was looking for. I pulled back around the corner and threw the empty whiskey bottle over the low roof of the houseboat, praying it would hit the stern deck. I wouldn't be able to hear it land, but I hoped I could tell by Portia's reaction if my stunt worked.

It did. Portia Bryson jumped a foot, then scrambled off the boat at a full run. I waited until she'd zoomed off on her motorcycle before I came out of hiding. As I'd hoped, she'd left so fast, she'd forgotten to close the door, let alone lock it.

I was inside in a matter of seconds.

A quick search of the place revealed that nothing much had changed since the last time I'd been there. I knew the sheriff had confiscated most of Jasper Coyne's papers. He'd left only a small collection of odds and ends. And lots of dust.

Jasper Coyne had been a pack rat—about more than just ashes, apparently. His drawers and cupboards were filled with useless objects. A collection of blank postcards were among the most interesting items. Especially when I flipped the cards over and found them all to be from the same alluring vacation spot: the Mystery Mansion.

Odd. I wondered why Portia didn't take them with her when she left? Because they meant nothing? Or because she hadn't found them?

Another drawer contained receipts from years past. Jasper Coyne apparently saved everything from his bar tabs to his grocery store tape. Some of the papers dated back five, ten, even twenty years, including a fishing license, an automobile repair bill, a receipt for a negligee from Frederick's of Hollywood, and a tuition statement from Levi Coyne's university. I wondered if the sheriff was coming back for all this stuff. Or was it all too old to be important?

It was clear I would not be stumbling upon any relevant clues left behind by a careless suspect or clumsy sheriff. Instead, I decided to do what I did best—read body language.

Or houseboat language, so to speak.

Houseboat language can tell you a lot about a person. What it mainly told me was that Jasper was not just a pack rat, he was a pig. There were no clean clothes whatsoever, only piles of dirty overalls and T-shirts strewn about the room. The floors, windows, and bathroom hadn't seen cleaning products since the chemicals had been invented. I had a feeling the smell had grown toxic since my last visit.

The bed, little more than a mattress with a soiled blanket gathered in a wad on top, looked about as comfortable as an army cot, only not as inviting. I shook out the blanket, hoping there was nothing alive inside, and watched a shiny piece of cloth flutter down to the floor.

At my feet lay a pair of women's underpants. I picked them up with the tips of two fingers, trying not to touch them, and realized I'd made an overstatement when I said a pair of women's underpants. This was little more than a scrap of fabric. There was no crotch, no visible means of support, and no way to hide your privates once you put these things on.

But then, they probably weren't worn for long.

It appeared Jasper Coyne had had a little romantic roll in the hay not long ago. I wondered who the lucky woman was.

Certain they were too small to be Del Rey's, I returned

the undies to the blanket so the sheriff could find them on his next visit and they could incriminate someone else. I turned my attention to the rest of the room, searching for more clues to Jasper Coyne's secrets.

But all I saw of interest were Levi's coveted trophies, which still stood lined up along one of the shelves, gathering dust.

Jasper Coyne must have been proud of his athletic brother. It appeared that Levi had received recognition for every major sport, from football to baseball to basketball.

All-around athlete. Now confined to a wheelchair. But according to Levi, he had conquered his self-pity. In fact, he'd gone beyond acceptance to meet the challenges of setting ever-higher goals.

The dates on the trophies spanned four years, then stopped abruptly five years ago, the time of Levi's accident. Same with the ribbons that had been tacked to the wall above the trophies. Hundreds of them, nearly all inscribed "First Place" or "Most Valuable Player" or "Highest Score."

Centered between the six trophies, in a dust-free space where a trophy once stood, was a faded snapshot of three men—Jasper Coyne, his brother Levi, and a man in the middle who looked vaguely familiar. Another brother?

I slipped the picture into my backpack and headed out with a last look around the houseboat, securing the button lock behind me.

I parked the Chevy behind the Penzance Hotel, where my newspaper office—and Dan's office—are housed upstairs, and walked a short distance down Main Street to the sheriff's department. Rebecca Matthews, Sheriff Mercer's elderly dispatcher, welcomed me as I entered. Of course, I would never call her "elderly" to her face. She might slap me or challenge me to arm wrestle.

Underneath her headset, she sported platinum blond hair, a radical change from last week's maroon. At eighty-four, Rebecca refused to grow up, let alone grow old. In fact, she was the one who'd taught me how to skateboard when Miah gave up on me. Her latest passion was apparent—the office was filled with a hand-painted ceramic plates, lining all the windowsills, filing cabinets, and countertops.

"Rebecca! Is this your latest project?"

I held up a large ceramic bowl painted to look like a watermelon. Next to it sat a smaller bowl that resembled a cantaloupe, another appeared to be a giant apple, and next to that, a bowl was painted like an orange. No doubt she wouldn't be done with this undertaking until she ran out of fruit.

"Yeah, Connor, how do you like my fruit collection? I'm thinking of doing vegetables next. Gets boring around here in the sheriff's office you know, between drug busts and sex scandals. Got to have something to occupy my mind and body."

She was being facetious about the drug busts and sex scandals. Too bad. They would have made great headlines. Although the discovery of the ashes—and Jasper Coyne's death—looked promising, I didn't have much to write about yet. If I didn't come up with more soon, next weekend's lead was going to be an in-depth report on Mama Cody's new Cornish meat pie.

So what was up with those ashes?

Sheriff Mercer rolled his eyes when I held up Rebecca's watermelon for his approval. He'd had to put up with a lot of his dispatcher's interests over the years. Last month she was planting terrariums. The month before that she was creating stained glasswork. I admired this woman who refused to rocking-chair her way through old age. Rebecca Matthews preferred rock and roll.

I set the faux watermelon down and sat opposite the sheriff in the interior office, watching him shuffle through his never-ending pile of papers. I thought I caught a glimpse of a colorful brochure under the usual glut of forms, and wondered if it might be information on a health spa or piece of new exercise equipment to combat whatever it was that had him so distracted. After his wife left him, Sheriff Mercer continually looked for new and improved ways to lose weight and tone up. But all I could make out was one-half of a familiar face: a nice-looking square-faced man with white hair and a gentle smile.

Bill Clinton? Nah. Sheriff Mercer was a die-hard Eisenhower Republican. I must have been mistaken.

"Any dirt, Sheriff?" I asked, pulling my eyes from the picture of the presidential look-alike.

"You tell me. I heard you been nosing around over to Sheriff Locke's."

"Did she say that? What a lie! I wasn't nosing around. I just stopped in for some friendly conversation, hoping to get better acquainted. Did she tell you I invited the two of you to dinner?"

"Yeah. What'd you go and do that for?"

"Because. I thought it would be nice to have you both over. Dan and I will cook for you."

"What do you want, C.W.?" The sheriff rubbed his eyes, as if tired of looking at me. I was losing him fast. Time to wake him up.

"Sheriff, I drove by Jasper Coyne's houseboat today, just to check things out—"

"You didn't go in there, did you?" I had his attention now.

"The door's locked! How am I supposed to get in if the door's locked? Besides, there's a police line. You know I'd never cross a police line, Sheriff."

He mumbled something I couldn't make out. I didn't ask for a repeat.

"Anyway, while I was driving by, somebody showed up. I thought you might want to know."

His tired eyes couldn't hide his sudden interest. "Who was it?"

"Portia Bryson. Do you know her?"

"Of course. She's one of Jasper's ex-wives. Runs that Mystery Inn over near Angels Camp."

"The Mystery Mansion. Yeah, I stopped by there, too."

The sheriff frowned. "What on earth for, C.W.? I told you—"

"Wait! She has a key—to the houseboat. She went in there today, while I was watching her, and I think she took something, but I don't know what."

That shut him up for a few seconds.

"You actually saw her go in?"

I nodded. "So what do you know about her, Sheriff?"

"Nothing much. Just what I told you. She's never been in trouble with the law, as far as I know."

"Guess who lives with her over at her Mystery Mansion?" I'd saved the best surprise for last.

"Levi Coyne. Jasper's brother," the sheriff said.

My face fell. It was my last attempt to show him what a great investigative reporter I was. "Yeah, well, did you know . . . there are two motorcycles at her inn?"

I was desperate and he knew it. I hated it when that happened.

The sheriff nodded. "She rides around on that thing all the time. It's a Harley. Bet you didn't know that, Ms. Lois Lane."

Like I cared. "So who rides the other one, Sheriff Andy Taylor?"

"I assume her brother-in-law. Ex-brother-in-law, that is."

"But he's—"

"I know. He's paralyzed. He's got it fixed up so he can ride it. The kickstand operates by a lever, which keeps him steady when he comes to a stop. The rest of the controls are all in his hands. The guy's always trying to improve things for the handicapped. You should see his wheelchair."

I winced at the word "handicapped." People who didn't know better still used that inaccurate term with me. To me, a handicap means there's something in the way that prevents forward progress. A disability means there's a bump in the road that has to be negotiated before progress can continue. In other words, one means "stop," the other means "figure out how to keep going." That's how I saw deafness. As more of an inconvenience than a hindrance. Except when it came to rap music. Then everyone envied me.

"Levi rides that motorcycle? Wow, I hadn't thought of that." When I'd noticed both motorcycles outside the inn, I assumed Portia had a boyfriend who rode the other one."

"Shame on you, C.W., of all people."

He was right. I knew my own disability inside and out, and found there were very few limitations. But when it came to someone else's disability, I could be rather ignorant.

I was wasting my time. The sheriff knew everything I

had to offer, except for the news that Portia had been by the houseboat. And the underpants.

"Are you going to question Portia about breaking and entering?"

"Illegal trespassing."

"Huh?"

"It's not called breaking and entering anymore. If you're going to be a wanna-be cop, at least learn the lingo. Besides, I thought you said she had a key."

"Yes, but, she went under a police line. What about that?"

"C.W., if I arrested everyone who ventured under a police line, you'd be the first to go to jail."

He was right. I stood up to leave.

Sheriff Mercer stretched back in his chair and folded his hands behind his head. "Don't you want to know what the ME said?"

Shit. I sat down. "Okay, what?"

"Arthurlene doesn't think Jasper Coyne drowned by accident. There was plenty of alcohol in his veins, but there was very little water in his lungs."

"But he had that gash on his head, the one that bled on the railing *before* he fell in. He could have slipped, cracked his head, and been dead by the time he hit the water."

"Arthurlene says it was too big to have occurred as the result of an accidental fall."

"You mean Dr. Jackson thinks someone hit him on the head . . . and then pushed him into the water?"

"At this point, she's not ruling out the possibility."

"Does she know what the weapon was?"

"Not yet. A heavy blunt instrument of some kind. Could be anything. We're still looking for potential weapons."

I was so puzzled by this latest news, I left without hinting at Jasper Coyne's recent romantic rendezvous.

Sheriff Mercer was no dummy. Small-town sheriffs have a reputation for being buffoons, too busy eating donuts to figure out what's going on under their chaw-filled jaws. But Sheriff Mercer was meticulous. He took his time to figure things out. He would be in no hurry to make an arrest. He'd investigate Portia's visit to the boat in his own good time, in his own way. And he'd find the underwear.

But what about the weapon? I had a hunch I knew what it was. I figured it wouldn't take long for Sheriff Mercer to notice the dust-free spot on the mantel, either.

I spent the rest of the day catching up on work at the newspaper. E. Clampus Vitus, a pseudomilitary group in the area that promised to help "widders and orphans, especially widders," was planning another Clamp ba be cue and beer brawl. After finishing a final edit on the article, I headed home for a romp with my signal dog Casper, a hot bath with extra bubbles, and a beer of my own. I hadn't seen Dan all day, but he'd be coming by for dinner at seven, if he hadn't forgotten.

My diner-turned-home was a welcome respite from the hectic day. Casper greeted me at the door with her usual tongue-licking reception. I poured her a bowl of gourmet dog food and served it in the large diner kitchen I'd restored to its original fifties look, while I downed a Sierra Nevada.

After refreshments, we went into the back room where I'd set up my living quarters. The large area houses my sofa bed, my TTY telephone, my captioned TV, and a wall full of my comic book collection. After kicking off my shoes and pulling off my clothes, I slipped into a bubble bath and read another chapter in Rick Riordan's San Antonio detective series. When I was clean and my skin had taken on the consistency of a very old prune, I changed into a fresh white T-shirt and comfortable jeans, then plopped down on the couch and sorted through a recent cache of Little Lulu, Richie Rich, and Heckle and Jeckle comics while waiting for Dan. I'd even found one of the first Beagle Boys recently, which I'd planned to hang in my bathroom.

At seven-thirty there was still no sign of Dan, so I decided to call him and see if he'd forgotten. Placing the receiver from the telephone into the coupler of the TTY, I dialed Dan's number. I paused, waited for a response, then read the words that flashed across my screen in bright red letters.

"Dan Smith here. That you, Connor? GA" It was my turn to "go ahead."

Unlike deaf people, who use all caps while typing, hearing people tend to use standard upper and lower case. I conform to the caller.

"Who else do you know that owns a TTY, I'd like to know? GA"

"Tons of people. I've got a lot of deaf friends you don't know about. What's up? Anything new on the death of that ash guy? GA"

"Ash guy? You have a way with words, Dan Smith. Want to come work for my newspaper? GA"

"Oh yeah. I'd love to write up recipes for Jell-O Surprise, or maybe do an in-depth report on Flat Skunk's latest bait controversy: 'Should we euthanize the worms before we hook them?' GA"

"Sounds great. You've got the job. In fact, why don't you bring a sample of your Jell-O Surprise when you come for dinner tonight? You haven't forgotten, have you? GA"

There was a longer-than-usual pause before the words appeared on the screen. "Nope, just lost track of the time. Sorry. I'm starving. You're making Westphal Hangtown fry, right? I hear oysters are an aphrodisiac. GA"

"You don't need anything more to get you in the mood. I think I'll substitute tuna. GA"

"I thought you said shrimp—"

Before the Go Ahead signal appeared, the glow of the red screen flickered and died.

And so did all the lights in my diner.

Casper?" I called out to nothingness. I felt like I'd fallen in a black hole. I swung my arms wildly, searching for my dog.

Something touched my leg. Again. And again.

"Casper!"

Her swinging tail swiped my calf. I bent down to hold her, but she struggled against my grasp, too agitated to be calmed. I felt her jaw snapping savagely.

"Casper, it's okay," I said, trying to steady myself more than my dog. I could feel the sweat break out on my back and forehead. "It's just the lights . . . and the phone . . ."

Although I couldn't hear her, I could feel Casper's seventy-pound body lurch as she barked to defend her home.

Against what?

My breathing double-timed as I sped through the possibilities.

I stood up, keeping one hand on Casper as I blindly explored the room. I tripped over something—my shoes?—on my way to the junk drawer next to my sofa bed. Reading the contents with my hand, I found what I'd been searching for—a heavy, two-foot-long metal flashlight. Snatching it up, I prayed for live batteries as I flicked it on.

Nothing happened.

I rapped it against the butt of my hand, the same way I fix most mechanical breakdowns.

Thank God! Light.

Frantically, I sent the beam around the room. The only thing moving was Casper, still snapping and jumping around like a mad dog. She was facing the far side of the room, her head moving furiously as she barked.

Abruptly, she stopped. She stood stiff and alert, ears peaked, her usual gentle grin pulled back in a tight grimace.

Then just as suddenly, she began the angry dance again. But this time she faced the back wall.

The only thing I could figure was that someone was out there. Casper could somehow sense—or hear—the movements through the wall.

Armed with my flashlight, I moved into the bathroom and stepped up on the tub rim so I could see through the tiny screened window. Holding up the light, I shone it around the dark backyard looking for any sign of movement. But I couldn't see anything in the brush, or beyond, in the inky landscape. There's nothing like the solid blackness of a country night to remind a person how truly alone she is. I'd liked the fact that there weren't any other houses or businesses near the diner when I'd first moved in. But there were times, after darkness fell, when I felt isolated, and vulnerable. Like tonight.

I stepped off the tub and slowly moved back into my living area. Casper had resumed her agitated movements once again—but this time she was facing the left wall.

Someone—or something—was circling my diner.

I shivered, standing rooted to the spot. I nearly had to force myself to breathe. I hoped Dan had realized the TTY was not functioning and was on his way over.

But I couldn't count on him.

I looked back at Casper. She was no longer barking wildly or swinging her tail like a snapping rope. She sat calmly on her haunches, tossing out an occasion bark, her tongue hanging nearly to the floor.

After a few more seconds of stillness, I took a breath and tried to relax. Maybe whatever it was, was gone.

"Come on, girl. Let's get you some water. Looks like the action is over."

Still wary, but trusting Casper's instincts, I followed her through the shadows made by the flashlight into the diner kitchen, my eyes constantly darting around the room. I refilled Casper's bowl of water, then helped myself to a glass, hoping it would give me the courage to take a look outside. Maybe, whatever it was—an animal?—had left footprints.

Or tire marks.

I refilled my glass—one last attempt to stall—and gulped the water down. Flashlight in hand and dog at my side, I cracked open the front door, which was still chained, and peeked out. The porch light was off, so I could see very little. But at least I found no one standing at my door waiting to grab me. I was fairly certain, based on Casper's calm demeanor, that whoever had come around was gone.

I unhooked the chain and slowly opened the door, my flashlight raised to break an unfamiliar skull should one appear.

Nothing.

I stepped cautiously onto the porch and scanned the deserted road and driveway with the flashlight. Nothing moved except a few treetops caught by the warm night breeze.

Staring into the darkness, I decided to wait and search the premises more thoroughly when I had more light—and some official company, such as the sheriff. Right now, all I wanted to do was get in my Chevy and drive to the sheriff's office.

I had just turned back to retrieve my keys when I stopped short. The flashlight beam allowed me a good look at the exterior of the front door. It still stood as I'd left it—ajar. But even in the dim light, the sight made my heart race.

The door was covered with blood-red splotches. For a second, I thought it *was* blood, and my stomach clenched. But as I shined the light over the door, and then the front of the diner, I realized what had happened.

Someone had attacked my home with a paint pellet gun.

I jumped as a bright light was reflected from the front of the diner. Car lights. I tensed and turned to see who had pulled up, hoping it was someone I knew, not someone returning to finish the job. But I was blinded by the brilliant glare. Holding my flashlight at the ready, I backed toward the front door, ready for fight or flight.

A dark figure emerged from the driver's side of the vehicle. As he stepped into the light, I saw his face.

Relief poured over me like water.

"Dan!"

"Connor. You all right?" I could barely make out his lips in the glow of the headlights. If he didn't say those words exactly, it was something close.

I rushed up to meet him, Casper close at my side. I gave him a kiss and Casper gave him a tongue bath. I wanted to give Dan a tongue bath too, but my mouth was too dry from fear.

"What happened to your diner?" Dan said, staring at the new paint job.

"What, you don't like it?" I managed to say, trying to sound braver than I felt.

"It reminds me of a Jackson Pollock, *Mad* magazine style. A little heavy on the red, though. Somebody trying to tell you something, Connor?"

"I'm an expert in body language, not paint language, but I'd say yes. There's definitely a message behind this. Unless it's been done to every place along this road. See anything unusual as you drove up?"

Dan shook his head. "No, but I wasn't really checking. Let's have a look around. Can't see much in the dark, but you never know."

Casper and I followed him around the side of the diner. Sure enough, that wall was covered with splashes of red, too. Lots of emotion, but no sense of design.

Circling around the back and the other side, we saw more of the same. Casper must have heard the shooter moving around the diner, blasting away at all four walls.

Dan scanned the area with his flashlight, focusing the beam on a metal box attached to the side wall. He moved in to get a closer look. In a matter of seconds, I could see beams of light shining through the windows of the diner.

"Circuit breaker was shut off. I just reset it." He knelt down. "And your phone wires were cut. You'll have to get the phone company out in the morning to repair them."

I always thought it would be awfully easy for anyone to shut off someone else's power. Even I knew where the circuit breaker was and how to operate it.

"How come nobody locks these things?" I asked.

"I guess so the utility companies can read the meter without too much trouble."

I shivered. That's got to change.

"Did you call Sheriff Mercer?" Dan asked.

I shook my head. "Phone's dead, remember? That's why the TTY shut off."

"I forgot you don't have a cell phone. Thought everyone did. I'll use mine and let him know. But I doubt if he'll come out until morning. There's not much to see in the dark."

Dan retrieved his phone from the car and followed Casper and me into the diner. The sheriff apparently wasn't in. I could tell Dan was leaving a message by the nonstop monologue. In the meantime, I made us mochas and cooked up the promised Hangtown fry as therapy.

"Who do you think did this, Connor?" Dan asked, after dinner was over and we were settling onto my sofa bed. I had filled him in on my recent activities while we ate, and now he held the "Bitch in 0–60 seconds" mug in one hand and my "Koko's Art" mug in the other.

"Maybe Koko?" I suggested, nestling in beside him and retrieving my mug.

"Who's Koko?" he asked.

"She's the signing gorilla from Stanford. Now that she's tackled sign language, she's marketing her paintings on coffee mugs and T-shirts to make money for her Gorilla Land home on Maui. I have the matching shirt, too."

"It does kind of look like those splatters of paint on your diner." He smiled, but he was trying to force me to be serious. "Can you think of anyone who has a grudge against you?"

"I really don't know. I haven't done anything to cause someone to destroy my property."

"What about Levi Coyne?"

"But why? All I did was ask him a few questions."

"Jasper Coyne's ex-wife, Portia?"

"Not a chance. I'm sure she didn't know I followed her to the boat."

"Maybe it was someone you don't know is involved yet. And if that's the case, you're at a great disadvantage. Everyone in town knows you're a reporter investigating this thing. It's possible there's someone out there who doesn't like your snooping around."

"Dan, it's not as if they were trying to kill me or anything. I mean, all they did was shoot up the diner with paint. I can hose it off in the morning. Maybe it was just kids running around with paint ball guns, looking for a fresh target, and my diner was handy."

"Well, I'm staying the night. I know you want your space, or whatever, but you're not going to be alone tonight. So let's make up the bed and get some sleep. We'll talk to the sheriff in the morning."

While he unfolded the sofa bed, I got out the blankets and threw them over the Underdog sheets that were already wrapped around the mattress. I left for the bathroom to change into my Cat in the Hat sleep shirt, and found Dan under the covers when I returned. I knew he hadn't brought pajamas—he didn't own any. The thought of what was under those sheets distracted me from the earlier terror.

I slipped in next to him and we wrapped up together, caressing one another for a few minutes, not saying anything. Then the lip-reading began—no words, just lips—followed by more body language. We didn't stop communicating for at least an hour.

The sheriff frowned when I walked into his office bright and early the next morning.

"Did you get Dan's message?" I asked without the usual pleasantries.

"Huh?"

I repeated the question. It was getting to be a habit.

"Yeah, I got it this morning. The message was kinda fuzzy. I think there's something wrong with the machine. Anyway, it sounded like you said someone painted your diner? I was just about to head out there. Been a little busy with this Jasper Coyne–Del Rey thing, you know."

"My diner wasn't *painted*. It was shot up with paint guns!"

The sheriff blinked at me. No wonder he didn't come running over to investigate. He misunderstood the message.

"And just what do you mean by 'this Del Rey thing'?" I continued. "There is no Del Rey thing!"

The sheriff sat back in his chair, looking tired. I could see the "Now look, lady" attitude he was about to cop.

"Now look, C.W., I know she's your friend. She's my friend, too. But Peyton—Sheriff Locke, that is—thinks Del Rey is more involved than she's letting on."

"And how's that, Sheriff?"

"Calm down. If you're too emotionally involved, then you'd just better back off."

"*I'm not emotionally involved,*" I said, then forced myself to relax. I took a deep breath. "I'm not emotionally involved. I'm just concerned about Del Rey."

"We all are. But you got to understand. Del Rey has no alibi for the time when Jasper Coyne died. And she was bitter about his treatment of their son, Andrew."

"But that doesn't even come close to—"

He cut me off with a lift of his hand. He looked like a traffic cop holding up a line of cars. "Sheriff Locke still thinks Del Rey was paying Jasper blackmail money."

"What do you mean?"

Sheriff Mercer shook his head. "Locke found more evidence that Del Rey's been making payments to Jasper on a regular basis, not just a couple of times."

"But I thought Del Rey explained all that."

"These payments are not only way above a reasonable amount for the distribution of the ashes, but they're too much to call 'helping him out in his time of need.' "

"Well, I still don't think she'd do anything illegal—or stupid."

The sheriff paused. He looked uncomfortable as he said his next words. "And then there's the panties."

You found them!"

The sheriff looked at me. "You knew about the panties?"

I blinked. "No, you must have misunderstood me. I said, you found some? I was going to ask where. Tell me about them."

Sheriff Mercer continued to eye me suspiciously, but he let it pass. "Sheriff Locke and I went back over to Jasper's boat this morning, after you told me about Portia snooping around. Found some ladies' panties wrapped up in the blanket on Jasper's bed."

"Wow. Whose are they?"

"Sheriff Locke thinks they're Del Rey's."

"That's ridiculous! Did you even look at them? Del Rey's a size—" Uh-oh. I'd said too much. "You're going to have them analyzed, right?"

He eyed me. "Don't suppose you'd know where they came from?"

"I have no idea! He could have been sleeping with anyone."

"Calm down, C.W. I meant, do you have any idea what store they came from? I thought maybe you owned a pair like that."

I'd have slapped him if I hadn't been laughing so hard. "Oh, yeah, can you see me in a pair of those—I mean, what did they look like?"

"Give it up, C.W. Why didn't you tell me about the panties?"

"First of all, women don't call their underpants 'panties.' Men call them that."

"What do you call them?"

"Underpants!"

"Okay, well why didn't you tell me you found them, instead of making up that story about Portia being out there?"

"Portia *was* out there. She happened to leave the door open and I just went in for a moment to see if she touched anything."

"And you found the panties . . . er, underpants."

"If there was enough of them to call them that."

"So where *do* you think they came from? What store?"

"How would I know? I don't wear stuff like that."

"Yes you do. I saw your underwear drawer one time, remember?"

I blushed. He was right. Someone had broken into my diner and fooled around with my underwear, and I'd had to have the sheriff come and check out my drawers, literally.

"Well, I get my underwear from Victoria's Secret, if you must know. But those things look like they came from Frederick's of Hollywood. Mail order. Why?"

"Just part of the investigation."

"Like hell it is! You're thinking of buying some, aren't you? For a certain sheriff . . ."

"Cut it out, C.W. Are we done now?"

"I want to know why you two still think Del Rey is a part of this in some less-than-honest way."

"Because of the money she's been paying Jasper."

"There are a billion reasons why Del Rey could have been sending money to her ex-husband. That doesn't make her involved in anything—"

I stopped ranting. I realized I had lost the sheriff's attention once again. He was studying a spider on his desk.

"Sheriff!"

He glanced up, looking almost startled. "Sorry, C.W. What were you saying?"

"Sheriff, is something wrong? You haven't seemed yourself lately. Is something on your mind?"

"Huh?"

I rephrased the question and spoke up, thinking maybe I was talking too softly. "I said, what is up with you?"

He shook his head. "Nothing. Just all that's been happening."

"What about my diner? Are you going to come look—"

The sheriff glanced past me and I turned around. In the doorway stood Sheriff Peyton Locke. Was that a little more blush on her cheeks today? I looked back at the sheriff and caught him tucking in the back of his shirt.

"Peyton! Come on in." He stood to greet her—something he never did for me.

"Hello, Elvis—Sheriff Mercer. Connor."

I nodded, then watched their conversation bounce back and forth as if I were viewing a pogo stick tournament. About the time I started to get a neckache trying to follow their speech, Sheriff Locke asked to see Sheriff Mercer alone.

"Sure. I need a break anyway," he answered. "How about a cup of coffee at the Nugget? You'll excuse us, won't you, C.W.?"

"But Sheriff, what about my diner and—?"

"I'm sure your dog will be fine."

I'm sure your dog will be fine? I didn't say "dog." I said "diner."

"I'll have my deputy take a look at your place this afternoon. After all, the vandalism has been done."

And with that, he escorted Sheriff Locke out the door.

I sat there for a few more minutes, trying to figure out what to make of Sheriff Mercer's suspicions about Del Rey. Or were they Sheriff Locke's suspicions and Sheriff Mercer was under her evil spell? With all the mistakes he'd been making, he had to be under some kind of spell.

With a quick glance toward Rebecca, who was busy talking on her headphones while trying to glaze a ceramic cauliflower, I leaned over the sheriff's desk and shuffled a

few of the papers. Maybe he'd left some evidence on his
desk that explained why he thought Del Rey was being
blackmailed.

Feeling like a sneaky kid in her mother's purse, I slid
some stuff around and tried to spot anything that looked
important. Most of the papers were standard police forms
that had nothing to do with Jasper Coyne. The sheriff always seemed inundated with paperwork. There were a few
stolen bike reports, a missing cat, a broken window at the
He's Not Here bar.

I moved deeper into the pile.

At the very bottom, hidden beneath the stack of official-
looking papers, was that damned picture of Bill Clinton.

Did Sheriff Mercer's recent odd behavior have something to do with the ex-president? I slid the photo out from
under the pile.

Suddenly it all came together. The reason Sheriff Mercer had been acting so . . . distracted. The lack of response
to some of my comments, as if he wasn't paying attention.
The countless repetitions I'd had to make. The blank look
in his face when I'd started a new subject.

The picture of the smiling politician was featured on a
flashy tri-fold brochure. Inside was an ad for the Presidential Hearing Aid 2000.

Just like Bill Clinton, who recently came out of the
closet as a hearing-aid wearer, and many others who were
getting on in years, Sheriff Mercer was losing his hearing.

I headed for the newspaper to try to get some work done.
Sheriff Mercer was obviously in denial about his hearing
loss, and it was something we needed to discuss. However,
now was not the time. At present, Sheriff Mercer was pre-
occupied with his investigation, not to mention Sheriff
Locke.

I peeked in on Dan at his office and found him at his
desk, rummaging through a stack of library books.

"Hey, Connor. About time you showed up for work."

I grinned as I sat across from him. My smile faded as I
scanned the titles of his research texts. *Dealing with Death.*
Funeral Planning for Friends and Family. Cremains of the

Day. And my favorite: *The American Way of Death* by Jessica Mitford. That book had changed the way I viewed the funeral business forever.

"Planning a party? Or taking up a new hobby?" I asked, snatching a bite of his smeared bagel and sipping a gulp of his egg cream soda. His New York habits would never die.

"Just checking on a few things."

"I don't suppose this has anything to do with those ashes?"

He shrugged.

"Anything new on your brother's remains?"

He flipped closed a book. "Not much. What's up with you?"

"The usual. Annoying the sheriff. Procrastinating at work. Recovering from incredible sex. Wondering what to do next for Del Rey."

"How's the recovery going?"

"I need a checkup."

"Come to Dr. Smith. Let me place my stethoscope on your—"

I laughed and missed his last word. Damn! But the thought of his stethoscope on my . . . "Doctor! You're making my heart race. Stop!"

He reached over, slipped his hand under my shirt, and felt my heart. It went into hyperdrive from his touch. I leaned over and kissed him. "We'll play doctor tonight. Right now, I've got to get back to work. Are you finding anything in those books of yours?" I stood up.

"Nothing yet. Just trying to learn about the process so I can get a handle on why Jasper Coyne might have done what he did. It's all so odd."

"Speaking of odd, have you noticed the way Sheriff Mercer has been acting lately?"

"Yeah."

"Do you know what's going on with him?"

"It's obvious."

My mouth dropped open in surprise. "You know?"

"He's in love."

"Oh, duh. That's not what I meant. There's something else going on."

"What's that?" Dan said, taking a swig of what I now considered my egg cream soda.

"He's going deaf."

It was Dan's turn to drop his mouth.

"You're kidding."

"Nope. He has all the signs. He misses words or sometimes whole sentences. He asks for repetition. He tells me I'm not talking loud enough and to speak up. And he seems disconnected."

While Dan thought about that, I finished the bagel before he could take it back.

"That's not good."

"What do you mean?" I asked, feigning anger. "I'm deaf. It works for me."

"Yeah, but you haven't spent the last sixty years hearing. This is a big deal for someone who isn't used to a disability. He's likely to go through those seven stages of acceptance I read about in what's-her-name's book, *On Death and Dying*."

"Kübler-Ross."

"What?"

"Don't tell me you're going deaf, too. I said, Kubler-Ross. Elisabeth Kübler-Ross."

"Yeah, that's her. I was just reading that the phases you go through are similar for everyone when they face death or some other traumatic experience. First you go through shock, then anger, then denial, then you finally accept it."

"You missed a few steps."

"Yeah, I forget the other ones. Anyway, you get my point."

"You may be right. I've been noticing his odd behavior for some time, but couldn't put my finger on it. If he's in denial, he may not even really believe it himself yet. Except for the fact that I found an ad for a hearing aid—the Presidential 2000 model. Maybe he's coming out of the denial stage. But he hasn't said anything to me, of all people."

"I don't blame him. He's probably terrified."

"Of not hearing?"

"Not just that. He's probably worried about losing his job."

"He can't be fired. It's an elected position."

Dan shrugged. "True, but if the community loses confidence in his ability to perform his office, they could vote him out. Not everyone understands that deaf and hard-of-hearing people can do any job that a hearing person can do."

I thought about this for a minute, while taking another sip of his egg cream. Odd-tasting stuff. Why was I drinking it, anyway? I looked around for a place to spit it out and could only find the cat dish. I was tempted. And where was Cujo, the attack cat Dan had inherited? Probably lurking behind the filing cabinet, waiting to kill and eat my foot.

"Well, you're right about one thing. I've never thought about the limitations of becoming deaf. My parents always taught me I could do anything. I was naive enough to believe it."

A light from the hallway bounced into the room. My phone light next door was blinking.

"Gotta run!" I dashed out of the room, jammed the key in my lock and shoved open the door.

A kaleidoscope of colors made my head spin.

"Oh, shit!"

I backed out and returned to Dan's office.

"Would you do me a favor?" I said, standing in his doorway. It was all I could do to keep from trembling openly.

He looked up, obviously surprised to see me back so soon.

"Right here? Right now?" He gestured to his desk.

I ignored his innuendo. "Would you call the sheriff for me?"

"What's the matter? You throwing me over for a man in uniform?"

"Maybe I will if you don't stop kidding around. Come here. I want to show you something."

"Now you're talking." Dan followed me to my office door. I opened it for him and stood back to allow him a full view. By now the phone light had stopped blinking.

"Wow!"

That was all he said, after seeing that my office was riddled with dozens of multicolored paint splatters.

Didn't you hear anything?" I asked Dan, as if the rainbow vandalism was his fault. "I mean, don't these paint ball guns make some noise?"

"They make plenty of noise. And I would have heard them if I'd been next door when they were shooting up your place. But I'll bet they did this last night, too."

I knew that. I just wanted to vent my frustration. I stepped in for a closer look. At first, the office massacre seemed haphazard. Some of the paint splatters were direct hits, but most were not. The back of my chair looked like a bull's-eye, but paint had only grazed the side of my computer screen. The framed Little Lulu comic book had caught some spray that hit the wall, and Miah's chair was highlighted in yellow dots. Yet the bookcase was heavily wounded, especially my AP style book and a couple of Nancy Drews from my collection. My favorite one, *The Secret of the Tolling Bell,* had survived unscathed, thank God. I pulled it from the shelf and held it as if it were the last book on earth.

"Are your Nancy Drews okay?" Dan asked.

"Most of them. I hope I can clean the paint off the rest. A couple look ruined, though."

"I can lend you a couple of Hardy Boys to fill in until you get them replaced," he offered.

I smiled. "Thanks, but those two boys are no match for Nancy."

I started to sit down, exhausted from looking at the mess, and realized my chair seat was stained. The paint had probably dried, but I didn't feel like testing it. Instead, I slid to the floor, cuddling my book.

"I'll call Sheriff Mercer." Dan started to dial but I raised a hand to stop him.

"He's not at the office. He's at the Nugget, flirting with Sheriff Locke."

"Rebecca will beep him for me." While Dan reported the information to the dispatcher, I scanned the room from my spot on the floor and noticed something interesting.

Several of the shots had hit underneath the two chairs.

God, who could have done this? I thought, overwhelmed at the message someone was trying to send me. It seemed to be getting more personal.

While Sheriffs Mercer and Locke investigated my office, Dan and I stepped into the hall to give them room. Sheriff Mercer still suspected kids were behind it, but I wondered if it might be related to my nosing around in the Jasper Coyne murder.

"How'd they get in here, Sheriff?" I asked.

Sheriff Locke pointed to the doorknob. "Jimmied the lock. Easy to do on these old-fashioned doors. Better update your security system. Looks like things are escalating. And you seem to be the primary target. Nobody else has reported anything like this."

I bent over for a closer look at the lock. Sure enough, there were tiny scratches. But I'd made half the marks just trying to get my own key inserted. How could Sheriff Locke really tell? Some kind of cop secret, I guessed.

As the two departed, Sheriff Mercer gave me a last warning to secure my home and office and watch my back. I returned to my empty office while Dan disappeared down the hall. I figured he was headed for the restroom. What I didn't figure was all the stuff he'd come back with. A bucket of water, a mop, a sponge, a couple of old towels, and some Mr. Clean.

"Ready to go to work?" he said. I wanted to give him a hug, but I hugged the mop instead and set about cleaning the room that someone had used for a canvas.

Two hours later Dan and I were sitting with mochas and BLTs at the Nugget, still trying to second-guess the intruder's motive and identity. When we hit another dead end and my brain was too tired to pursue the matter, I changed the subject.

"So you read the Hardy Boys when you were a kid?"

Dan nodded. "Had the whole collection. But my mom sold them all at a garage sale when I left for the police academy. I've never forgiven her for that."

"Which one were you?"

Dan looked at me blankly.

"Frank or Joe? Who did you identify with more?"

He laughed. "Both, actually. Frank cause he was smart, always took his time to think things through. Joe because he was cool, loved to take action, always ready to blast ahead."

"Aha!"

"Which one did you like?" Dan asked.

"Both. I liked Frank cause he was hot. I liked Joe cause he was a babe."

A shadow fell over the table. I glanced up.

"You talking about me again, C.W.?"

Sheriff Mercer scooted in beside me. I would have preferred he sit across from me so I could read him better, but apparently real men don't sit next to other real men. Not in Flat Skunk, anyway.

"So you hear me clearly if I call you a babe, but you don't hear me when I tell you my diner has been shot with paint?" I stared at the Sheriff.

Sheriff Mercer frowned. "I always hear you, C.W. Unless you mumble, which you've been doing a lot lately."

I continued to stare at the sheriff. He began to squirm.

"What?" he asked, his frown deepening.

I glanced at Dan, who looked away, obviously not wanting to get involved in the upcoming confrontation. He pulled some bills from his pocket and slid out of the booth.

"I'll leave you two to discuss your business. I've got some work to catch up on. See you later, Connor. Bye, Sheriff."

The sheriff turned to face me. "What's on your mind, C.W.? You got something to say? Spit it out."

I turned my head and deliberately spoke to the wall. "On the contrary, Sheriff. I think you have something to say to me. About the ad I found on your desk."

I faced him again, in time to see him say: "What? Would you speak up? I can't hear you."

"Exactly."

It took him half a second to realize what I meant. His face flushed a deep red, and he suddenly seemed to find Dan's empty mocha mug fascinating.

"Sheriff?"

He looked up. "You've been snooping around my desk again, haven't you, C.W.? You saw the brochure. Well, my desk contains official business. I could arrest you for trespassing. I could—"

"Knock it off, Sheriff. Tell me about your hearing loss."

The sheriff ducked his head, then surreptitiously glanced around the room.

"Hush, C.W., will you? Someone might hear you!"

"Well you don't—at least half the time. Tell me what's going on. Of all people, I'm the one you should be able to confide in about this, Sheriff."

He flapped his hands to quiet me. "Okay, okay. But keep it down." He squirmed a little more, then signaled Jilda for my check. I had apparently spoken too loudly, even for a man with hearing loss. A few heads at the surrounding tables turned, but quickly lost interest when they realized I had nothing further to say.

Except one man, sitting at the counter. Chunker Lansky, Del Rey's new handyman.

Although I couldn't see his face, I could tell by his body language he was paying attention to my conversation with the sheriff. His head was turned slightly toward us, and he'd stopped eating the plateful of food in front of him.

I nodded toward him, alerting the sheriff. Chunker caught the signal. Stuffing a grimy hand into the pocket of his overalls, he pulled out a wad of wrinkled dollars and some change. He spread the money on the counter, adding it up carefully. Reclaiming a few extra coins, he stood and left the diner without looking back. His Hangtown fry was untouched.

Sheriff Mercer and I watched him shuffle past the outside window with a quick glance in our direction. He tried to make it seem casual, but we both knew he was checking us out, too.

"What's up with him?" I asked.

The sheriff frowned again. "This isn't for your newspaper, yet, C.W. If you're willing to go off the record, I can tell you a little. But if I read any of this in the *Eureka!*, it'll be the last bit of police information you'll ever receive, understood?"

I nodded. "Come on, come on. Tell me!"

The sheriff ran his tongue under his lip and glanced around for eavesdroppers. "All right. I ran a check on Chunker Lansky. He has a record. He was just released from Folsom Prison a few days ago. Got a parole officer in Angels Camp keeping an eye on him."

"What was he in for?" I pictured the guy burglarizing a fast-food joint or stealing a fancy car.

"Attempted manslaughter."

I sat up. "Whoa. I would never have guessed."

"It was five years ago. Prison can take a lot out of you. Anyway, I'm supposed to get a full report faxed to me this morning. Now, the only reason I'm telling you this is 'cause I want you to keep an eye on Del Rey. As soon as the report comes in, I'm going to go talk to her, let her know about this guy. If you want to take a walk to my office, I'll check and see if it's come in."

I was out of my seat before he finished his sentence.

Sheriff Mercer turned to face me as we headed down the street toward the station. It's tricky, walking and lip-reading at the same time. I nearly stepped off the wood-slatted sidewalk.

"Tell me about your hearing loss," I said, now that I had the chance to ask him without an audience.

"All right, all right. It's true. I haven't been hearing as well as I used to. Too many gunshots without ear protection, too much Elvis Presley at full blast in my youth, too much noise pollution in general, I guess. Anyway, doc says I have a forty percent loss in my right ear, and a twenty-five percent loss in my left."

I nodded, encouraging him to go on. I knew it wasn't easy for him to talk about. Watching his lips intently, I bumped into a couple of tourists carrying bags from Aunt Tickwittie's antique store. I brushed off the shoulder slam, missing his last few words.

"Are you worried about losing your job?" I asked.

Apprehension was clearly written on his face.

"The position of county sheriff is elected, you know. If I can't do my job because I can't hear, people won't trust me anymore, and they won't vote for me come Election Day. You know folks around here don't understand handicaps the way you do, C.W." He sounded just like Dan.

"First of all, it's not a handicap. A handicap is something you can't overcome—like a biased attitude, not a hearing loss. And I really don't see how it will interfere with your ability to function fully as a police officer."

"What about answering the phone?"

"You can get an amplifier that fits onto the receiver."

"What if I misunderstand somebody and make a big mistake? I've already made a few minor ones, but thank God I haven't done anything really disastrous."

"There are classes, books, videos, that will help you learn to make up for your hearing loss. I wrote a couple of articles for the *Chronicle* on presbycusis—elderly hearing loss."

"Oh, now I'm not only losing my hearing, I'm *elderly*."

"Sorry, I meant 'late onset hearing loss.' Anyway, you'll learn to keep your eyes on the speaker and how to find the person who's talking in a multiple conversation, things like that. Kind of like how to fill in the blanks, which isn't too different from police work, really."

"I suppose . . ."

"And you'll learn to explain to people that you have a hearing loss. You have to ask them to speak more slowly, to face you, and make sure you've understood them."

"I can't do that—"

"You can, and you will. We'll work together on some techniques I learned from my speech therapist. And we'll check out that hearing aid you've been looking at. They've got some new digital ones that are supposed to be extremely sensitive."

The sheriff shook his head. "I hate the idea of wearing a hearing aid, C.W."

"Why, Sheriff? If it will help you hear better?"

" 'Cause, like you said, it means getting old. Well, not in your case. But for me, it's a symbol that I'm not as young as I used to be. And I hate that."

I nodded. I promised to say no more about it, after Sheriff Mercer promised to visit a hearing aid dealer with me sometime next week. But I also decided to write an article for the *Eureka!* on the subject of hearing loss. It was time to educate the gold country public.

Sheriff Mercer entered the office and hung up his jacket.

"Sheriff, you got a fax," Rebecca called from behind the dispatcher's desk. She was painting grapes.

"Thanks, Rebecca," he said, heading for the fax machine. He lifted the paper from the tray and read over the information.

"What does it say?"

"According to this police report, Chunker Lansky was arrested at a bar in Angels Camp. He admitted he'd been drinking heavily and got into an argument. He supposedly knocked some guy out, although he denies that part."

The sheriff glanced at a second faxed sheet, then handed it to me. It was a copy of Chunker Lansky's mug shot, front and side, with a long series of numbers across the bottom, just like in the Beagle Boys comics. But this wasn't one of Walt Disney's creations. It was a photo of a scruffy, long-haired convict who barely resembled the handyman at Del Rey's mortuary. In fact, he looked just like the guy in the photograph I'd taken from Jasper's mantel. The man standing between the two brothers.

"What's Del Rey doing hiring an ex-con? Do you think she doesn't know about his record? Del Rey does have a soft heart."

"That's not all. Oh, you're gonna love this, C.W." The sheriff grinned smugly.

I waited for the punch.

"The guy he knocked unconscious? Seems he fell down

some stairs and ended up with a C-four break in his spinal column. When he woke up, he couldn't move his legs."

My stomach tightened. The sheriff met my wide eyes.

"Looks like Chunker Lansky's the one responsible for Levi Coyne's paralysis."

"Where are you going?" I said to the sheriff, as I watched him slip into his official jacket and hat. The gunbelt remained in place around his waist.

"I got business to do, C.W."

"Are you're going to Del Rey's now? To warn her?" I was thinking about Chunker and how he'd watched Courtney that day. Del Rey had never responded to my message about that.

He said nothing.

"Don't pretend you don't hear me. I'm very familiar with that trick and it won't work with me."

"You're not coming."

"Yes, I am."

"No, you're not. This is official business. Now go write one of those do-it-yourself mysteries for your newspaper and let me handle this."

"You know I'll follow you there."

"Goddamn it, C.W. You'll just be in the way. All I'm going to do is ask Del Rey a few questions about this handyman she's hired."

"You don't think she's involved with Chunker in some sinister way, do you?" I stood staring at the sheriff.

"I didn't say that. I just said—"

"You do! You think she knows something about this guy and what he's done!" I was so furious at the sheriff for even considering this, I slammed out of the office without letting him say another word.

Sheriff Mercer and I arrived at the mortuary about the same time, him in his patrol car, me on my bike. We both stomped up to the front door of Memory Kingdom, not saying a word. I knew he was angry with me for interfering, but I was angry with him for his lack of faith in Del Rey.

When Del Rey opened the door, she appeared to be angry with us both. Although I should have been the one angry with her, for all the secrets she seemed to be keeping from me.

"What are you doing here again? I thought I'd explained—"

Sheriff Mercer held up his hand. "Sorry, Del Rey, but something else has come up." The sheriff glanced at me, then back at Del Rey.

"What now?" She stood her ground, not opening the door any farther.

"Is your handyman around?"

Del Rey gave the sheriff a blank stare, as if it took her a moment to process what he was saying. She collected herself and stammered, "Uh . . . yes, I suppose . . ."

"May I see him?" Sheriff Mercer continued.

"What for?"

For a moment, I couldn't help thinking it was a little odd that Del Rey was being protective of her new handyman.

"I just want to talk with him."

Del Rey pulled the door wide, allowing us to enter. Sheriff Mercer glared at me as I followed him in, but he didn't try to stop me. Maybe he realized I could serve as a cushion between Del Rey and him.

Del Rey stopped in the middle of the mortuary parlor and faced us. "What's he done?"

"Could you ask him to come in, Del Rey?" the sheriff said, ignoring her question.

Del Rey frowned, looking as if she might refuse. I was ready for an onslaught of rage, but instead tears welled in her eyes.

"Del Rey—" I rushed to her side to comfort her, surprised at her response. "What's wrong?"

She blinked back the tears, refusing to let them fall. "Sheriff, I want to know what's going on."

"Actually, this doesn't concern you, Del Rey. It's police business. I'd just like to ask the guy a few questions."

"He hasn't done anything."

I looked at Del Rey, again surprised at her defensiveness on behalf of a man she barely knew. I flashed on the picture of the Coyne brothers, with Chunker standing between them. Maybe she did know him better than I thought.

"Del Rey, what do you know about this man? You only hired him a few days ago," the sheriff continued.

"I know that he's a good man who needs a job. A man who works hard and is trying to start a new life."

The sheriff nodded. "I'll bet you didn't know he was just released from—"

"Prison," she broke in. "Yes, I did."

"He told you, then?" I asked, surprised. She was too smart to hire just anyone off the streets. But an ex-con working for a woman who lived alone with her two kids— that didn't seem so smart.

"Do you know what he was in for?" Sheriff Mercer asked.

"Attempted manslaughter. He served five years at Folsom and now he's out on parole. Part of his parole obligation was that he had to find and maintain a job. And that's what he's doing. Yes, Sheriff, I'm well aware of his history. But I'm not one to judge a person by his past. And I hope others would do the same for me."

What did she mean by that?

"But Del Rey," the sheriff said, "he's an ex-con. He could be dangerous. If he gets drunk or mad, there's no telling what he might do to you and the kids—"

Del Rey's face flared with color. "Stop it, Sheriff! Chunker Lansky wouldn't hurt a fly. He got caught up in that fight years ago because someone attacked him first. He was only trying to protect himself. He had nothing to do with—"

She stopped abruptly, the color draining from her face.

"Looks like you been talking to him quite a bit, Del Rey. Did he tell you all that stuff?"

"Listen, Sheriff. Chunker shouldn't have gone to prison. That drunken ex of mine and his shitfaced brother attacked Chunker, and Chunker did what he had to. Otherwise, *he'd* be in a wheelchair today. Or worse."

"So you knew he was involved with Jasper and Levi Coyne?"

Del Rey nodded. She glanced at me, but all I could do was force a smile that was meant to be understanding. I wasn't sure how it came across, but there was something in Del Rey's eyes that seemed almost . . . desperate.

"Del Rey, I hate to say this, but don't you think it's awfully coincidental that as soon as Chunker Lansky is released from prison, one of the men who testified against him is found dead?"

"No, because I know Chunker wouldn't commit murder."

"But Del Rey, you *don't* know him!" the sheriff insisted. "That's just it. You only hired him a few days ago. You know how you are. You have that big old heart that goes out to every stray animal or man who comes along. I don't think you're seeing him for the person he is."

"Oh, but I am. It's you who's not seeing him for what he really is, because of your preconceived ideas about a person who has spent half a decade in prison."

"And what gives you such insight into this man's character, Del Rey?" the sheriff asked.

"Because he was my second husband."

"I'll go get him," Del Rey added, without further explanation. She passed through the heavy velvet curtain that led to the back of the funeral home.

The sheriff and I looked at one another in disbelief. After a few seconds, Sheriff Mercer said, "C.W., you keep your mouth shut and let me do the talking or you're outta here, is that clear?" He exaggerated his lips as he spoke. I guessed he was whispering so Del Rey couldn't overhear him. Hearies often distort their lips when they whisper, thinking it helps with the lip-reading. It doesn't.

After a few moments Del Rey appeared from behind the curtain, followed by Chunker Lansky.

I could smell fresh dirt on the handyman's grimy overalls. Grave-digging? I wondered. This time he held his Forty-Niners cap in his hand, freeing his sparse, oily hair and revealing a tanned and freckled pate. He stood staring at the floor.

"You wanted to see me, Sheriff?" Chunker said. At least that's what I thought he said. It's easier to lip-read people when they look at you, but I did my best.

"Are you Charles Kirkham Lansky, aka Chunker?"

The man glanced up. "Yes, sir."

"I'd like to talk with you, Chunker, if I might."

"Yes, sir."

"Alone." The sheriff looked at Del Rey, then at me. Del Rey indicated a room through the curtain. Chunker ducked behind the partition, with the sheriff close on his heels.

As soon as they were gone, Del Rey headed for the mini-refrigerator and grabbed two Sierra Nevadas.

"A little early to get tanked, isn't it?" I said, watching her guzzle six or seven swallows.

"I'd say it's a little late."

We plopped into a couple of velvet wingback chairs and worked on our beers—she with gusto, me with the knowledge that I'd have to think clearly later on and this wouldn't help.

"You seem awfully upset. What's up, Del Rey? Are you still in love with him?"

Del Rey took a deep breath, then another long swallow of beer. Resting the bottle on her knee, she paused, as if trying to find the right words.

"No, Connor, I'm not in love with him. I got over that in record time, once he started drinking nonstop. I should have known better than to get involved with one of Jasper's buddies. They're all alike. But I thought Chunker was different. He seemed so sweet at first."

"And he changed? Did he ever become violent?"

Del Rey's eyes flashed. "No! He drank, but he never raised a hand to me and I never saw him physically fight with anyone. But I realized after we were married that his friendship with Jasper had changed. I think that's what caused his drinking to get worse."

"So when you divorced Jasper and married Chunker, it caused a problem between them?"

Del Rey shrugged. "Even though Jasper and I were divorced, he didn't like the idea of me marrying Chunker, especially since it was so soon after I left him. I think it bruised his ego. But I didn't figure it would cause him to carry a grudge the way he did."

"What did he do?"

"He started harassing Chunker, calling him names, getting in his face, you know?"

"So why didn't Chunker stay away from him? Why was he at the bar that night when the fight broke out?"

"They both liked to hang out there. I think it was something territorial, kind of like their attitudes toward women. The two of them were totally wasted. Jasper probably said something stupid to Chunker, and all hell broke loose. But Chunker swears he didn't hit Levi. All he did was protect himself."

"And you believe him? Why?"

"Because I know him. I know what he's like. He's not violent." Del Rey sat still for a few moments, then shook her head. "No, Sheriff Mercer is dead wrong on this."

"And Jasper is just plain dead, Del Rey. You can't blame the sheriff for considering the coincidence that he died right after Chunker was released from prison. Where, I might add, he was sent because Jasper's testimony swore Chunker struck a blow that ended up paralyzing his brother."

Bolting from her chair, Del Rey walked swiftly to the hidden mini-refrigerator and helped herself to another beer. She didn't even offer me one this time. When she turned back to face me, I saw tears in her eyes again.

"Del Rey, all of this is such a surprise to me. I thought I really knew you. I assumed your kids were from your marriage to Mario Montez—your third marriage, apparently. Since Mario died, what, a little over four years ago, after all those years of marriage, and you and the kids still talk about him, I just figured he was the father of both kids. And you certainly never suggested anything different."

"I'm sorry, Connor. My first two marriages were so

long ago, and so brief, they're not something I like to talk about. It's not that I've avoided telling you, it's just that they didn't seem important, until now anyway."

I nodded. "So Andrew has always believed that Mario was his real father?"

Del Rey nodded. "He adopted Andrew right after we were married, when Andrew was still a toddler. He never knew. And I didn't see the point in telling him that his real father was a drunken bum. He loved Mario, and Mario loved him."

"Is there anything *else* you haven't told me that might be important?"

Del Rey took another sip of beer, and another deep breath. Then she stared straight at me. "Okay. There's one more thing. But Connor, you can't tell anyone. I mean it."

I nodded.

"Chunker Lansky is Courtney's father."

I downed the rest of my beer faster than you could say "Holy shit!"

After I recovered from the initial shock, I tried to make some sense of the tangled alliance between Del Rey, her ex-husbands, and her children.

"You mean to tell me that Andrew is the son of your first ex-husband, Jasper, who is now dead, and Courtney is the daughter of your second ex-husband, now suspected of murdering your first ex-husband, and both your ex-husbands were once best friends, but they both married you . . ."

Confusing myself, I stopped. Del Rey's relationships reminded me of those logic puzzles I hated. I could never figure out if Abelard, the ex-husband of Heloise, whose brother's sister married her step-aunt Cleopatra, who once divorced Caesar, but is now living in sin with Nicholas after secretly giving birth to triplets while in a coma . . .

"Connor?"

I looked up at Del Rey's wave.

"Sorry, I was trying to do the math in my head and, as you know, that never works."

"It's really not that unusual to fall in love with your ex-husband's best friend, you know. Happens all the time."

"I guess," I said absently, still trying to tie down the

loose ends. "So Courtney and Andrew have different fathers . . . and Mario isn't one of them."

Del Rey nodded.

"Well, as of the other day Andrew knows who his real father is. Does Courtney know who her father is?"

Del Rey shook her head. "Like I said, they were both so young when I left their fathers, they don't remember much about them. Since I was already pregnant with Andrew when I married Jasper, and we were married so briefly, I never discussed him with Andrew. The fatherhood question just never came up with Courtney—and when Mario came along, he wanted to adopt them both."

"So you let them grow up thinking Mario was their real father."

"It seemed simpler at the time."

"Jesus, Del Rey! That's not a little white lie, like the tooth fairy gives you money when your teeth fall out or carrots will make you see in the dark. This is a whopper!"

"I know that, now! But at the time I didn't want my kids to have such alcoholic losers for fathers. I thought it might scar them, psychologically, you know. I was reading all these child care books and they were saying things like, 'Don't yell at your kids too much or they might grow up to be serial killers.' I was worried that if Andrew and Courtney found out the truth, they'd have some serious problems. And I didn't want them to know they weren't full-blood relatives. I thought it might distance them. They needed each other, you know?"

I didn't, but I nodded and gave her a pat on the leg. What made sense to other people often didn't make sense to me. With her eyes welling up again, Del Rey seemed to need reassurance. And I felt for her. I certainly don't know what I would have done in her position, back in my youth. I've learned that most people don't start thinking clearly until they're at least thirty-seven. My age.

"You didn't think Jasper would mind that you were going off with his best buddy?"

"Remember, Connor, it wasn't working out with Jasper and me. He and I wanted different things. When we broke up, Chunker was there, trying to console me. He was the only friend I had at the time."

I was beginning to imagine how it could have happened. "But Chunker started drinking, too."

Del Rey shrugged. "Like I said, it got worse. I didn't notice it at first. He was on his best behavior. But after we got married, he changed. He brooded about something but he never told me what it was. My guess is he felt disloyal to Jasper but couldn't help himself. Anyway, I quickly realized that marriage wasn't working either, so I left."

"And you were pregnant again?" I said gently.

Del Rey nodded. "I didn't know it at the time, but I found out soon after I left him. I was granted my divorce a month after Courtney was born."

"What did Chunker say about the baby?"

Del Rey looked at me steadily and said nothing.

"Del Rey?" I insisted.

"I never told him."

"What? How could you not—"

"I didn't see Chunker much after that. I moved to another town, joined a codependents group, 'Women Who Love Drunks Too Much,' and stopped getting involved with alcoholic men. I just wanted a clean slate. I wanted to start over fresh, with no baggage. That's when I met Mario."

"But Chunker had a right to know about his daughter."

"Just having sex with someone doesn't give him the right to raise a child, Connor. He wouldn't have been anything to my daughter except trouble. When he went to prison, I put it all out of my mind—forgot about him, really. My kids were *my* kids. That was that."

I had to go along with her there. I wouldn't have wanted alcoholic men involved in my kids' lives. I thought about Chunker and how he'd watched Courtney so intently. He must have known the truth, at least by then.

"I think he knows Courtney is his daughter."

Del Rey nodded. "When he came to work for me, he remarked on how much Courtney looked like his sister. I wasn't prepared for his comment and didn't say anything. He figured it out right then."

"I just wish you'd told me some of this, Del Rey."

"I couldn't, Connor. I'd pushed it away to a dark place and tried to forget about it. Besides, I'm sure there are things you haven't shared with me. These things take time."

She was right. There were some things I hadn't shared with anyone, not yet.

"So what makes you think Chunker didn't kill Jasper the minute he got out of prison?"

Del Rey stood. "Because! I told you—he's not a murderer!"

Maybe. Or maybe Del Rey couldn't face the fact that the father of her daughter may have killed the father of her son.

"Why did you hire him at the mortuary, if you wanted him out of your life?"

"I was starting to have regrets about what I'd done. I wanted to see if he'd changed, and maybe give him a chance to get to know Courtney, now that Mario is gone. Besides, he needed a job."

"Are you going to tell the sheriff?"

Del Rey's eyes flared. But she wasn't looking at me. She was staring at something behind me. I turned to see Sheriff Mercer and Chunker Lansky standing in front of the draped doorway.

"Tell me what?" the sheriff asked.

Del Rey and I glanced at each other.

"I . . . was just telling Connor that Chunker has been doing a great job here at the mortuary. He's been no trouble at all. I haven't seen him take a drink. I don't see how—"

Del Rey stopped talking and stared at the sheriff. He felt around his belt, and for a moment, I thought he was going to pull out his gun, but he whipped out his cell phone instead. I wondered if he had the fastest cell phone in the West.

"Yeah," Sheriff Mercer said. I couldn't make out the rest of his words with his mouth obstructed by the receiver. But by the look of Del Rey's and Chunker's widened eyes, I had a feeling something serious was up.

The sheriff frowned and closed the phone. As he replaced it he unhooked a pair of handcuffs.

"What—?" Del Rey started to demand.

"Charles Kirkham Lansky, you're under arrest for the murder of Jasper Coyne . . ."

If the sheriff read Chunker his Miranda rights, I missed

them. Del Rey required my immediate attention. She had become hysterical.

While the sheriff led Chunker to his patrol car, I managed to calm Del Rey by reassuring her Chunker could be out on bail in a matter of hours. I told her I'd do what I could to help her, and we'd pursue this together. Moments after Del Rey stopped crying, Courtney came in through the front door.

"Mom? I saw the sheriff taking the handyman away. What's wrong?"

Del Rey visibly perked up with her daughter by her side. Courtney, dark-haired like her mother, but with the round eyes and full lips of her father, stroked her mother's back as Del Rey began to tell her some of what had happened. It was obvious the two cared about each other very much and that Del Rey had done a great job of raising her children without the help of their real fathers.

I left the two of them to talk, wondering how much Del Rey would tell Courtney about Chunker.

After a quick stop at home to feed Casper, change clothes, and grab a bite to eat, I arrived at the sheriff's office about an hour and a half after Chunker had been taken away in the patrol car. I found Sheriff Mercer filling out forms at his desk. He didn't look up until I was standing in front of him. He started when he saw me.

"C.W.! Don't sneak up on me like that. You about gave me a heart attack."

"Awfully jumpy, aren't you, Sheriff?" I slid into the chair opposite him. Now that I knew the sheriff had a hearing loss, I'd have to remember to make some noise when I got close to him. I knew what it was like to be startled, with no sound to warn me of someone's presence.

"What do you want, C.W.? I'm pretty busy here." He didn't look at me. He didn't really want to know.

I leaned in to make sure he heard me. "Where's the prisoner?"

Sheriff Mercer met my eyes. "In the back."

"Can I see him?"

"What for?"

"Del Rey asked me to look in on him."

"What's it to her?"

Assuming he didn't know yet, I said, "Uh . . . she's just concerned about her employee, that's all. You know how emotional she gets."

"No, you can't see him. It's not visiting hours. Besides, his lawyer's due soon."

"Why did you arrest him? You didn't have enough to go on when you went over there. What was that phone call about?"

The sheriff said nothing, just continued with his paperwork. He didn't seem to be accomplishing much, though. Going through the motions, it looked like to me.

"Sheriff! I can't help Del Rey if you won't tell me what you have. Please. You don't want her involved in this either, so give me some support here. What did you learn from that phone call?"

The sheriff set down his pencil and faced me square on. "I'll tell you, if you promise to leave me alone for a while."

I nodded. He knew it was useless, though. I'd never leave him alone.

"It was Peyton. I mean, Sheriff Locke."

"What did she say?"

"She found an eyewitness."

"Eyewitness to what? Jasper's murder?"

The sheriff leaned back in his chair and laced his fingers behind his head. He did that whenever he felt confident. "Not exactly. But someone saw Chunker in the vicinity of Jasper's houseboat on the night Jasper was killed. I'd say that's enough to give Chunker opportunity. Along with motive, it's not looking too good for him."

"But you don't have the weapon!"

"We have a good idea what it was. We're going to get a warrant to search for it."

"So who saw him there?"

"Can't say. Gotta protect the witness, you know."

I shook my head. "Are they sure it was Chunker? I mean, it was dark. And Chunker's only been in town a few days. It seems unlikely he could be that easily identified by someone who lives at the lake." Okay, so it was a cheap effort, but Sheriff Mercer either fell for it or indulged me.

"The witness didn't live there. She—or he—was there

to see Jasper. And the witness knew what Chunker looked like."

"Well that's pretty convenient. But can *she* prove it?"

"I didn't say it was a woman."

"Yeah, right. Well then, can *she* or *he* prove it?"

"The witness is willing to stand up in court and swear to it. I'd say that's enough to make a case on our boy."

Shit. It wasn't looking good for Del Rey's second ex-husband. He'd be lucky to get bail at all, being on parole with a murder charge now hanging over him.

"Sheriff, do you really think—

One of the buttons on his desk phone lit up. He picked up the receiver and gave his usual greeting: "Sheriff's office."

He gave a few "uh-huhs" with some head nods, then stopped talking and pressed his lips together. The last words I read before he slammed down the phone was "Goddamn it!"

"What's wrong?" I asked, as Sheriff Mercer leaped from his seat and headed for the hook where his jacket hung.

"Goddamn it to hell!"

I stood in the doorway, sensing his next move. He wouldn't get past me without an answer.

"Sheriff! What happened? Is it Del Rey? Is she all right?"

The sheriff stood at the doorway, his face red, his eyes gleaming.

"That was Peyton again."

"What's wrong?"

"Portia Bryson is missing."

This wasn't the news I was expecting. It didn't compute. "What do you mean?"

"I mean, goddamn it, our eyewitness is gone!"

Portia Bryson was your eyewitness?" I was more surprised at this news than the fact that she might be missing.

Sheriff Mercer either didn't hear me or ignored me. It was getting tougher to tell. "Levi called Sheriff Locke after he discovered Portia didn't come home last night. He says she never does that."

"Maybe she has a new boyfriend," I suggested.

Sheriff Mercer gave me a look. "Peyton found her motorcycle, over at Jasper's boat. It's Peyton's jurisdiction but since we're working together on this, I told her I'd join her. C.W., can you do *me* a favor for a change?"

"What do you mean, for a change? I always do you favors. Don't I make you look like a hero in my newspaper?"

He rolled his eyes at me.

"Okay, what do you want?"

"I want you to go over to Del Rey's place and wait for me there. I know she's going to try to make Chunker's bail as quickly as she can, and I don't want her to be alone with him. Will you do that?"

"You think he'll make bail? What about Portia's disappearance? Won't that complicate things a little?"

"No—now that our eyewitness is gone, we won't be

able to get the judge to deny bail. I don't suppose you could talk Del Rey out of springing him?"

"I doubt it. You know Del Rey. Soft heart, but a strong will."

"I know. But see what you can do. I'll be there as soon as I can."

I knew what he was really after. He wanted me out of his way while he did his investigation. Fine. I had another idea I wanted to pursue.

When I arrived at the mortuary on my bike, I found a late-model Lexus parked in front of the double entrance doors. I didn't recognize the car, but the bumper sported a "Golden Years Retirement Center" sticker. The door to the driver's side was ajar.

I headed inside the mortuary and spotted an elderly man rapping his fingers on the front desk. Del Rey was nowhere in sight. The old man turned around to face me as I stepped up behind him.

"Is Del Rey here?" I asked. His face resembled a dried apple doll, with crinkles accenting his forehead, eyes, and cheeks. I guessed him to be in his seventies, a nature lover by the looks of his dry, suntanned hands and face. He didn't seem to be hurting for money. Both hands sported gaudy gold rings. In his plaid pants, cardigan sweater, and roadster cap, he looked like he'd just come from the country club golf course. And I assumed that car outside was his.

The man glared at me. "She better be. I want a word with her."

Del Rey appeared from behind the heavy drape looking surprised to see us both. She didn't seem to know which one to address first.

"Mr. Samuels? Connor? What are you—"

She didn't get a chance to finish her question. Mr. Samuels interrupted with a string of accusations that stunned Del Rey into silence. I missed the first few words, but the body language was clear. Mr. Samuels was upset about his wife.

". . . you've destroyed my life, is what you've done. With your bungling and lies. You and that money-hungry, grave-robbing maggot. Any peace I thought I might have after my wife passed away is gone . . ."

I'm not sure he meant it exactly that way, but figured he was too angry to make himself clear. He must have been referring to the recent discovery of the cremains, and his wife must have been in one of those boxes stored in Jasper's locker.

As if Del Rey didn't already have enough to handle, now she was hearing from irate relatives as they realized their loved ones weren't exactly laid to rest. Although local gossip had already done alot to spread the word, I had a hunch the morning issue of the daily-except-weekends *Mother Lode Monitor* had headlined the story, beating me once again to the news. But what can you do when your newspaper only comes out once a week?

Mr. Samuels' tirade was growing more belligerent. Spittle sprayed from his mouth and his fingers jabbed the air with each accusation. The noise must have alerted Del Rey's kids. They appeared in the doorway looking concerned. I turned back to Mr. Samuels.

". . . paid good money for those services and I trusted you to see that my wife's last wishes were carried out. How could you take my money and . . ."

He was beginning to close in on Del Rey, who was trying to back away. I reached out and grabbed his gesturing arm.

"Sir, this is not Del Rey's fault. She—"

Samuels jerked his arm away, spewing his venom my way. "You stay out of this. You have no idea what this woman has put me through." He whirled back and began jabbing his finger into Del Rey's shoulder. I knew she wasn't going to take that for long.

Whack! She slapped his arm. I could feel the sting myself.

That did it. The old guy started flailing on her with both hands. She flailed back, but he was relentless. It took me several seconds and all the physical strength I could muster to pull them apart.

"Stop it!" I yelled. I could feel a scratch on my face. I reached around and tried to bend the elderly man's surprisingly strong arm behind him. He might have been old, but he was no ninety-eight-pound weakling. All that golfing must be paying off.

In the confusion, I hadn't noticed that Andrew had disappeared, but I could see Courtney out of the corner of my eye, waving her hands frantically.

Seconds later, Andrew reappeared.

He was carrying a rifle.

Aiming the gun at the old man, Andrew cocked the barrel.

The rest of us froze.

"Get away from my mother!"

Mr. Samuels relaxed in my grip. I felt my heart beat double-time. Del Rey stood still, ready to protect herself in case Samuels came at her again. I glanced at Courtney; she was crying.

Andrew held the gun firmly. "I said, get away from my mother!"

"Andrew!" Del Rey said. "That's . . . not necessary!"

Andrew ignored her. "Now get out of here before I shoot you for trespassing, harassment, assault and battery, and plain stupidity."

"Andrew!" I said. "Put the gun down."

I looked at Mr. Samuels, praying he'd just turn around and leave. When he didn't seem to be going anywhere immediately, I spoke up. "Sir, you can't just come in here and attack someone like that. If you have a grievance, talk to Sheriff Mercer and he'll do what he can to help you. Del Rey had nothing to do with this. She hired Jasper Coyne with the best intentions, fully expecting him to carry out his job of distributing those ashes. She was as shocked as you were to find out he'd been deceiving everyone. I'm sure—"

The man spat on the ground, spun around, and left the mortuary. He didn't even let me finish my speech.

It was several moments before we could breathe again. I think I was the first one to exhale. Del Rey was the first one to speak.

"Andrew Montez! Where did you get that gun?"

I stepped over and took the rifle from Andrew's hands. He didn't resist. Nor did he say anything.

"Andrew! I said where did you get that gun? You know I don't allow guns in my home."

"It's not yours?" I asked Del Rey.

She shook her head, but kept her eyes on Andrew. "I refuse to have a gun in this place. I've read too many reports about people shooting themselves or their family members with their own guns. Now answer me, Andrew."

"I don't know. I got it from one of the guys."

Del Rey looked dumbfounded. "What guy? And for God's sake, why?"

He shrugged. "I wanted it. It was cheap. I thought we could use it for protection. You're here all by yourself most of the time. At least you will be when Court goes back to school and I get my business started. I wanted you to be safe."

"So you bought me a rifle but you didn't tell me about it."

"I was going to. I just got it a few days ago."

"Is a gun that easy to get?" Del Rey asked. She looked back and forth between Andrew, Courtney, and me.

I shrugged. Courtney looked away. Andrew looked defiant.

He said, "Anybody can get one, if you know who to ask."

"Illegal, then?"

He shrugged.

"Aren't they expensive?"

"Not really."

"Wow!" I guess I shouldn't have been surprised. After all, we lived in the country. Guns were much more common around here than in the city—at least, they used to be. The city was catching up.

Courtney spoke up. "It's true. A bunch of the guys have them, mostly handguns, some rifles. One guy even has an AK-forty-seven."

Del Rey and I said nothing for a moment. Finally she slumped down into a chair, shaking her head. "Oh, my God. What is going on around here?"

Andrew moved to her side. "Mom, you're overreacting. There are some real weirdos out there today. More people are getting guns for protection."

"But for kids to be able to get weapons so easily! And illegally! It's just not . . ." She couldn't seem to finish her sentence.

I thought about the recent spate of shootings by local kids and wondered if Sheriff Mercer could be right. Maybe the paint ball attacks were related.

"While we're talking about guns, Andrew, do you know who might have shot up my diner and my office with paint pellets?"

Del Rey looked surprised. "You're kidding! You didn't tell me someone shot up your place. What happened?"

I told the story, briefly, then prompted Andrew for an answer.

"Don't look at me! I have no idea. I told you, I just have this for protection. And it's not a paint pellet gun."

I didn't really think Andrew had anything to do with my new paint jobs, but the world of young people has its own grapevine, and I had a hunch he might know something, if it was done by kids.

"Andrew, I'm not accusing you. I'm just asking if you have any idea who might have done it."

He shook his head. Del Rey reached out for the gun and I handed it to her. She disappeared from the room. I suspected she was hiding the weapon so Andrew wouldn't be able to find it next time he wanted to shoot someone.

I turned my attention to Courtney. "What about you, Courtney? Do you know anything about the paint ball attacks?"

She shrugged. "It's Freedom."

"Uh, right. Sorry." I glanced back and forth between the two of them. "All right, you guys. I need help. And so does your mother. But guns aren't the way to do it. Cour— Freedom, maybe you could ask around at that tatoo place you're working at, see if any of the kids that come in there know anything about these paint pellet attacks?"

She shrugged again.

"Andrew. See if you can find out where kids are getting these guns so easily. I'll get Miah to do some Internet searching. Maybe together we can figure out what's going on around here. You never know. It may tie in to Jasper Coyne's death. These things all seemed to start up at the same time."

They both nodded. Andrew turned to see if his mother had returned, then said, "Okay, the gun—Don't tell Mom, but I got it from one of the guys who runs the paint ball games. I don't want to get him in trouble, but if it will help my mom in some way . . ."

I thanked him and told him I wouldn't say anything to the sheriff just yet. I thought about the paint ball game I'd played the other morning, and tried to picture who was there. Jeff Pike ran the business, and doubled as referee. Any chance he sold real weapons on the side?

My thoughts jumped to another scene at the paint ball field—the fight between Andrew and the camouflage-wearing Berkeley Mondshane, the other mortician in the Mother Lode.

I wondered if that had anything to do with Andrew getting a gun.

I'd have to find out.

After the kids took off, Del Rey and I shared a couple of Sierra Nevadas.

"You all right?" I asked, after the first couple of swallows of beer hit my bloodstream. I was still on edge from the recent assault by the old man, but the alcohol was beginning to help.

"Yeah, I'm all right. It's been quite a day. And I don't think I've seen the last of Zack Samuels. I've been getting so many calls from people who are extremely upset about the discovery of those stored ashes. Some of the calls are about loved ones who died ten or fifteen years ago. Most of them just want to know why they weren't distributed at sea. But I can't give them an answer."

I sipped the beer. "It's such an emotional reflex. People get very protective of their dead relatives, sometimes even more than they were when the relatives were alive. There's something superstitious about it."

"Oh, there is. Some people don't walk on top of graves. Or they put stones on the markers. Or they won't speak ill of the dead. We haven't come that far from the pyramid days, when the mummies were ceremonially prepared for the afterlife, then their servants were sealed up in the burial chambers to protect the dead."

"But Mr. Samuels—he seemed a little beyond grief. Think there's some kind of guilt behind all the dramatics? How did his wife die anyway?"

Del Rey thought a moment. "Uh, let's see. I handled her cremation a couple of weeks ago. His wife's name was Holly. She drowned. They were out camping at Lake Miwok and he said his wife took a midnight boat ride, after drinking several glasses of champagne. Early the next morning he found the boat with her clothing inside, but she was gone. It took the marine patrol several hours to find the body."

"Ugly way to die," I said, wondering what would possess a woman to take a midnight ride—alone. Alcohol, I suspected.

"Anyway, I expect there will be more and more calls and visits like that one. And now I can add Andrew's new gun hobby to my growing list of problems."

"Well, I've got your kids working for me now. I figure if they put all their energy into solving this puzzle, they're less apt to get into trouble, and it'll keep their minds off the mortuary problems. But the accessibility of guns for kids around here is really bothering me."

"I'd like to find out exactly who gave Andrew that gun and get him behind bars."

I didn't say anything, remembering my promise to Andrew. Besides, I didn't really know who it was. After I had some proof, I'd turn the information over to the sheriff.

"And speaking of people behind bars, I've got to get over to the bail bondsman and pick up the cash. It should be ready."

"You're really going to bail Chunker out of jail? Do you think that's a good idea?"

"I don't even know what a good idea is anymore. But I do know this: Chunker Lansky doesn't belong in that jail."

I returned to my office, after offering to join Del Rey at the jail for Chunker's release. She'd declined my invitation, saying she wanted to do this by herself. I said I'd come by later to see how things went, and thought about catching up on my much-neglected newspaper work. But I couldn't concentrate. Exhausted from the excitement, I decided to take a break. I picked up Casper and the two of us took a long walk around Lake Miwok, giving me a chance to think about all that had happened. While Casper chased squirrels, I chased dead ends.

After returning Casper to the diner and freshening up, I thought about paying a visit to Berkeley Mondshane, the other mortician in the Mother Lode. Something about the man bothered me, and I wanted to ask him a few questions. But after checking my watch, I had a feeling Del Rey would be back with Chunker, and I wanted to be there for moral support, if not physical protection.

I was on my bike headed for Memory Kingdom, taking a shortcut through the cemetery, when I noticed a trailer parked among some trees. That was new: Chunker's? Maybe I'd make a detour to check it out after I made sure Del Rey was okay. I pulled up to the parking lot and parked the bike. Del Rey's car wasn't in the lot. Still dealing with the bail bondsman? Perfect. With nobody around, I could check out the trailer now, uninterrupted. But first, better to double-check to see if she was in.

I entered the funeral home and called out for Del Rey. No one appeared from behind the curtain, so I began shifting things around on the registration desk, searching for a key that looked like it might fit the trailer.

Someone tapped me on the shoulder.

I jumped a foot, nearly wetting my pants. A handful of papers tumbled to the floor.

"Jesus! I wish you people wouldn't do that!"

"What people? Do what?" Andrew said, looking startled himself.

"You hearing people. You're always creeping up and scaring the bejesus out of me. It's especially unnerving in a place like this." I glanced around to see if any corpses had appeared.

Andrew frowned. Apparently he was so used to living among the dead, the mortuary didn't cause him the least bit of concern.

"What are you doing here?" he asked, glancing down at the papers I'd dropped on the floor. I bent over and picked them up, mumbling something about how I'd just been neatening up the stack, then faced him.

"Andrew, you know that trailer that's parked at the back of the cemetery—does it belong to your new handyman?"

Andrew nodded. "Yeah, why?"

"I wondered if your mother might have a key to the place."

"I don't know," he said, frowning. "Why?"

He was worse than a three-year-old, with all the "whys." Hadn't his mother taught him "because!"?

"I thought I might take a quick peek inside. See if there's anything that might tie him to Jasper Coyne."

"Sheriff's already been there."

"Maybe he missed something." I gave him my coyest smile.

Andrew's eyes narrowed, but he said nothing.

Coy wasn't working. I needed to be more direct if I wanted to get a look inside that trailer. "Want to come along?"

After a momentary pause, he pulled open a cabinet door on the wall behind him. Inside hung a row of keys, each one labeled across the top in black felt-tip pen. All but the last one. He removed the unlabeled one from the hook, examined it, then held it out to me. "This one looks new."

I tried to take the key from his hand, but he wouldn't let it go.

"So why do you want to go in there, exactly?"

I took a deep breath. "Andrew, your mother is in more trouble than she's letting on. The sheriff thinks Chunker is involved in Jasper Coyne's death. Since your mother is bailing Chunker out of jail as we speak, I thought it might be a good idea to learn a little more about him—for her protection. After all, he spent the last five years in prison." I deliberately made no mention of Courtney's parentage. It was not my place to spill that particular secret, if he still didn't know.

Andrew gave me a long look, then nodded. I plucked the key from his fingers and we started for the door. Courtney met us as we stepped outside, wearing such baggy pants, I wondered how they stayed up. Her hair was sprayed orange on one side and maroon on the other. For a moment, I almost couldn't read her lips. The new stud in the middle of her tongue distracted me from her words.

". . . didn't know you were still here. I thought you left with Mom. Where are you guys going?"

"Hi, Courtney."

"It's Freedom."

"Uh, yes, I mean Freedom. Uh . . . " I looked guiltily at Andrew. "We were just . . ."

Andrew took the reins. "We're going out to Chunker's trailer to snoop around. Wanna come?"

So much for secret conspiracy.

"What for?"

"Mom's in trouble, Court, or whatever you're calling yourself this week. We're going to find out if this handyman has any secrets. Now, do you want to come or not?"

"What kind of trouble?"

Uh-oh. I took over, forcing myself to use her preferred nomenclature. "Freedom, when Sheriff Mercer found those ashes in the storage warehouse, some of the boxes were traced back here. The sheriff is investigating all the possibilities—"

Andrew cut me off. "Yeah, and he thinks Mom is in on this in some way."

"No, she's not! That's so lame. I'm coming with you guys."

This was turning into a field trip. I'd begun to regret including either one of them.

"Maybe you two should wait here. You know, guard the area and make sure the coast stays clear."

Andrew rolled his eyes. "Shit, you sound like we're playing cops and robbers. We're not children, Connor. We're coming with you."

I'd have to think of something other than helping me with my investigation to keep these kids busy or they were likely to get into real trouble. Too late now.

"All right, but if we're caught, I'll disavow any knowledge of your—"

"Quit the *Mission: Impossible* act," Andrew interrupted. "Let's go."

Andrew and Courtney led the way through the Pioneer Cemetery, across the expanse of grass that gave the grounds a parklike feeling, rather than just a final-resting-place kind of look. One young mother sat on the lawn with her three children enjoying a picnic. While her toddler tried to climb up a jungle gym, the two older kids bounced up and down on a teeter-totter. The nearby graves went unnoticed.

After crossing the area of flat markers, where more recent citizens of Flat Skunk had relocated, we reached the older part of the memorial park. Here there were carved granite headstones, weathered by age and the elements, decorated haphazardly with plastic flowers, toy windmills, and tiny American flags.

The area had been renovated by the Pioneer Cemetery Preservation Society, a volunteer group dedicated to restoring and maintaining the historic markers. But there was still an air of unseen decay and longtime neglect that hung about like cobwebs. It was here that my great-grandparents, Sierra and William Westphal, were buried back in the late 1800s.

My parents grew up here, then moved to San Francisco so I could attend good schools for my disability. I hesitated a moment at my great-grandparents' monuments, thinking about how often my mother had said I took after my determined great-grandmother.

Chunker Lansky's small motor home sat at the back of the historic cemetery. Andrew had walked on ahead, but stopped when he realized I hadn't followed him. He turned, waved his arms, and said, "You coming?"

I nodded, and caught up with him at the dilapidated trailer. The dwelling was teardrop-shaped, and looked as weathered and abandoned as the decomposing markers that surrounded it. Outlined in rusted faux-chrome, the chipped silvery paint laced the exterior like irregular snowflakes, revealing a layer of headstone gray aluminum. Slatted windows were covered on the inside with what looked like mismatched old rags. A few of the slats were cracked and repaired with duct tape. The door featured simulated-wood Con-Tact paper, peeling at every corner.

I couldn't wait to get inside.

With Andrew and Courtney-Freedom standing behind me, I stuffed the key in the door handle lock and gave it a twist. As the door opened, the pungent smell hit me like a bullet.

"Whew!" I said, trying to catch my breath. "Did something die in here?" And then for a second, I really thought I might be right.

Andrew fanned his face in an effort to clear the air around him. "Smells like a skunk!"

"A dead one," Courtney said, pinching up her face.

"With garlic breath," I added.

"You go in," Andrew said to me. "I'll wait out here and stand guard like you said."

I smiled at him.

"Chicken," Courtney said.

He made a face. "I'm not chicken. It stinks to high heaven in there. The smell will stick to my clothes the rest of the day." He turned away, ostensibly to begin his lookout.

I took a deep breath of clean air, then headed up the two rickety metal stairs and went inside, trying not to exhale so I wouldn't have to inhale again. Courtney followed me, holding onto the back of my waistband as if she were being led into darkness. Once inside, she released her grip. We both stood in the middle of the tiny room, taking it all in.

Funny about smells. You get used to them quickly. I'm especially sensitive to odors. I can tell what Dan has had for lunch, how recently the sheriff has sneaked a cigar, and what flavor of gum Courtney was chewing at the moment—watermelon. As I glanced around the shabby living quarters, it didn't take long before the smell of skunk dissipated. I hardly noticed it for the sight. Chunker Lansky hadn't been around long enough to unpack entirely, but, oh, what he had already done with the place.

First of all, he apparently had a fascination for photography. Pictures of Lake Miwok, the Mother Lode country, and her historical towns hung on the walls and sat framed on all available surfaces. A collage of photos from what looked like a long-ago camping trip was strung along one wall. In the middle of the collection he'd placed several "look at me with the big fish" photos.

Another series of pictures lined the opposite wall, featuring mostly portraits, everything from old prospectors with missing teeth to young children playing in the park. One photo caught my eye—a picture of three men poised on a fishing boat, arms wrapped around each other, all holding beers in their hands. I recognized the three faces at once: a younger Chunker flanked by Levi and Jasper Coyne. It wasn't exactly the same picture—the poses were slightly different—but it had been taken at the same time as the one that hung on the wall of Jasper's boat.

Underneath it was an old picture of Del Rey and Chunker, in their happier days. Next to it, one picture of Courtney. Recent.

"That's weird," Courtney said, staring at the snapshot of herself practicing skateboarding tricks on the mortuary driveway. I recognized her outfit in the photo from the day I had spotted Chunker watching her—surfer shorts and a tank top, with elbow and kneepads as accessories.

"I wonder when he took that picture? I don't remember him having a camera or anything." Courtney stood closer to the photograph, as if that would help jog her memory.

But something else had distracted me from the photograph. On the tiny kitchen table was a postcard from the Mystery Mansion bed-and-breakfast.

I lifted the postcard and flipped it over. On the back, written in a feminine hand, were the words: "8 P.M., THE MINE." It was unsigned.

The Mine? Did the writer mean an old gold mine—or The Mine, a popular redneck bar in Murphys? Located between Angels Camp and Flat Skunk, it was the closest hangout to Lake Miwok.

The same bar where Levi, Jasper, and Chunker had gotten into that fight five years ago.

Wow, Sheriff Mercer must have really been distracted to have missed this. I had a hunch Portia was the one who'd written the message on the back of the card—after all, it came from her inn. If so, Chunker must know Portia, Jasper's second ex-wife. So far, it had been an awfully small world.

I checked for a postmark; nothing. I wondered which night Chunker had planned to meet Portia. The night she disappeared?

I didn't have time to think it through. Andrew thrust his head inside the door, looking frantic.

"You gotta get out of there, fast! Someone's coming!"

A posse of sheriffs was headed up the path.

I must have dropped the postcard in my hurry out the door. It wasn't in my hand when I dove behind Septimus Penzance's headstone. I was moving on blind instinct—fight or flight. Flight was preferred over trying to explain my actions to Sheriff Mercer, which would have turned into a fight.

I looked behind me and spotted a hand gripping another gravestone. Andrew's. Behind it I could see the top of Courtney-Freedom's maroon and orange spiked hair. I wondered if their hearts were beating as fast as mine. Then I wondered if I could be arrested for contributing to their delinquency.

I didn't have time to think about life in prison at the moment. I was too busy trying to hide from the suspicious eyes of Sheriff Mercer and Sheriff Locke as they hurried toward the trailer. Andrew had done well as a lookout, but even so, we'd barely cleared out in time for their arrival.

The two sheriffs were talking, but I couldn't make out anything they said. Sheriff Mercer surveyed the trailer, trying to peer in the windows as he moved around the back and came out the other side. Sheriff Locke tried to poke something into the lock, but didn't have any luck. Apparently I had remembered to shut the door on my way out, and it had locked itself. I still held the key.

When Sheriff Mercer appeared at the front of the trailer again, Sheriff Locke indicated she couldn't open the door. I still couldn't read their lips, but from Sheriff Mercer's body language, I could tell he had a plan. Forcing up one of the window slats on the door, he reached in and unlocked the handle from the inside.

I felt a sharp pain in my back. I turned just in time to take another hit in the shoulder. Someone was throwing rocks at me!

I strained to see where they were coming from and spotted Andrew's head popping up from behind his headstone like a jack-in-the-tomb.

"Quit it!" I mouthed, hoping he could lip-read a little.

Andrew gestured wildly in the direction of the mortuary, where the two sheriffs had come from. In the distance, moving between the pine trees, came Del Rey.

Even from afar, I could tell by her gait she was upset. I knew I would only make things worse if I was caught hiding, so I decided it was time to show myself. To Andrew and Courtney's horror, I stood up and tried to act as if I had just arrived at the trailer. I waved to Del Rey but she didn't return my welcoming gesture.

When Del Rey reached me, puffing and out of breath, I saw that streaks of tears covered her face.

"Del Rey! I . . . was just looking for you—What's wrong? And where's Chunker?"

"Sheriff Mercer is here?" She looked even more upset.

I nodded. "And Sheriff Locke. They're in the trailer."

"They had no right to take that key . . ." was all I caught. Her face and lips were so distorted from crying, she was nearly impossible to read. It wasn't the time to set her straight about the key.

She stamped up the small steps and pushed open the flimsy door. I was right behind her. And so was that smell.

"Del Rey," Sheriff Mercer said, looking startled. In his hand he held the Mystery Mansion postcard. He was fanning away the odor with it. Behind him, Sheriff Locke held a dead skunk wrapped in old newspaper. They'd apparently made a major discovery—the source of the smell. Sheriff Locke ducked outside with her cache.

Before I could say, "How the hell did that get in here?" Del Rey lit into Sheriff Mercer. "What are you doing in Chunker's trailer? You have no right! This is private property and you can't just storm in here as if—"

She stopped abruptly, her attention caught by Sheriff Locke, who had returned to the trailer skunk-free. At least, mostly skunk-free. She was waving a handful of papers—and a lingering aroma—at Del Rey.

"We have a warrant, Del Rey," she said. And Sheriff Mercer added, "Sorry, but we've got to look around Chunker's trailer again and see if there's anything that connects him to Jasper Coyne. He seems to have a real eye for portraiture—especially for pictures of his ex–best friend. Who's now dead."

He said nothing about the postcard in his hand. But it didn't slip by Del Rey. She gazed at the colorful picture in horror. A moment later she ran from the trailer. I watched her hurry down the path, not even noticing her own children, who had come out from behind their hiding places.

"What's wrong with Mom?" Courtney asked as I came down the steps.

"I don't know," I said, feeling helpless. Courtney glanced back at the trailer, then turned and ran after her mother. Andrew sidled up to me, repeating the question Courtney had asked.

"I have no idea, Andrew. She went into the trailer saying the sheriffs had no right to be on her property. Then Sheriff Locke waved a warrant at her and she fled. She's terribly upset about something. More than I expected, even if she was once married to this Chunker guy."

Andrew blinked. "What did you say?"

Uh-oh. Didn't mean for that one to slip out.

"C.W. Come in here." My jumbled thoughts were interrupted by Sheriff Mercer. He waved me inside, and Andrew followed me in.

"Sheriff, where's Chunker? Why is Del Rey so upset?" I asked.

The sheriff didn't appear to hear me. Instead, he asked, "C.W., have you been in here? Tell me the truth."

"I . . . uh . . ." I looked to Andrew for a quick lie but he had nothing to offer. He showed me with a shrug of his shoulders.

"Goddamn it, C.W.! Did you touch anything?" Sheriff Mercer said. Sheriff Locke stood next to him, her hand on her gunbelt, looking as if she was about to practice her quick draw.

"No! I swear I didn't touch anything . . ." and I meant it, until I remembered the postcard. "Except that postcard. I may have picked it up—"

The sheriff was too steamed even to curse. Exhibiting remarkable control, he asked me to show him where I found it. I did.

"It was right there on the table."

"Well, I found it on the floor," he said, looking exasperated.

"I . . . I must have dropped it—"

"In your haste to get out the door, no doubt."

I pressed my lips together, hoping they wouldn't let anything else out of my mouth.

"You got something more to say?" Sheriff Mercer demanded.

"No! Honest."

I stood still, giving the sheriff a few minutes to calm down. He turned his back and said something to Sheriff Locke that I missed. I looked to Andrew for a possible interpretation. Andrew shook his head.

"Sheriff, can you tell me why my mother was so upset just now?" Andrew said instead.

Again Sheriff Mercer ignored the question. Andrew tapped him on the shoulder and repeated it.

Sheriff Mercer glanced at Sheriff Locke. Neither said anything for a few moments, but Sheriff Mercer looked as if he was trying to find the right words to say to Andrew.

"Sheriff?" Andrew demanded.

"Look, Andrew. Things are kind of complicated. I haven't got anything to tell you right now—"

Andrew exploded. "Fuck that, Sheriff! I have a right to know if my mother is in trouble. Now tell me what's going on!" His face reddened as he spoke, and the veins on his neck pulsed visibly.

"Calm down, Andrew. And watch your language. Look, it's not specifically about your mother. It's just that . . ."

"What?" I asked.

Sheriff Locke spoke up. "We found another body." She glanced at Sheriff Mercer for approval. He nodded almost imperceptibly.

Andrew turned white. I held my breath.

"Was it Chunker?" Andrew said, barely moving his lips.

Both sheriffs looked at each other.

"No," Sheriff Locke said finally. "It's Portia Bryson. She was found an hour ago, drowned in Miwok Lake."

Portia's dead?" I stared at the sheriff. The woman I had only just met, the woman who was once married to the same man as Del Rey, no longer existed today? Portia Bryson had drowned?

A wave of dizziness swept through me along with a horrible thought. It was one thing for Del Rey to be in trouble, what with her connection to Jasper Coyne. But what if her life was now in jeopardy? Someone was on a killing spree—and Del Rey could be next. As I reached for the support of the wall, I knew in my gut Portia's death had not been an accident.

Sheriff Mercer turned to say something to Sheriff Locke, but I missed the words. That gave me a moment to try to collect myself. When the sheriff faced me again, I asked him what happened, although I dreaded the details.

"Don't know much yet. Body's been taken to the county coroner. Arthurlene should have something back to me in a few hours."

Dr. Arthurlene Jackson was certainly competent at her job, but I had a feeling she wouldn't have all the answers to this one—like who did it and why. And I knew she wouldn't appreciate all the questions I'd be asking her—but she was used to it. We had a respectful relationship, but I drove her crazy with my inquisitiveness on behalf of the *Eureka!*

"Is that why Del Rey was so upset? Because she found out about Portia?" I asked Sheriff Mercer.

He stared through me with a blank look I couldn't read. Sheriff Locke motioned for his attention and he turned to discuss something with her. I left them to their private conversation and headed for the mortuary. At this point, I was worried about Del Rey's mental health—and her physical safety. I was also wondering why she'd gone to bail Chunker out of jail and come back alone—could Portia's death have something to do with it? That postcard . . .

Andrew caught up with me on the path. "Where are you going?"

"To see your mother."

"Connor, why are you doing all this for my mom?"

"When I first got to Flat Skunk a year ago, after leaving my job at *The San Francisco Chronicle,* some of the people here were a little afraid of my disability, as if my deafness meant I couldn't communicate with them at all, so why should they bother. But Del Rey just introduced herself to me here in the Memorial Park, when we were both walking our dogs, and we talked for two hours."

"Two hours! What about?"

"She talked about growing up with her sister, the one who's blind. I talked about growing up deaf. We found we'd had some similar experiences. We've been good friends ever since."

"But she never told you about . . . about Jasper being my . . . her husband?"

I paused, wondering if he had talked with Del Rey about what he'd overheard. "No. But some things are harder to talk about than others. It doesn't mean we're not good friends. Now that she's in trouble, I'd like to help her out as much as I can."

Andrew nodded. If he said something, I didn't catch it. When we reached the mortuary parking lot, Andrew started to veer off.

"Aren't you coming? I'd imagine your mother needs you right now."

Stuffing his hands in his pockets, Andrew looked

distracted. "Naw . . . I got something to do. You can handle it. I'd only be in the way."

"Andrew, you're her son! You're not in the way."

"You're better at this than me, Connor. I . . . gotta go."

With that he hopped into his beat-up Volkswagen bug and drove off.

Entering the foyer, I saw no signs of Del Rey, or Courtney-Freedom. I searched the halls, peeked behind closed doors, stopped by Del Rey's office, and even checked the embalming rooms. Nothing. I headed upstairs and knocked at the door of her living quarters. Nobody home. Apparently the only bodies currently in the place weren't among the living.

I returned to the reception area and was about to jot down a note asking Del Rey to contact me, when one of the three phone lights went on. Figuring her voice mail would pick it up, I watched, hypnotized by the blinking light, until it became a solid red glow. I placed a hand on the answering machine to see if it had taken the call. No vibration.

Someone must have answered the phone.

I double-checked the parking lot for Del Rey's car, but her Honda was gone. I retraced my steps throughout the mortuary, but again found no one. Who had picked up the phone? Before I could think it through, movement at the window caught my attention. The two sheriffs were headed for the mortuary. Locke carried a handful of papers. Sheriff Mercer was pushing a bicycle. My Peugeot.

"Thanks, Sheriff." I stepped out to greet him. "Guess I forgot my bike."

"No problem," Sheriff Mercer replied. What he meant was, *Now you don't have to go back to that trailer and snoop around again, C.W.*

"Del Rey in? Looks like her car's gone," Sheriff Mercer said.

"I don't know where she is. I . . . gotta run."

Without a backward glance, I hopped on my bike and headed for my office. I was anxious to find Del Rey, but since I didn't have any leads, I thought I might catch up on some neglected work. One thought still bothered me, though: if no one was home, who had picked up the phone at the mortuary?

I stopped by Dan's office and found him at his desk staring at a box. I couldn't see the contents from the doorway, but he looked as if it contained the secrets of the universe. A deep frown etched his brow, and he sat rubbing his beard like a scientist.

"Got lunch?" I asked, hoping it was food. Since there was no smell, I had a pretty good idea I was out of luck.

"Ashes," he said simply, as he pushed himself back in the chair.

"You looked like you were reading them, sort of like tea leaves."

"I wish I could. Do deaf people know how to read dead body language as well as they can read live body language?"

"Let me have a look." I peeked into the box. Sure enough. Ashes. "Where'd you get these?"

"Found them," he said mysteriously. I knew it was a lie, and he knew I knew, but I didn't question him further. If only the sheriff would let me get away with mysterious responses like that.

"Whose are they?" I was hoping they weren't his brother Boone's.

"Unidentified."

"What are you doing with them?"

"Working on an idea."

"What?" I asked.

"Look at them for a moment."

I did. I didn't get any ideas.

He stuck two fingers into the center of the ashes and pulled out his key ring. "They're the perfect hiding place."

"You lost your keys in there?" I still didn't quite get it.

"No, I dropped them in, a few minutes ago. They practically disappeared."

"So you're saying, if someone wanted to, they could hide something in a box of ashes?"

Dan nodded.

"Like what? Keys?"

"Anything small, lightweight . . . and illegal."

I took in a breath. "Drugs?"

"Anything."

"But why? And didn't the sheriff check the ashes in the warehouse? He didn't find anything hidden inside."

"True. Like I said, it's just a theory I'm exploring." As he returned his attention to the box of ashes, I slipped out the door, wondering what Dan expected to find out. When I entered my own office, I found Miah cropping a photograph on his computer screen. He started when I tossed my backpack on my desk.

"Shit, you scared me!"

"You were expecting someone else?" I signed.

"Yeah, the guys who did this." Miah picked up a handful of the Polaroids I'd taken for evidence before Dan and I cleaned the office, and fanned them out in front of me. "What happened in here?"

"What do you think of the new-wave chaotic modernist look? If you liked it, we could do it again. We'll just have the next paint ball game here."

"Someone actually shot up the office with paint pellets? Shit!"

"Hey, where were you on the night of the murder, anyway?"

"I have an alibi. I was . . . in church, yeah, at the time of the incident in question."

"You don't even know what a church is."

Miah feigned a pout that was adorable on him. "Well, I'm hurt that you consider me a suspect in this, *cheif*." Trouble with finger spelling is, you can tell when someone can't spell.

"I suspect everyone, and no one," I said, trying to look hardboiled. I think it came out a little too cozy. "And don't call me chief. Besides, you spelled it wrong. Where'd you learn finger spelling? Hooked on Foniks?"

He flipped me a sign that didn't need clarification. "Seriously. Any idea who did it?"

I shook my head and pointed to him. "Do you?"

He shrugged, the universal sign for "I have no clue."

"The same decorator stopped by my diner last night, too."

Miah's young face grew tight, his signs forceful. "Con, you could really be into some deep shit." He signed his favorite word by pulling his right thumb out of his left fist. I knew it was his favorite sign because he used it all the time. And he had taught it to all his friends.

"I'm being careful."

"Did you tell my dad?"

I nodded. "Speaking of your dad, have you noticed his hearing loss?"

"What?"

"Your dad is losing his hearing. I wondered if you knew. Apparently not."

"You know, I suspected it, but half the time he seems like he can hear fine. I thought he just wasn't paying attention or he was ignoring me. Wow. How's that going to affect his job?"

"It shouldn't, if he gets hearing aids. That's the next step. Better watch out when you listen to that alternative-grunge-punk-ska music you love to turn full blast. You'll be wearing a hearing aid some day."

"That's okay. I already know sign language."

I shot him a look, then changed the subject. "How's the photo of the Annual Clamporee coming?"

"Okay. Got a great shot of Cleatus MacMath hanging a historical plaque at the cemetery, and one of him pouring beer down Augie Aleksy's throat using a funnel. First comes the ceremony, then the party. Which one do you want to use for the front page?"

I gave him a very-funny smile. He nodded and returned to his computer screen to detail the finishing touches on the first MacMath shot. I put in a call to the sheriff to see if he'd heard anything from the ME.

"YEah cw what do you want ? GA" I could always pick Sheriff Mercer's typing style out in a TTY lineup. He had a habit of holding down the cap key a little too long, not to mention doubling his letters while leaving others out completely.

"Hi Sheriff. Anything back from Dr Jackson yet? GA"

"ITs only been an hour Cw. COould you let me get some work done herE?"

I waited for the go ahead but as usual, he'd forgotten it. I went ahead anyway. "I was just checking. By the way, did you find Del Rey? GA"

"YEah, she came by to connvince me I was rong about CHunker. GA"

"Did you tell her about Portia? GA"

"Yeah, she seemd pretty stunned. GA"

"Is Chunker out?! GA"

"NOope hes still here pending the further investigatoin of new circumstances. Hold on a sec CW. FAx coming in."

I waited, watching the red letters on the small TTY screen. I was thankful the sheriff had finally gotten his own TTY. Communication with him was so much easier now, at least for me, even if he did have a unique typing style. Just about the time my eyes were growing heavy from staring at the hypnotic glow, the letters began to dance again.

". . . its from ARThurlene."

"What's it say, Sheriff? GA"

There was no response. The screen went dark.

Damn! I removed the receiver from the coupler and hung it up. I'll bet he didn't get in more than half a dozen curses before I was there to lip-read his words in person.

"What took you so long?" Sheriff Mercer asked. I had a feeling his voice was loaded with sarcasm. His expression certainly was.

"Where's the fax?"

"Right here in my official hands."

"So what does it say?"

The sheriff shared the highlights without actually letting me read the information.

"Portia Bryson drowned."

"We knew that, didn't we? Of course, that's what you thought about Jasper and it turned out—"

"There was water in her lungs."

"Was it murder?"

"We don't know yet."

"Were there any other signs of—"

"No other marks were found on the body, no bruises, lacerations, or bumps, except for one nearly healed bruise on the side of her right leg."

"What about drugs or—"

"Toxicology reports won't be in for another couple of days, so I can't confirm whether or not there were any foreign substances in her system."

"Where's she going to—"

"The victim's body will be released to the Memory Kingdom Mortuary according to the wishes of her closest relative. It was also her posthumous request, verified by her attorney."

Sheriff Mercer seemed to have a gift for anticipating my every question. Did he know what I was about to ask next?

"So who's her closest relative?" This time he didn't cut me off. In fact he paused before he answered.

"Levi Coyne."

My mouth dropped open. "You're kidding! She didn't have anyone else?"

"Apparently not."

"And after she's embalmed by her ex-husband's first ex-wife, she's going to be buried in Pioneer Cemetery. This is getting bizarre."

"Who said she was going to be buried?"

I stared at him.

"What do you—oh God! You mean, after all this business with the ashes, she's going to be—"

"Cremated. Yep. Those were her wishes."

I had a feeling she'd made that decision long before Jasper Coyne was murdered. I had one more question.

"So it's still possible that Portia drowned accidentally?"

The sheriff shrugged. "Like I said, Arthurlene doesn't know for sure yet. Portia was found floating in Lake Miwok, right near Jasper Coyne's boat. She could have slipped and fallen in. Could have been a suicide. Grief over her ex-husband's death."

But the answer was obvious to me, and I'm sure the sheriff was thinking the same thing. Portia Bryson was murdered.

I made my suspicions known. "You know Portia was murdered, don't you, Sheriff."

"I have nothing to say to the press at this time," the sheriff replied. But his eyes confirmed that he suspected the same thing.

"What else did Dr. Jackson say?"

"Nothing I can tell you right now."

"Is there any indication that Chunker might have been involved in her death?"

"No comment."

"Why not?"

"I don't have to have a reason."

"Then can I see him?"

Sheriff Mercer frowned. "Who?"

I nodded toward the jail.

"What for?"

"I just want to talk to him."

"Why?"

"Do I have to have a reason?"

"What do you want to say to him?"

"Sheriff! Come on. I might be able to find out something from him. He may be more apt to talk to me than to an officer of the law. He knows I'm a friend of Del Rey's, so he might open up. At least give me a chance. It can't hurt."

Sheriff Mercer mumbled something incoherent as he pulled himself up. All I caught was ". . . see if he'll see you . . ." Hoisting the key from his waistband, he unlocked the door to the back room where the holding cells were. With a swing of his arm, he ushered me in, leaving the door open after I passed through.

Two cells stood side by side, one empty, the other occupied by a blurred shadow. I could see what looked like a pair of feet on the floor. I stepped closer, and Chunker Lansky came into view.

He lay on the cot, his hands behind his head, staring up at the chipped paint on the ceiling. He wore the same clothes I'd last seen him in, only they looked dirtier. He didn't appear to see me until I stood close to the bars, peering in. Pulling his hands from his head, he sat up and faced me, smoothing down his oily hair. He said nothing.

"Hello, Chunker. I'm Connor Westphal. I'm a friend of Del Rey's. We met at the mortuary . . ."

He eyed me suspiciously.

"I wondered if . . . we could talk for a moment."

Chunker abruptly rose up and stepped to the bars. Reflexively, I moved back, then forced myself to stand still.

Up close he looked distraught. His lined face softened as he spoke. "How is she?" he said.

"Del Rey's fine . . . you know, as well as can be expected. But she's very concerned about you. She tried to get bail for you, but . . ."

He waved my words away. "I know, I know. I told her not to bother about bail, but . . . she's stubborn. You probably know that. And Court—the kids. Are they okay?"

"Yes, they're fine. They're trying to help out the best they can, too. How about you? Do you need anything?"

Chunker hung his head and said something I couldn't make out. I asked him to repeat it, and he just shook his head. I went on.

"Chunker, I wondered if I could ask you a few questions." I paused, waiting for a sign he was willing to talk. His eyes met mine and I took it to be the go-ahead.

"What exactly happened the night Jasper Coyne died?"

"Christ, I'm tired of that question." I waited. He took a deep breath and shook his head. "I swear to God, I have no idea. I got a call asking me to come to the boat to talk with Jasper about something . . ." he hesitated.

"What did he want?"

Chunker shrugged. "I don't know. He said it had something to do with Del Rey. He knew that would get me there. I was supposed to meet him on his boat at eight o'clock."

"And?"

"And he wasn't there. The place was deserted. I waited awhile, then I left. End of story."

"Except now you're in jail on suspicion of murdering two people."

"Yeah, and they're going to try to pin the drowning of that woman on me. I'm an easy target. Ex-con with a grudge. Only I didn't do it. I didn't kill Jasper Coyne." Another sigh.

"What do you think happened to Portia Bryson?"

"How the hell should I know? I didn't kill her, I know that. They're saying . . ." He stopped, then pressed his fingers to his eyes. I waited while he collected himself again.

"Look, lady, I didn't even know Portia Bryson. Jasper married her after we stopped being friends. I don't know why they think I'd have anything to do with her death—"

"Except for the fact that she saw you on the boat the night of Jasper's murder. She was the eyewitness."

"I know that now. The sheriff told me." Chunker shook his head. "Well, I never saw anyone."

"That's not the point. The point is, she said she saw you. What about the postcard she sent you? The sheriff found it in your trailer."

Chunker paled. "Hope he had a warrant to go snooping around my private property," he mumbled. At least, that's what I thought he said. Mumbling is hard to read.

"You've got quite a collection of photographs. Including a few of the Coyne brothers."

"How do you know? Shit, did Del Rey let you into my trailer, too?" His face stiffened as disbelief began to turn to anger.

I said nothing.

"I don't have to explain nothing to nobody. I didn't do

nothing." He turned away and plopped down on his bed, his hands laced behind his head. I paused, knowing I had to phrase my next few questions carefully if I wanted to restore the conversation.

"Chunker, I'm really trying to help you. If you can give me something to go on, I might be able to figure out what really happened. You can't do much sitting in that jail cell."

His feet flapped nervously. I could tell he was agitated, but he didn't respond. I tried another approach.

"The postcard said something about meeting Portia at eight o'clock at The Mine. Did you go there?"

Chunker sat up and turned toward me, looking defeated. "Yeah, but I never found out what she wanted. I told the sheriff the same thing."

"You don't have any idea?"

He stood up and faced me at the bars again, grabbing the metal tightly in his hands. "I honestly don't know. I . . . I figured it was something about Jasper, so I went over there to find out. But she never showed. So I left. The next thing I know, I've been arrested for murder."

My brain was tired. I needed a good workout with my dog, Casper, followed by a good beer with Dan. And maybe another workout of a different kind.

When I got home, I left him a message to come by after he'd finished his work, and set about making a chicken salad with homemade croutons for dinner. Around seven, the light on the TTY lit up.

"Connor Westphal here. GA" I typed on my TTY.

"This is Dan Smith here."

"Hi Dan. It's about time. Don't forget to use the GA when you're finished typing. GA"

"O.K. What are you doing? GA"

"Not much. Waiting for you to come eat this wonderful chicken salad I just made. Got beer for dessert. Are you coming? GA"

"Yes. I'll be over soon. Are you alone? GA"

"Yes, except for Casper, of course. Bring your pajamas. GA"

"O.K. Got to go now. GA"

I stopped typing and hung up the phone, my hand resting on the receiver. Dan didn't appear to be in a very playful mood. He always had a bit of witty repartee ready when I asked him to bring his pajamas. I wondered if something was on his mind. He didn't even remember to use SK—Stop Keying signal—to end the call.

I didn't have time to guess. Out of the corner of my eye, I saw the fax machine come to life. As soon as the paper came through, my computer screen signaled an E-mail alert. And then my TTY light flashed again.

Setting the receiver on the TTY coupler, I typed in my greeting. Maybe Dan was calling back for some reason. To cancel? While I waited for the response, I leaned over and removed the fax from the tray. Before giving it a glance, I swiveled around to the computer and punched the keys to pull up my E-mail. I felt like a multitasking Super Secretary.

I glanced back at the TTY screen, expecting to see his usual greeting of "Dan Smith here." I was poised to type a response, but the words on the screen caused me to freeze.

"Not paint," was all the cryptic message said.

"Not paint?" I said aloud, waiting for the "GA."

I lifted the headerless fax and scanned the print: "Real bullets."

Turning to the computer screen, I read the message that had appeared from an anonymous server. There were two words: "Next time."

I repeated the message, looked again at the fax, then read the TTY letters, this time in a different order.

"Next time."

"Real bullets."

"Not paint."

Uh-oh.

"Casper!" I screamed. I hoped some sound came out. Must have. Casper appeared at my side in seconds. "Let's get the hell out of here."

I grabbed my backpack on the way out the door and the two of us hopped into my Chevy. Reaching into the bottomless pit of my backpack, I came up with candy bars, tampons, birth control pills, half a dozen pens, a few coins, and a hairbrush, but no keys. Shit! Where had I left them?

Glancing out the car window every few seconds to see if anyone had appeared, I dumped the contents of the backpack in the seat and fished around one last time. Still no goddamn keys.

I opened the car door and made a dash for the diner, commanding Casper to wait there. As I ran, I checked the darkness for signs of movement. Reaching the front door, I twisted the knob. It slipped through my sweaty grasp. Damn! I'd forgotten I'd set it up to lock automatically.

With the Fort Knox bolts I'd recently installed, there was no way I was going to get in. I had no choice. I'd have to ride my bike into town.

Retrieving my backpack and dog from the Chevy, I hauled my bike from the side yard into the porch light so I could read the numbers on the combination lock. My hands shook as I fumbled with the dial. It took me three tries to open the damn thing. Hoisting on my backpack, I started out on the five-mile trek to downtown Flat Skunk in the nearly pitch black. By the dim light of my dying bike headlamp, I could barely see my silver-white dog at my side.

We didn't pass a soul the first few minutes. I couldn't see a thing and practically had to feel my way down the road, veering off the shoulder every few minutes into the gravel, dirt, weeds, or gutter. At least if a car had passed by, I would have had some decent light for a few moments. But what if it was the person who'd threatened me? He—or she—could put my lights out forever.

Casper kept up well, considering my frantic pace, an erratic mixture of desperate speed and terrified caution. In the dark it was nearly impossible to tell how far I'd come or how much further I had to go. At one point, I wondered if I was on the right road, headed in the right direction.

After endless surprise bumps and swerves, I caught sight of a pair of headlights coming toward me. A car. I stared at the oncoming beam as I pedaled, my hope of rescue tempered by the fear that this might be the person who had sent me those threatening messages.

As the car approached, it decreased its speed. The slower it drove, the faster I found myself pedaling. Just as the car was about to pass me, I ducked my head and pushed forward, racing toward an imagined finish line like an Olympic contender gone mad.

The car kept going. Thank God.

Sweat on my back and chest cooled me as I flew down the uneven pavement, wondering how much longer before I reached town. In the daytime I knew this road like the back of my hand. In the dark, it seemed strange and unfamiliar. Every few minutes another car passed by, causing a repeat of the terror.

Would this one stop?

Would this one have a gun?

Just as I was running out of air and my aching legs were

about to give out from the demands of pedaling, I saw the
glow of the neon blue Sheriff sign up ahead. I brightened
momentarily, until I remembered Sheriff Mercer always
left the outside lights on, whether he was there or not. If he
wasn't there, I'd head straight for Dan's office.

What if he wasn't there either?

I slowed my pace, sat upright, and stretched out my
back, so engrossed in my plans for salvation that at first I
didn't notice Casper's agitated behavior. And I didn't see the
car that had sneaked up behind me. The headlights were
off, and of course I didn't hear it.

It wasn't until the bumper of the car hit the back of my
bike frame that I knew I was in trouble.

The jolt catapulted me off my bike. I flew head over
heels into the dirt, skinning everything on my body that was
exposed, from my chin and nose to my elbows and knees. I
lay sprawled on the side of the road, gasping for breath, the
wind knocked out of me. When my air finally returned, I
felt dizzy and nauseated. I rose up on my hands. The impact
had caused my vision to blur, but I could make out Casper
snapping wildly at the car that had slowly moved on down
the road.

The car stopped. It made a U-turn.

"Casper! Come on!" I yelled, pulling myself up on
aching legs. I shook my head to clear my vision, but that
sent a jolt of pain through my temple. The sting of my scrapes
and bruises faded into numbness as the threat of more bod-
ily harm loomed ahead.

Abandoning the twisted bike in the middle of the road, I
scrambled into the nearby field, searching the shadows for
someplace to hide. In the hot daylight sun, the gently
rolling hills were blanketed with golden grain. But at night
the mounds were colorless and flat, except for the occasional lava rocks that jutted up like scattered tombstones. I
headed for the largest rock I could see and signaled Casper
to follow.

As I crouched behind the boulder, I remembered the
landscape behind me, where the small dry meadow met
the Miwok Reservoir, which reached from Flat Skunk to
Angels Camp. Although it served as a cool respite from

the parched terrain of the summer, it currently posed a logistical problem. If the person who had hit my bike decided to chase me on foot, the reservoir blocked my escape. There was a twenty-foot cliff overlooking the pool of water.

In other words, Casper and I were trapped.

Out of the corner of my eye, I thought I saw something moving behind another one of the lava rocks. A mountain lion? There had been a couple reported in the area lately. I should know—I wrote up the report.

Hunkering down farther, I waited for the attack from both sides. As the menacing car approached my abandoned bike, I prayed a hungry cat wouldn't charge me from behind.

Without the headlights, I couldn't see exactly where the car was. But Casper's body language made it clear: the car was getting closer. Her head-snapping stopped abruptly, and for several seconds Casper didn't move at all. She stood frozen to the spot like a topiary statue. Then she resumed her agitated dance.

I could see the car now, just barely, ten feet from the road. All the driver had to do was park and run after us with a flashlight—and a gun. With Casper's barking, we were sure to be caught.

"Hush, Casper!" I whispered, but she wouldn't calm down. I pulled her close behind the rock and held her still, hoping her yelps wouldn't give away our location.

Breaking out in a sweat, I watched as the car pulled up to the side of the road just opposite us, only a few yards from my hiding place. Whoever it was knew my location, I was sure of it. I stared, tense, ready for flight at the first sign of the door opening. But the car didn't move. It just sat there, waiting.

I strained to see who was inside, but it was too dark even to make out the type of car. All I could see was a general outline. It was a small pickup truck. Not that it would help much in identifying it later. There were many more trucks than cars in the Mother Lode.

I squatted, holding my dog and wondering what the driver planned to do. As I readied to make a run farther into

the darkness and face leaping into the reservoir, or worse—
like fighting a mountain lion—I inhaled sharply. Something
in the truck caught my eye. A flicker of light glowed behind
the driver's window. A second later the window opened a
crack. I blinked several times, but what I saw was clear
enough.

The tiny red glow dropped from the crack in the window to the dry ground below. Another match was struck inside the truck. It, too, fell from the window. And another.
And another.

Within seconds the parched weeds burst into flames.

The truck moved slowly along the rim of the road,
dropping lit matches every few feet. When it reached the
end of the field, it idled for a few more minutes, probably
making sure the fire had taken hold. Then it sped off down
the road, leaving Casper and me to deal with the danger of a
major grass fire.

"Oh, my God!" I'm sure I said the words aloud.

I ran out from behind my shelter. The fire had already
spread along the perimeter of the field, blocking the opening to the road.

On either side, about a hundred feet apart, were two deserted buildings, one an old barn, the other what had once
been an Esso station. They'd both flare up big time any
minute. I'd have to run through the flames in order to reach
the road—and risk catching myself on fire, not to mention
Casper.

I had no choice but to run to the reservoir. Casper followed behind me, as I stumbled in the darkness. Pausing
momentarily at the edge of the rocky cliff, I lifted Casper,
took a deep breath, and jumped in.

I let go of Casper just after we hit the ice-cold water. I
knew she could swim, and would save herself. As I rose to
the surface, I felt the scrapes and scratches all over my body
light up as if on fire. But I had no time to wallow in the pain.
I swam to the edge, pulled myself out of the water, and
made my way up the carved-out path as quickly as I could,
calling Casper to follow.

When I reached the top, I ran across the field trying not
to think about what I was about to do. Still dripping wet, I

took another deep breath, and ran as fast as I could—right through the three-foot-high border of flames.

I made it without a singe! Bent over to catch my breath, I looked up for Casper.

She hadn't followed me. I should have known she wouldn't! Dogs are terrified of fire, more so than humans. I should have carried her through the flames.

"Casper! *Casper!*"

I couldn't see her behind the looming wall of fire. Where was she?

I'd have to go back and get her.

And right then I saw a streak of white sprinting out of the old barn, just before the building went up in flames.

"Casper!" She had managed to find a hole and wiggle through.

I gave her a hug, but she leaped out of my arms and barked, too agitated to be comforted. It was time to go for help.

My bike lay in the middle of the road looking like a metal pretzel. The sheriff's office was still half a mile down the road. By the time I alerted him—if he was in—the fire would be completely out of control.

I had no choice. There was no way to tell when help might come along. I had to walk into Flat Skunk.

That is, if I could make it. My legs had stiffened and I could barely bend my knees. My right shoulder felt as if it had come loose from its socket.

"Casper, come on!" I started limping down the dark road like a peg-legged pirate, screaming, "Fire! Fire!" every few seconds, in between gasps for air.

As I hobbled forward, the pain in my right shoulder increased, but I could barely feel my knees anymore. Focusing on the sheriff's sign helped. So did groaning, wincing, and grimacing. But I constantly had to turn back to check the spread of the fire.

My bones felt bruised and my skin stung by the time I reached his office. Pounding on the door with my good arm while screaming at the top of my lungs, I looked around for any signs of life in the small town.

I started when the sheriff finally opened the door. "C.W.! What the—"

I bent over in the doorway, trying to catch my breath.

"Sheriff . . . fire . . . there . . ." I said between puffs as I pointed down the road.

Sheriff Mercer caught on immediately. He went back into the office to alert the volunteer fire department.

Good thing. I couldn't talk anymore.

The sheriff headed for the scene of the fire, leaving me behind in the confusion. Forgetting I was bruised and skinned
up from head to foot, I limped over to my office building
and took the stairs, using the rail to pull me forward.
Casper followed right behind me. I needed Dan to give me a
ride back to the fire. I knew he'd be headed that way, as a
volunteer firefighter.

He met me as I was about to try his doorknob.

"Connor! What are you doing here?" Dan had already
donned the thick yellow jacket and was holding a large
flashlight.

"Dan! I need a ride back to the fire."

"You look like you need a ride to the hospital. What the
hell happened to you?"

"I'll tell you on the way over. Wait a second!" I hobbled
to my office, unlocked the door, and grabbed my camera. I
wasn't going to miss this *Eureka!* moment.

"Let's go!" Dan helped me down the stairs to his
truck, and I called Casper to join me on the front seat. Dan
kept asking me questions, but I was too worried about the
fire to talk.

We arrived at the chaotic scene in minutes. The fire truck was already hosing down the flames that had nearly reached the reservoir's border. Volunteers had hastily thrown their yellow jackets over their sleepwear. I took pictures, recognizing several members of the quasi-organization E. Clampus Vitus. Dan joined in, and soon he'd disappeared into the billowing smoke.

"Casper! It's all right!" I tried to soothe her as she snapped at the firefighters, the flames, the streams of water. The old barn had burned down completely, but the Esso station still stood, charred and smoking. I sidled over to get some closer shots, but the firefighters wouldn't let me near the place. Something about the danger of collapse. I tried to cross the blackened grass, still smoking and hot although it had already been doused, but again I was rebuffed and sent to the sidelines.

All I could do was try to calm my dog and snap a few shots of the periphery.

The firefighters had most of the flames out in less than thirty minutes. With highpowered lights from the fire truck shining on the charred field, I could see the weeds smoldering like some primordial swamp. Beyond the smoke was movement. There was something near the cliff of the Miwok Reservoir.

Casper! How had she slipped away from me?

Forgetting my injuries, I ran through the hot embers in my Doc Martens, evading the reaching arms of a firefighter in my path. But when I reached the cliff, I saw that someone already held her. She was dripping wet and covered with soot.

"Andrew!"

I was stunned to see Del Rey's son. He, too, was wet and sooty. And he wasn't alone. With him were Miah and several of his friends from the paint ball team, all of them climbing slowly out of the reservoir.

"What—?"

The sheriff took over before I could get the question out of my mouth. I read his lips by the headlights of his patrol car. "What in God's name are you boys doing here? And what do you know about this fire?"

They looked sheepish and their clothes were soaked. They were wearing camouflage T-shirts and shorts, and a couple of the guys had on some kind of headband gizmo. Spotting a similar headband on the ground, I picked it up. I held what looked like an eyepiece up to my eye and peeked through. Everything turned green.

"These are night-vision goggles, aren't they, Andrew?" I said.

The sheriff scowled at me. Apparently I had interrupted him. He lifted the headpiece from my hands and took a look.

"What are you guys doing with these?" he said.

The boys stood on the edge of the cliff, squeezing the excess water out of their shirts and pants. Casper shook off her latest bath, giving us all a shower in the process. The sprinkle of water felt great on my hot skin.

"Son." The sheriff turned to Miah. "You have some explaining to do."

Miah nodded, embarrassed at being caught by his dad, not to mention being lectured in front of his friends. As much as I felt for him, I wanted to know what they'd been doing there, too.

"We were playing a night game," he said, shrugging, as if it were no big deal to be out shooting one another in the dark.

Miah bent over and picked up a paint ball gun that had apparently been dropped on the run to the lake.

"You were playing paint ball at this hour? Why?" The sheriff's frown deepened.

" 'Cause it's fun. One of the guys at the paint ball games got us these night-vision goggles, so we thought we'd give them a try."

"So you were here playing war games when the fire started?" I asked, trying to put together the sequence of events.

Andrew spoke up. "Yeah. Then we saw someone running in the field—we didn't know it was you at first. We hid behind some rocks so we wouldn't get caught—part of the fun, you know. Then all of a sudden we smelled smoke, and then you go jumping into the reservoir with your dog, and then before we can say anything to you, you start climbing back up the path. Miah and I followed you and saw the flames. Then we saw you running through the fire, and started yelling at you, but you didn't hear us."

"By then the fire was really picking up. We had no choice but to turn around and jump in the reservoir," Miah added. "After the fire trucks arrived, we were too scared to get out. We thought we might get accused of setting the fire. But somehow Casper must have sensed we were in the water and jumped in, too."

I rubbed Casper's back, feeling the damp fur. She sat up, tongue practically hanging to the ground, as if she knew she had done something important. I'd have to rent a Lassie video for her sometime.

Some other kid spoke up, but he wasn't as easy to lip-read in the shadowy light, especially with that chaw in his mouth. I kept my attention on Casper, promising her a special dinner and a thorough behind-the-ear massage when we got home.

Home. I'd almost forgotten why I'd left home in the first place.

After things calmed down, and the sheriff had interviewed the boys, he took down everything I had to say, and asked me to stop by the next morning to sign the report.

After Dan drove Casper and me home, he picked the lock on the diner's front door and let us in. It's great having an ex-cop around when you can't get into your own home. I set about soothing all my ouchies with Neosporin, Bactine, and Mercurochrome, while Dan made medicinal mochas with shots of brandy and prescribed them for internal use. Then he decorated my worst scrapes and scratches with Tweety Bird Band-Aids. Finally, he insisted on spending the night, especially after I told him about the threatening notes, the attack on my bike, and how the fire was started.

"You got another fax," he said, after looking over the notes I had received earlier.

A chill ran through my aching body. "Oh, God. You read it and tell me what it says."

Dan lifted the paper from the tray and read it over before saying anything.

"Is it another one?" I asked, bracing myself with another sip of mocha.

He shook his head and handed it to me. "I think you might be interested in this one."

I read the handwritten note aloud:

"Hi Connor. I got something interesting for you. A guy down at the tattoo parlor said Jasper Coyne tried to sell him his truck once, about five or so years ago. He remembered cause it was the day after Jasper's brother got hurt. They were at a bar together and Jasper was real drunk, and saying things about his 'damn truck.' Anyway, Harrison—he's the tattoo artist—he was kind of interested but before he could take a look at it, Jasper changed his mind. Said it had a dent in it and he needed to get it fixed. Harrison said Jasper was pretty incoherent the whole time. Harrison figured he was getting tanked cause he felt bad about his brother getting paralyzed. Anyway, that's it."

The fax was signed "Freedom."

I looked up at Dan. He said, "So what do you think?"

"I have no clue. How about you? Did you turn up anything more about your brother's ashes?"

"Not exactly. But I did find out something about Jasper's business. The sheriff let me read over his log. According to his notes, he made a trip twice a week through the delta to the bay. And that's where he claimed he scattered the ashes."

"But we know he didn't," I replied.

"Right, but according to his records, and the Coast Guard confirmed this, he *did* make that trip twice a week."

"That's odd. Why would he even bother if he wasn't going to distribute the ashes?" I asked.

"Good question. In fact, one time the Coast Guard made a routine stop and checked the boxes of ashes."

"What did they find?"

"Ashes."

"So he took the boxes of ashes, went to the bay, pretended to pour them overboard, then returned home and stored them in a warehouse. It doesn't make sense."

"Not unless you think about why he might do that."

"Why?" I asked.

"As I was saying earlier, using the ashes to transport something—to hide something—could be the perfect cover. No one would suspect you. And if they checked, like the

Coast Guard apparently did, they wouldn't find anything but ashes."

"You think he was smuggling drugs or something?"

"I would, except there's been no indication he was into that."

"Still, it's possible."

"My thoughts exactly."

I was too tired to think anymore. We showered. Together. To save water. I crawled into bed and pulled the covers up to my neck, relishing the cool sheets and soft comforter against my scraped skin. Dan did the same, substituting my breast for his pillow. It was about the only place that didn't hurt.

"Ow," I said when he stroked my arm.

"Ow," again when he ran a hand up my inner thigh.

And again when he touched my sore shoulder, my ragged knees, and my bruised hip.

"You all right?" he finally asked. "I'm afraid to touch you."

"I'm fine, really. It only hurts when I have sex."

But he did a little detective work and found a number of spots that responded to his gentle handling. I found a few of his too, and we both fanned the flames before the fire was completely put out that night.

The flashing light of the TTY woke me from my pirate dream. But this time I'd been on a houseboat, not a pirate ship. And I was cooking and cleaning for all the men instead of being ravished. What a nightmare.

Dan was still out cold, exhausted from putting out all those fires—literally and figuratively. I rolled out of bed and placed the receiver on the coupler, then waited for the response to my typed greeting. The all-caps style, standard for deaf TTY users, told me it was someone familiar with the TTY.

"THIS IS CALIFORNIA RELAY OPERATOR 51 CALLING FOR ANDREW MONTEZ. GA"

Andrew was calling me? Did he have more to say about last night's events?

"HI ANDREW. HOW ARE YOU THIS MORNING

Q RECOVERED FROM LAST NIGHT I HOPE Q GA" I
used "Q" to indicate a question. It would be interpreted by
the relay operator for Andrew.

"HI CONNOR. I HOPE U ARE ALL RIGHT TOO. I
DID SOME CHECKING ON THE QUESTION YOU
HAD. GA"

"WHAT QUESTION Q. YOU CAN SPEAK FREELY.
THE RELAY OPERATOR IS REQUIRED TO KEEP
EVERYTHING CONFIDENTIAL. GA"

"OK. WELL, I TALKED TO THE GUY WHO GOT
ME THE YOU-KNOW-WHAT AND HE TOLD ME
WHERE HE GOT IT. CAN WE MEET SOMEWHERE—
NOT AT THE MORTUARY SO MY MOM DOESN'T
FIND OUT Q GA"

"SURE. HOW ABOUT MY OFFICE IN AN HOUR
Q GA"

"I'LL BE THERE. DON'T TELL MY MOM, OK Q
OR THE SHERIFF YET. GA"

I promised him secrecy and we signed off. The gun information was certainly important, but my mind was occupied
right now by other matters—like the fire, the threatening
notes, and the death of Portia Bryson.

I made a mental note to show the threatening fax and
TTY printout to the sheriff after I talked with Andrew. And
I wanted to see if Arthurlene Jackson had discovered any-
thing more about Portia's death.

Maybe I'd pay another visit to Chunker Lansky, too.

After showering, feeding Casper an extra-special breakfast and giving her a belly massage, I left Dan asleep on my
sofa bed and headed for the office. I had to drive my Chevy,
since my bike was beyond repair. It would take me a while
to find another one I liked as much as the Peugeot.

Andrew was in the office when I arrived. Miah had apparently let him in. The two boys were engrossed in a computer version of War Games that even the smell of fresh
cinnamon raisin bagels couldn't break. It was another five
minutes before Andrew threw up his hands in defeat, while
Miah shot his up in victory.

"Lose another battle?" I asked Andrew, who shook his
head in disgust at Miah. Miah took the opportunity to rub
it in, as guys do. I turned on my computer screen and checked

my E-mail while they argued over who was really victorious. There was another message from the generic E-mail address that had sent me the threat last night.

"If you play with fire your going to get burned."

My first thought was he'd spelled "your" wrong. It was the newspaper editor in me. But the second thought hit home. Someone was going to hurt me if I continued to investigate this story.

"Miah!"

Miah broke off from the playful argument to sign "What?"

"Can you find out who sent this note?"

Both young men leaned over my screen and read the message.

"Shit!" Andrew said. "Somebody trying to scare you?"

Miah signed an answer to my question. "Sometimes you can go back to a clearinghouse that holds links but sometimes it's kept anonymous. Let me take a look."

"What are you guys talking about?" Andrew said. I realized we'd been excluding him from the conversation with our signing, not using our voices. The feeling of exclusion was something I experienced with hearing people all the time.

"Sorry, Andrew. I was just asking Miah if he could trace the E-mail. While he's working on that, let's talk about the latest news. You said you found out something for me?"

Andrew nodded as Miah went to work at my computer. I pulled up another chair opposite Del Rey's son so I could read him clearly.

"I found out who's providing the guns. It wasn't easy—they're so gung-ho about all this secrecy, you know. Anyway, this guy, he's got AK-forty-sevens, all kinds of militia gear, a lot of it left over from Vietnam, a lot of it new. He sells it out of his bedroom, if you can believe that. Everything's hidden under the floorboards, so his parents won't find out about it. He's got a fuckin' arsenal there."

"Who is he?"

"Name's Jeff. He's one of the skinheads who runs the war games."

I knew exactly who he was—the guy who'd refereed our paint ball game. In fact, I'd suspected as much. Now I needed to find out who was supplying *him* with the illegal weapons.

Miah sat back in his chair, flashed open his fist beneath his chin, and shook his head.

"Nothing."

One path opened while another one closed.

I knew I was taking a risk going to see Jeff Pike alone. He could easily have been the one who shot up my diner and office, or the one who knocked me off my bike and set fire to the hillside. After all, if he thought I was investigating his gun dealing, he might do anything to stop me.

But I figured he wouldn't hurt me in broad daylight with a bunch of people standing around. Besides, I wanted him to know I wasn't afraid of him. A lie, of course.

I found him in at the paint ball field, refereeing another game. A number of wanna-be soldiers were stalking the perimeter of the battlefield, hoping to avoid being shot while capturing the opponents' flag. The players with the red armbands currently outnumbered the ones in blue.

I marched up the dry hill to where Jeff stood and nodded hello, the way young guys do. He nodded back, then returned his attention to the game. I stood so I could read his lips and glance now and then at the action.

"Who's winning?" I asked, attempting to ease into the interrogation.

"Clampers—the guys in red. They're beating the crap out of the Moose Lodge."

"You do this seven days a week?" I asked after witnessing a hit. Some guy with a blue armband now sported a splotch of yellow paint on his khaki vest.

Jeff nodded. "During the summer. It's usually just weekends during the winter. People come from all over to play here. We've got the best setup, the fastest guns, and the biggest battlefield."

"Business is really booming, then. Must be nice, not having to work at some boring job when you can do this full-time."

"Beats washing cars and selling burgers, that's for sure."

"That's what you did before you got into paint ball games?"

For the first time since he greeted me, he met my eyes. "You're full of questions today. What's up? You planning to open your own field?"

"God, no. I thought I'd do an article on the paint ball games—and how you got involved in them. I thought I'd personalize it a little and include your background."

He nodded and glanced back at the field, which currently looked deserted. Apparently everyone was hiding from everyone else. I wasn't even playing the game and still I could feel the tension rising.

"So what do you want to know?"

"Well, how did you get into this?" I pulled my notebook out of my backpack for effect, and jotted down notes as he spoke.

"Like I said, it beats those minimum-wage jobs. I read about paint ball in one of those survivalist magazines, and the games sounded like a kick. So I organized a couple of battles up here for my buddies, and got into it. That was three years ago. Now I've got my own small business."

"Do you really make enough to live on?"

Jeff gave me another side glance. "It pays the bills."

I scanned the parking lot and spotted a new Harley Davidson in the space closest to the trailer office. Blue with lightning stripes, the hog was as big as a Volkswagen. But it probably cost three times as much.

"Nice bike. Is it yours?"

He shrugged.

"I thought you drove a truck. Sidestep pickup. That was new, too, wasn't it? I know the kids were drooling over it the other day."

"Yeah, I still got it."

"You must be making the big bucks."

"Like I said, it pays the bills. But I don't discuss the financial aspects of the business. You understand."

I nodded. "Wish I'd thought of something this lucrative. I barely get by with the newspaper. If it weren't for the ads, I'd have to figure out another way to make money, moonlighting."

He shot me a look.

"Jeff, I've been . . . well, harassed lately. I'm kinda worried about my safety. I hear you know a lot about guns. Maybe you could tell me what kind of weapon I should get to protect myself."

Jeff stared at the battlefield.

"A friend of mine said you might know where I could get a gun. I don't need anything really fancy—"

He whirled around. "Who said I knew where to get a gun?"

"Just a friend. He asked me not to give his name. As a reporter—"

"Well, he must not be a friend of mine. I don't know nothing about getting ahold of real guns. Whoever said that is mistaken. I'm strictly paint ball weapons. That's it."

"Sorry, I didn't mean to upset you. I just thought you might be able to help me."

"Go talk to the sheriff if you want protection. He's your buddy, isn't he?"

"I don't think he'd like it if I got a gun. He thinks I might shoot myself or something."

"Yeah? Well, you might. Better listen to his advice."

I sensed this conversation had reached an end. Jeff wasn't going to tell me anything about his side job.

"Thanks for the information. I'll see if I can work up some kind of follow-up story. Can I stop by if I have any more questions?"

"Sure," he said, smiling for the first time. "But I think I've told you everything I can. Sorry I can't make it more interesting."

"Oh, it's been very interesting." I returned his smile, and headed back to the parking lot. I didn't need to look back to know he was watching my every move.

I checked to see if Dan was in his office, but the door was locked. Still investigating those ashes, I assumed. Wish I had the free time to just snoop around all day, like he did. But I had a newspaper to produce. Dan seemed to be at loose ends, after his temporary employment at the mortuary ended. This ash scam investigation was the first thing I'd seen him get excited about in a long time. The cop in him was still there.

I spent the rest of the day adding to Miah's story about the increase in vandalism at local schools—mainly bullet holes. The Mother Lode area had also experienced more break-ins and destruction of property lately, and no one seemed to be able to account for the recent trend. After using the relay system to interview a school psychologist, two principals, and a custodian regarding possible reasons for the damage, I had enough to fill a half page—all providing conflicting theories. What I had didn't seem substantial enough to balance the many police reports I'd pored over.

A little depressed from doing the homework and not coming up with answers, I stopped by Dan's office again to see if he wanted to share dinner, but he still wasn't in. I swung by the sheriff's office to see if anything more had come in on Portia's drowning, but he wasn't in either. I finally headed over to the mortuary, to see if Del Rey wanted to go to lunch. I had a feeling she might need some cheering up. When I arrived, I found her at her desk, staring off into space.

"Del Rey?"

She started at my words. "Oh, hi, Connor. I didn't hear you come in."

"Happens to me all the time. How're you doing?" I sat across the desk from her, in a cozy overstuffed antique chair covered in blue velvet.

"I'm okay. You heard about Chunker? The court won't release him. In fact, now they're thinking about charging him with Portia's murder. This whole thing is out of control."

"I know. Sheriff Mercer told me."

"And here's irony for you. Portia is scheduled to come here for cremation! Not only does she get my ex-husband accused of murdering my other ex-husband, but she makes me handle her disposition."

"You don't want to handle it?"

"Not especially, but—"

The door burst open. Red-faced with anger, Berkeley Mondshane stormed in. He held a wad of papers in his hand and was shaking them violently at Del Rey. Right behind him came Andrew, who also looked angry and upset.

"Mondshane! I told you. Get the hell out of here—"

"What's the meaning of this?" Berkeley Mondshane screamed at Del Rey. He looked ready to attack her at any second. With his attention on Del Rey, I surreptitiously lifted the desk phone and punched 911.

When I looked back, Mondshane was still raging. ". . . you have no right to handle Portia Bryson's body! With all the damage you've done to this community, all the piss-poor handling of loved ones' ashes, you're nothing but an incompetent fraud. And you're ruining the reputation of legitimate mortuaries like mine! I've worked hard to show customers the reliability of my services. Never would I allow someone connected with my mortuary to misplace ashes!"

I think that's what he said. His lips were distorted by his anger, but I had a feeling I got the gist of it. I hoped the sheriff had too. I'd been holding the phone at my side, turned to pick up Mondshane's diatribe.

Berkeley turned to me. "What the fuck are you doing?" He wrenched the receiver out of my hand and slammed it down. "Who do you think you're calling? Get the fuck out of here before I—"

Andrew was all over him, just like he had been at the paint ball games. The two tussled to the floor. Berkeley hit his temple on the edge of the desk in the fall. Andrew whaled on him until Del Rey and I both pulled him back.

He had calmed down and had Berkeley under control by the time Sheriff Mercer arrived.

"Sheriff! You heard the call!" I said.

Sheriff Mercer yanked Andrew off Berkeley and pulled the mortician to his feet.

"I didn't, but Rebecca called me and told me to get over here. What the hell is going on? What in God's name are you doing, Andrew? You wanna kill the guy? Jesus! Am I going to have to throw you both in jail until you can cut it out?"

Andrew flushed. "He . . . attacked my mother!" he sputtered.

Berkeley pushed himself up and brushed off his light summer suit. "I did not! I didn't lay a finger on her!"

"You verbally attacked her—"

The sheriff held up his hands. "Stop it! Both of you. Mondshane, what the hell are you doing here? A grown man, a professional in the community, and here you are arm wrestling with a kid half your age."

Berkeley Mondshane grew indignant once again. "Sheriff! How can you let Portia Bryson's body be turned over to this shady establishment when you know about their illegal involvement in that warehouse discovery? It's immoral, blasphemous, and downright criminal!"

I saw Andrew's fists tighten, and I stepped between him and Berkeley.

The sheriff continued. "Look, Mondshane, Del Rey hasn't been charged with anything and until she is, she has every right to carry on her business. It was Portia's wish that she be cremated at the Memorial Kingdom Mortuary and I'm here to make sure her legal request is carried out. You got that?"

Berkeley turned to Del Rey, glowered, and stormed out of the room without even a "you're going to regret this!" That was the first surprise. The second came after the rest of us headed out through the foyer.

In the middle of the ornate Persian carpet stood a heap of gray soot. Someone had dumped a pile of ashes on the floor.

After the sheriff drove back to his office, Del Rey and I cleaned up the ashes. Neither one of us wondered aloud where they had come from. I hoped it was newspaper ash, but I couldn't be sure.

Del Rey accepted my invitation for mochas at the Nugget Café. Andrew declined to join us, saying he had things to do. I worried what those things were, but said nothing. Del Rey didn't need the extra stress.

Jilda took our orders and brought our mochas. We sat for a few minutes, saying nothing.

"Idiot," I said, after a few minutes. I emphasized the word with a sign, hitting my forehead with a fist.

"Moron," Del Rey added.

"Asshole." I ran my index finger around the letter "O."

"Jerk."

"Butthead." I twisted a "V" at my forehead.

Del Rey burst into laughter. "Butthead? That's the best you can do?"

"I need a thesaurus. I usually stop after 'asshole.' "

Grinning, Del Rey and I sipped our mochas.

"He's something else, that Mondshane," I said.

"He's always been so competitive. Always felt threatened by Memory Kingdom. I wouldn't put it past him to have a hand in this. He'd like nothing better than to see my mortuary fold up and die."

"Think that's possible?"

"That the place will close?"

"No, that he could be involved."

Del Rey shrugged. "I just don't know what's what anymore, Connor. Nothing makes sense. All I know is, my first ex-husband is dead, my second ex is in jail, my kids are a wreck, my business is suffering, and I've got to do a cremation tomorrow that I'm not looking forward to."

"Why not turn it over to Mondshane, if you don't want to do it?"

"Because I respect the wishes of the deceased, whether anyone believes that or not. But I do have a problem."

"What's that?"

"With Chunker in jail, I'm shorthanded again. Any chance Dan might consider a part-time job cremating bodies?"

I shivered. "I doubt it. Don't you have anyone else?"

She shook her head. "I could hire a temp, I suppose. Some guy came around yesterday looking for a job. At the time, I told him I didn't need anyone. I might have to give him a call."

"So it doesn't take much skill to cremate someone?"

"Nah, not these days. I can show him what to do. Basically, you lay out the body in a combustible container, like pine or even heavy cardboard, so it doesn't pollute. Then you place it on the conveyor belt, point the body toward the retort—"

"The what?"

"The retort. The oven. Then you turn on the heat to about two thousand degrees, and three hours later, you've got an oxidized body. After that you collect the ash, transfer it to the proper container, and sign a paper that you witnessed the proceedings, that's it. It's not difficult. I could do it, but I'll be busy with the memorial preparations and guests and all that."

"It sounds simple enough."

"It is, but you have to watch out for a few things. If the body has a pacemaker, the lithium batteries could explode, so it has to be removed. We use an electromagnet to remove any metal. And you have to pulverize the bone fragments when you're done, so it's all a fine powder. Also, you have to be careful about air pollution. We use afterburners and scrubbers to take care of that."

"Is this a big trend today—cremation?"

"It's growing, cause it's quick, clean, cheap, and easy— and there's no danger of being buried alive." Del Rey grinned. "It's also a great way to hide a murder. It destroys all the evidence, except some poisons. But it's still not the primary way people want to go. Eighty-five percent prefer to be interred."

"Why?"

"Religion. Tradition. Superstition."

I had a thought. "How much do the ashes weigh?"

"Anywhere from three to nine pounds, depending on the size of the body. The average man weighs about seven pounds, a woman is usually six."

"Do you ever have trouble with cremains robbers? Guys who steal gold crowns and jewelry, either before or after the cremation?"

"I did once. Fired his ass the next day. It wasn't difficult to figure what he'd done. Sluice has been helping me ever since. But he's gotten so flaky."

"Well, before you hire anyone else, you might want to do a background check. You never know. He might end up being another ex-con."

Del Rey downed the rest of her mocha.

I was awakened by my TTY light the next morning. Stumbling out of bed, guided by the blinding flashes, I clumsily placed the receiver in the coupler and sort of typed a greeting: "CONNOR WESTPHAL HEAR. GA" I was too tired to correct the ironic spelling and let it go.

Seconds later the display lit up with an introduction from California Relay: "DEL REY MONTEZ CALLING CONNOR WESTPHAL. GA"

"HI DEL REY. WHAT'S UP Q GA"

"CONNOR I'VE GOT A PROBLEM AND NEED YOUR HELP. CAN YOU GET OVER HERE RIGHT AWAY Q. GA"

I waited a few seconds to see if there was more, then typed, "WHAT'S THE MATTER DEL REY Q GA," hoping for a good reason to get dressed and leave the comfort of my diner at the ungodly hour of 6:00 A.M. Instead, I read the words: "YOUR PARTY HAS DISCONNECTED. GA SK."

And then I had a disturbing thought. Was it really Del Rey who had called? What if it was the wise guy who'd been leaving me threatening messages?

I replaced the receiver and sat at my desk, wondering if

the call was legit. One way to find out. Call her back. I dialed the California Relay operator, gave her Del Rey's number, and waited for Del Rey to come on the line.

"THERE'S NO ANSWER. GA," came the typed response. "DO YOU WANT TO LEAVE A MESSAGE ON THE ANSWERING MACHINE Q GA"

I declined, hung up, then dialed another number. After waiting what seemed a lifetime, a familiar typing style appeared on the screen.

"YEeah what is it cW? What are you doing up so early"

I waited for the signal to go ahead. When it didn't come, I gave up, and typed in hearing style. "Sheriff, I just got a strange call from Del Rey. At least I think it was Del Rey. It came over the Relay, so I guess it could have been anybody. Anyway, she said something has happened and she wants me to come over. I wondered if you'd like to come along, just in case. GA"

"ANY idea whats going onn GA"

"No idea. But I think we should check it out. When I called back she didn't answer her phone. I'd say that's odd, if she just called me. GA"

"Come on over. I'll drive you to the mortuary and we'll check it out. Got any of those mochas you make yourself every morning"

Forgot the go-ahead again. "I'll mix one myself at the Nugget after we check on Del Rey. I'm leaving now. GA SK."

He GA'd and SK'd me and I hung up the phone. It took me five minutes to pull on the same clothes that still lay in a heap next to my bed from yesterday—my maroon jeans and my blue T-shirt that read "Deaf—Not Dumb" in fingerspelled letters. I sucked on the toothpaste tube, ran a brush through my hair three times, and headed out the door with barely a word of explanation to Casper.

The light was just breaking in Flat Skunk as I drove my Chevy into the sheriff's parking lot. Every little bump in the road reminded me of my sore shoulder. *I should really have that checked*, I thought as I got out of the Chevy. The sheriff must have seen me, because he was outside by the time I got out and slammed my car door.

"It's too early for a wild goose chase, CW," Sheriff

Mercer said, just before he climbed into the driver's seat of his patrol car.

"It's too early to live," I responded, after sliding into the shotgun side. I loved riding in his patrol car. It made me feel like I was a cop. I wanted to be a cop once. Thought I could, too, until I found out about the hearing requirement. That is, you have to be able to hear.

"Full lights and siren?" I asked, as he backed out onto the street.

He turned on the rotating red and blue lights, and I watched them give Main Street a horror movie glow. "What about the siren?"

"It's on," he said, shifting in his seat.

"Liar."

He looked at me. "How do you know?"

" 'Cause that's one of the sounds I can hear. High and low noises are my specialty."

He grinned. "I sometimes wonder if you really are as deaf as you lead me to believe. No siren—too early for the hungover residents of Skunk."

We pulled up to the mortuary and knocked on the door. Andrew, wearing an untucked white T-shirt and flannel boxers, opened it wide to allow us both in. "Hi, Connor, hey, Sheriff," Andrew said. Rather than looking sleepy, he looked nervous.

"Where's you mother, son? C.W. here got a call that Del Rey had a problem. What's up?"

He ran a hand through his tousled hair. "I think you better follow me."

Andrew led us barefoot through the mortuary, out the back door, and into a windowless building constructed of heavy brick. We passed a large sign that read, "Crematory," with a small sign underneath that warned: "No admittance. Biohazard." I shivered as the door closed behind me.

"I've never been inside here before," I said, as I followed behind them. If they gave a response, I missed it.

"In here," Andrew gestured, as he held open the door to a tiny room painted in soft pastels. Along three walls sat decorative brass, copper, silver, and gold-plated urns on mahogany shelves, each one labeled. "The Legend." "The

Keepsake." "The Memento." "The Voyage." Something for everyone's view of eternity.

Del Rey sat on a cotton candy pink sofa flanked by two sky blue wing chairs. Lemon yellow and sherbet green cushions rested on the sofa. Del Rey stood as we entered, leaving a small box of ashes on the seat. In one hand she held a file folder; her other was a tight fist.

"Connor! Thank God you're here. Hi, Sheriff."

"I hope you don't mind—" I started to say, but she cut me off.

"No, I was going to call him myself eventually, after I talked with you. Sheriff, the body you sent over, Portia Bryson? You said she drowned, right?"

The sheriff nodded.

"And there were no other signs of foul play, according to Arthurlene Jackson's autopsy report, right?"

"That's correct. What's this all about, Del Rey?"

Del Rey turned toward the door and called out something I couldn't lip-read. In a few seconds a young man with a shaved head, studded jeans, and a black Marilyn Manson T-shirt appeared at the door. "Sheriff, this is Keith Melton. He's my new temporary assistant."

The sheriff nodded, and Keith nervously returned the greeting. I figured the police just made some people skittish, the way dentists and tax auditors did.

Del Rey held out her arm and opened her fist. In her palm rested a small, mushroom-shaped piece of metal.

"What's that?" I asked.

"It's a bullet," Sheriff Mercer replied.

I bit my tongue to keep from saying, "Duh," and went straight to, "I *know* that. I mean, what's it doing there?" I pointed to Del Rey's hand.

"Good question. Del Rey, what's this all about?"

"Keith found it. After he cremated Portia Bryson's body."

The sheriff said nothing at first, just looked back and forth between Del Rey, Keith Melton, and the bullet. Finally he said, "That's not possible."

"Not according to the coroner's report," Del Rey agreed. "But here it is."

"But Arthurlene didn't find any evidence of a bullet wound."

"I understand that. Nevertheless, let me repeat, this is what we found in Portia's ashes."

While the sheriff rubbed his chin, I did a little mental chin rubbing. Could the ME have overlooked a bullet wound? Not Dr. Jackson. She was too good. The sheriff must have read my mind—he pulled out his cell phone and dialed what I assumed was the county coroner's office. After a few minutes of double and triple checking, he hung up the phone, shaking his head.

"Arthurlene confirms it. She said there were no bullet wounds found in the body. And she's too careful to miss something like that."

"But . . ." Del Rey began, then she stopped speaking and fell back into the sofa. Her face was pale and beads of perspiration had broken out at her temples. Her expression changed from incomprehension to horror. "You know what that means, then . . ."

The sheriff stated the obvious aloud. "It means, if Portia Bryson didn't swallow a bullet before she died, the body you just cremated wasn't Portia Bryson."

"Then who . . . ?" Del Rey seemed unable to complete her sentence.

I said it for her. "Then whose body was cremated?"

The sheriff voiced my next thought. "And where is Portia Bryson's body?"

It was too early in the morning for a beer, but we all could have used one. The five of us gathered in Del Rey's kitchen and sipped coffee in silence, mulling over the possibilities of this new wrinkle.

"All right. Here are the facts," Sheriff Mercer began. "Portia Bryson's body was supposedly picked up by one of your staff, Del Rey, and brought to the Memory Kingdom Mortuary, correct?"

Del Rey nodded, still looking dazed.

"Keith, you collected the body from the coroner, with all the proper documents, I assume."

Keith nodded.

"Then you prepped the body for cremation, according to Del Rey's instructions, right?"

Keith nodded again.

"You didn't know what Portia Bryson looked like, so you wouldn't have noticed whether or not the body you collected was really hers, correct?"

Keith, looking wide-eyed and confused, said, "I sure hope I didn't do anything wrong. It's my first day on the job and I really wanted to make a good impression. I liked the last job I had but they laid me off 'cause of lack of business. I was real lucky to get this one—"

"Okay, Keith." The sheriff cut him off. "Simmer down. You haven't done anything wrong. I'm just trying to figure this thing out."

No one said anything for a moment, then Andrew spoke up. "Well, someone must have switched her body at the county morgue. That's the only explanation. Someone's going to have to check it out."

"If that's true, son, then not only is the county in trouble for mishandling the body, but we've still got to account for the fact that someone else was cremated instead of Portia."

Del Rey began to weep. "And you know what that means. I'm out of business for good. I can't make it through another scandal. No one will ever trust this mortuary again."

Andrew angrily pulled a tissue from a box on the counter and thrust it at his mother. "Shit! I know who did this. Somehow, Berkeley Mondshane is behind this. For months, he's been trying to run us out of business and take over the whole industry in the Mother Lode. Well, he's not going to get away with it!"

Andrew stormed out of the room before the sheriff, Del Rey, or I could grab him.

I was staring at my computer, pretending to work, when Dan stopped in to question me about the latest development. The news about Portia's missing body was spreading like a windblown grass fire.

"Sheriff get any info from the coroner yet?" Dan asked, perching on my desk. He stared out the window as he spoke.

I explained the bullet Del Rey had found in Portia's ashes that morning. Dan didn't seem to be paying attention.

"What are you looking at?" I said, standing so I could see out the window, too.

"Nothing. Thought I saw Levi Coyne drive by in his truck. Could have been anyone. There are so many trucks in this town."

"Beat-up gray with a red hood?"

Dan nodded.

"Damn. I'll bet he's headed for Del Rey's." I snatched up my backpack and headed for the door. Dan caught me by the arm.

"Whoa," he said. "If you're going over there, you may need some company. This guy could be really pissed."

"I can handle him," I said, frowning at the insinuation I couldn't. "He's in a wheelchair."

Dan stopped in his tracks.

"What?"

"Connor Westphal. You of all people, underestimating the disabled."

He was right. I had my own biases and I couldn't seem to shake them. I'd deal with them later.

Dan and I arrived at the mortuary in time to see Levi Coyne enter via the handicapped ramp. He'd left his truck in a blue-curbed parking space near the front. The door to the mortuary stood ajar.

I dashed inside with Dan right behind me. Sure enough, Levi was not in the best of moods. He seemed to be shouting through the curtained doorway, but he had a hand at his mouth, so I couldn't tell what he was saying.

Del Rey appeared a moment later, looking perturbed.

"What's going on here?" Del Rey demanded. Her hands were covered with rubber gloves. She removed them as she glanced from Levi to Dan and me.

"That's what I'd like to know," Levi said. "Where's Portia?"

"Calm down, Mr. Coyne. As I said in my message, there's been a slight problem, but I'm sure we'll get to the bottom of it."

"Where's my sister-in-law's body? I demand to see it!" The veins on Levi's forehead pulsed with every heartbeat.

While Del Rey tried to calm Levi, I saw Dan slip through the curtain and down the hall. I hoped he was on his way to Del Rey's office, to call the sheriff. I turned my attention back to Del Rey, and caught her midsentence.

". . . sure her body will turn up. It seems that someone else was sent over instead of Portia, but we're looking for her. Just calm down—"

"If anything has happened to her, I'll . . . I'll . . ." He stopped and pinched his eyes. "For the love of God, how could you do this to me? On top of everything that's happened, now you've managed to lose her . . ."

Suddenly Levi's anger dissipated, replaced by tears he could no longer hold back. He buried his face in his hands.

Dan reappeared in the doorway and exaggeratedly mouthed the words: "Sheriff is coming." I nodded, but Del Rey didn't see our communication. She was staring at Levi, looking helpless and near tears herself.

I squatted in front of Levi and placed a hand on his arm. He ignored it for a few seconds, then looked up at me. I reached for a tissue from the desk—the mortuary was full of tissue boxes—and passed it to him, giving him a few minutes to collect himself. He seemed to be reacting more to Portia's death than to his own brother's.

When I thought he was composed, I said, "Levi, was there something more between you and Portia?"

He glared at me. "Of course there was. She was my sister-in-law! She did everything for me, and now she's been killed by that ex-con, drowned . . . and her body's gone . . ." Tears lined his eyes again.

I didn't see the sheriff come up behind me, but I smelled his mints. Altoids. He ate them all the time, in case he's ever in a position to kiss someone, he'd once told me. Sheriff Locke, perhaps? I stood up and faced him.

"What's the problem now, Del Rey?" Sheriff Mercer seemed to be growing tired of the constant drama.

Del Rey shook her head. Levi filled in the conversational gap with another tirade about the misplacement of Portia's body. The sheriff listened patiently, his hand resting on his gunbelt.

"I understand your concerns, Levi. And we're looking into it, believe me. The county's doing their part—"

Levi tried to interrupt, but the sheriff wouldn't let him. He went on, speaking calmly.

"Now you go on back to your place and I'll contact you as soon as I know anything. That's a promise. I know this is hard on you—it's hard on us, too. We all want to get it resolved as quickly as possible. But if you keep interfering with the investigation, like you are now, it just slows everything down, you understand?"

Levi eyed him but said nothing, although his clenched jaw was working at hyperspeed. The sheriff continued his soothing but generic words about checking the county morgue and finding nothing out of the ordinary. No shooting victims who had mysteriously gone missing. When he was finished, Levi backed up his wheelchair, spun around, and rolled out the still open door. Dan closed it behind him.

"Thanks, Sheriff." Del Rey looked relieved as she dipped under the desk and pulled out four Shastas in four different flavors. Dan and I grabbed one each, following Del Rey's lead, but the sheriff just stood there, as if listening to some other voice in his head. Something was still on his mind. Or was it his hearing loss?

"Sheriff? What is it?" I said.

He rubbed his chin.

"Sheriff?" Del Rey echoed.

"Del Rey, do you own a gun?"

Del Rey flushed, then nodded.

"Mind if I take a look at it?"

We all stood there for a moment, saying nothing. Then Del Rey broke the silence. "Why do you need to see my rifle?"

The sheriff rubbed his chin again. He was going to rub a hole in it if he wasn't careful.

"It's just routine. I need to do a little checking. Now could I have the rifle? Please."

Del Rey whirled out of the room. I didn't know how much more stress she could take. If it had been me, I'd have jumped in Lake Miwok by now.

"What's this all about, Sheriff?" I asked, but he waved me quiet. I glanced at Dan, but all he did was shrug. Some help he'd turned out to be. I wanted answers.

Del Rey took her time returning. After five or so minutes of Dan's sipping his soda, my pacing the room, and the sheriff's rocking back and forth on his heels, she finally appeared at the door. But she was no longer upset. The fire had gone out of her.

"What's wrong, Del Rey?" I asked.

"The rifle's gone."

Andrew was nowhere to be found. A thorough search of the mortuary turned up a puzzled Courtney-Freedom, but no sign of Del Rey's son. I went looking for the new guy, Keith, but he'd left a note saying he'd gone to lunch. No one had any idea where Andrew—or the rifle—might have gone.

Dan left with the sheriff, but I stayed with Del Rey until she asked me to leave so she could get on with her work. She sent Courtney out to Andrew's haunts to look for him. Reluctantly, I headed back to the office, my stomach growling. Still worried about Andrew, I took a detour and entered the Nugget, starved for a BLT, a double mocha, and maybe a bag or two of potato chips. It would give me time to think.

Levi sat in the first booth, his wheelchair tucked into a nook to one side. He was stewing over a strawberry milkshake, staring down at a tall old-fashioned glass. I decided to join him and make it a party.

He looked up as I swung myself into the opposite side of the booth.

"What do you want?"

"That's not a very welcoming greeting. Just thought you might want company."

"Well, I don't." He took a big suck on the straw and swallowed the mouthful. Pink peeked out from the corners of his mouth.

I signaled Jilda for a mocha, then folded my hands in front of me. In a few minutes Jilda brought my coffee. I ordered a BLT and asked Levi if he wanted one, which he declined.

I took a sip of the mocha. "I'm sorry about everything that's happened to you," I said, hoping the icebreaker wouldn't break anything else.

"I don't need your pity."

"I didn't mean it that way. I don't want anyone's pity either."

Something melted in him, I could see it in his eyes. He said nothing, but the two-by-four seemed to fall from his shoulder. "Someone's going to pay for all this, I swear it. If it weren't for Del Rey and Chunker, none of this would have happened."

"What do you mean? Del Rey didn't do anything. If you want to blame someone, try your brother. He's the one who—"

"You keep my brother out of this. He changed after she left him. She's the one who made him give up on life and drink himself into a stupor every night. And she's even the one who caused the fight that night."

"What are you talking about? Del Rey wasn't at the bar. She had nothing to do with it."

"Oh, you can go on believing she's Little Miss Innocent, but the fight was all about her. It's really all her fault."

"Levi—"

It was too late. He'd worked himself up again and wouldn't listen. I watched him retrieve his wheelchair, then scoot himself out of the booth and into the well-worn leather seat of his chair. He pulled on his fingerless gloves and guided the wheelchair out the door, held open by Dan. He even stiffed me with the bill.

Dan and I talked things over while he ate a BLT and a bag of cheddar chips. I sat with him, occasionally mustering up the hunger for another chip. He hadn't found out anything new about the ashes, but had plans to go to the library and do some more research. I told him about the weight of the ashes after cremation, but he already knew. After the sandwich, I headed back to the office, while Dan went to the library.

I spent the rest of the afternoon working on a piece about accessibility for the disabled in Flat Skunk—or the lack of it. As I packed up at the end of the day, I left Miah to lay out the back page of the *Eureka!*, including reports on two more shootings—one in Feather Camp and one in Silver Creek, both reported by Sheriff Locke. The sheriff who didn't believe in gun control.

I hopped in my Chevy, looking forward to decompressing at my diner. I needed a good romp with my dog, a nice plate of leftover pesto linguine, and a distracting murder mystery on captioned TV to bring me peace of mind.

But fate had other plans. As I drove up to my diner home, I was greeted by another not-so-subtle message. Once again my diner had been shot up.

And this time, the bullet holes looked real.

Shit!"

I stamped my foot and threw my backpack into the driveway.

"Shit! Fuck! Goddamnittohell!"

I screamed the words at the top of my lungs. I could tell because my throat was hashed after I shut up. I hoped to God the shooters heard me.

I thought about not going inside. Maybe they were in there, waiting for me. Nah. If they wanted to surprise me, they wouldn't have left their calling card first. These were bullshit cowards, trying to scare a deaf reporter into backing off. Fuck that.

I jammed the key into the front door lock and called Casper, certain she was hiding under my sofa bed. But a quick search of the place revealed no sign of her. I ran out back where she likes to play when I'm not home. She has a pass-through door that allows her in-and-out privileges so she can come and go as she pleases. The backyard is au naturel—no gardening required to maintain its indigenous beauty. A bed of pine needles padded my steps as I searched behind bushes and trees for my dog.

I spotted the doghouse. She never used it. I'd bought it for her when I first got her, but she preferred the master's quarters over her own condo. But if she was frightened, maybe . . .

A tail stuck out from the small opening.

"Casper!"

The tail wagged once.

"Casper! Come on girl, it's okay. I'm here."

The tail went into full swing. I could have washed my car with the motion. She backed out of the hole and jumped up as I squatted beside her. Her enthusiasm nearly knocked me over.

"You had a bad scare, didn't you, girl?"

She licked my face, my hair, my hands, and my T-shirt. I wouldn't need a shower tonight.

After I calmed her down and reassured her she was safe again, we went inside the diner for drinks—a light beer for me, a large water for her. Then I dialed the sheriff.

An hour later the sheriff was finished with his official investigation of the shootings at my diner. His deputy, Marca Clemens, had taken pictures, prints, and even a cast of tire marks, while Sheriff Mercer asked me questions I couldn't answer. Casper and I followed him to his office to fill out a couple of forms, but I had a hunch it wouldn't be easy finding enough physical evidence to catch these guys.

"The only thing we have to go on are these bullet casings, C.W. And they probably came from an unregistered weapon. That causes me concern."

"Are you worried about me, Sheriff?"

"Course I am. I know how you hate that, and I *know* you can take care of yourself, but this guy is serious."

I glanced at the slugs the deputy had extracted from the wall of the diner. To me, bullets all look the same. Deadly. Still, this one looked a lot like that bullet Del Rey had found in the cremated ashes. Kind of flattened, distorted. Same guy, I wondered?

I picked up one of the bullets from the diner and examined it closely. "Sheriff, what kind of gun did this come from?"

"A rifle," he said simply. I waited for him to give me more details, but he suddenly looked uncomfortable.

"Okay, Sheriff, what's up?"

"C.W., why do you always think there's something when there's nothing?"

" 'Cause you're an open book when it comes to reading body language."

"Oh yeah? Well then, why don't you tell me what's on my mind?"

I stared at him, trying to read the thoughts beyond his expression. "You know something and you're not telling me. What is it?"

"C.W., I happen to be an officer of the law. That means I don't have to tell you everything there is to know about everything."

But he gave it away as soon as he glanced at a small envelope on his desk marked "Portia Bryson."

I picked it up.

"Put that down," he said sharply.

I felt the outline of the bullet. The bullet taken from Portia's—or whoever's—ashes.

"I said, put that down."

"All right, then show me."

The sheriff frowned and opened the envelope. He shook the bullet onto the desk, careful not to touch it. It looked like the ones that had been taken from my diner.

"They're the same, aren't they?"

The sheriff shrugged. "Can't tell without a ballistics test."

"But we can make a tentative assumption here, can't we? The guys who shot up my diner are the same ones who shot and killed Portia—or whoever was cremated in Portia's place."

"You can't make that assumption, C.W. Not without a lot more proof." The sheriff blinked nervously. What was going on behind those eyes?

"There's something else, isn't there! Tell me!"

Sheriff Mercer slid the bullet back into the envelope and set it aside. I watched his eyes for clues. Sure enough, he glanced at a report that had been hidden under the envelope. I picked it up. The sheriff tried to snatch it out of my hands.

"Give me that, C.W. Now!"

I did. I didn't want to be arrested for obstruction of justice or whatever. "What is it, Sheriff? Maybe I can help."

"If only you could, C.W. But I'm afraid it's gone beyond that now."

"What's happened?" My heart began to beat double-time.

"I got the report back on that bullet, the one found in the ashes."

"You did! What does it say?" I could feel the hairs on the back of my neck rise up.

"The bullet came from an unregistered, illegal weapon."

My face fell. "Well, then, we're back to square one."

The sheriff rubbed his chin. "Not exactly. This time we found the rifle that matches the bullet."

"That's great! Whose gun is it—"

I stopped short. Sheriff Mercer didn't have to answer that. I already knew.

"You found Andrew's rifle."

But my brain simply could not accept the fact that Andrew could be violent. My mouth took over.

"Sheriff! Andrew can't be involved in all this! He's just a kid. And he's a good kid. Have you forgotten he's disappeared? He could be in jeopardy himself—"

The sheriff cut me off. "C.W., all I have to go by is the physical evidence. I can't say a person is guilty or not guilty based on how old he is or how nice he is. I think your vision is being skewed by your emotional involvement. I won't let my personal feelings affect my judgment. What kind of sheriff would I be then, huh?"

I shook my head. "The physical evidence doesn't say who pulled the trigger." Emotional involvement or not, I knew Andrew couldn't have shot up my diner. Nor could he have shot another human being. At least he didn't drive a truck. The sheriff would have nailed him for sure.

So the sheriff didn't like hunches, huh? Well, I had one that wouldn't go away. Andrew was still missing. And someone was out to discredit Del Rey and her mortuary. That someone could only be one person: Berkeley Mondshane, owner of the competing mortuary in Angel's Camp. But was it enough to kill for? It was time to pay Mondshane another visit—first thing in the morning.

. . .

In the midmorning fog, the Mondshane Mortuary looked more like a small-scale antebellum plantation than a house of mourning. It stuck out like a nugget among fool's gold, nestled alongside the California ranch–style dwellings that flanked it. The two-story, four-columned building stood back from the road, secluded and surrounded by large pyracantha bushes and towering Sierra pines. I half expected Butterfly McQueen to greet me at the door with a mint julep. It was obvious Mondshane wanted to attract the discerning deceased—those with dollars.

I slipped by the secretary in the outer office and found Berkeley in his own office. He was talking to an elderly woman who dabbed at her eyes every few seconds. He had taken her hand and was patting it as if trying to burp the thing. While all this empathy was occurring on top of his desk, underneath I could see his shiny oxfords tapping away. Was he mentally singing along to a tune, or just plain bored?

He spotted me in the hallway and jumped up to close the door in my face. I sat down in a nearby wooden chair and waited for him to finish his hand patting and toe tapping. In a few minutes, he escorted the old woman out, now holding her around the shoulders as if she were an invalid trying to walk. I wanted to gag.

He returned with a less-than-empathetic look on his face for me.

"What do you want? I'm not giving any interviews."

"Well, I was thinking of doing a feature on your mortuary, but if you're not interested . . ."

"Nice try, Ms. Westphal, but we all know where your loyalties lie. Now, if you'll excuse me . . ."

"Actually," I said to his back, something that wouldn't have worked if he'd tried it with me. "I do have a couple of questions for you, Berkeley, before I talk with Sheriff Mercer . . ."

He spun around.

"What questions? I have nothing to say, I told you." Again he turned to leave. Again I spoke to his back.

"I was just wondering where you were the night Jasper

died. And the night Portia died. It seems to me that you'd be the one to want them out of the way."

He turned around slowly this time, and folded his hands in front of him. "Oh, really? And why is that?" He spoke with a smirk I was tempted to slap off his face.

"Because if you discredit the Memory Kingdom Mortuary, then you stand to gain all of the mortuary business in the area. It's a wealthy vein of gold when it comes to dying around here. And maybe Jasper and Portia somehow found out what you were doing. Maybe they were threatening to expose you. With all these retired people moving in, you must be in the largest growth business in the Mother Lode next to panning for gold, wouldn't you say?"

"So what? I have plenty of business. Why would I want to take over Del Rey's little operation?"

"Sorry if I didn't make it clear. Being a writer, I should be better at coming up with the right vocabulary word. I'm talking about greed."

He forced a laugh. "Ridiculous."

"I don't think so."

"Del Rey has already dug her own grave. I don't think there's much hope of resuscitating her business."

"I love your metaphors. How about this one? You killed Jasper when you found out he was going to expose your plan to hurt Del Rey—maybe he still had a soft spot for her. Then you made it look like Chunker did it, because he was easy to frame with his criminal record. You bribed Portia to act as a material witness to Jasper's death, but something went wrong, and you had to kill her, too. Then you made Del Rey look even worse by somehow mixing up the bodies—"

"A brilliant investigation, Ms. Westphal. Is this how you write your articles for that little paper? Frankly, I'm tired of this, and I have clients to take care. A business—a legitimate one—to run. See yourself out, would you?" He turned and headed down the hall.

"So did you find out about Jasper's secret stash before or after you killed him?" This time he didn't turn back when I called out. But from his misstep, I had a feeling he heard me.

Instead of leaving by the front door, I paused to check for a side exit. Glancing back down the hall to see if the coast was clear, I picked up a mortuary brochure from a hall table, tore off a corner, and headed outside, pausing to leave something for later.

After a quick stop at Portia's bed-and-breakfast—where I was in and out in seconds without disturbing a soul—I pulled off the highway at Miwok Lake Road and drove on toward Jasper's boat, which was still moored in its berth. Did it look even more dilapidated?

The police line was still up, sort of. One end dangled down into the water. Had someone else been aboard? I entered the front door using the key I'd sneaked from Portia's pegboard.

The smell hit me first. I wanted to gag, but held my nose and tried not to breathe while I thought about air fresheners and deodorants. Whew! Apparently no one had taken out the garbage. What a great deterrent to crime—fetid air. You'd have to be desperate to go in here—or nuts. Which one was I?

I preferred nuts, I decided. Then I began opening drawers and cupboards and checking cubbyholes. There was nothing new. The same paperwork, the same printed forms, the same canceled checks from various vendors. Most of the checks had been made out to Cash, which I figured was the easiest way for Jasper to deal with his finances. But could there have been another reason?

I pulled out Jasper's makeshift ledger and several envelopes filled with miscellaneous papers. Although the sheriff had been through everything—and had taken most of the good stuff—I wanted to check once more to see if anything stood out now that I knew more about the man and his bogus business. But there was nothing.

Something had to be here. And if Jasper didn't want it found, he'd have hidden it well, not tucked it into one of these drawers. But where? I searched for half an hour—it didn't take long to cover a place this small—and found nothing of any real value. The only things that appeared to have meant anything to Jasper were his brother's trophies.

I returned to the small wooden mantel that held the trophies—there was still one missing. The dust had begun to settle over the spot, but the only thing that had been added was fingerprint powder. The sheriff had had the place dusted for prints, and two sets of four fingers were clearly visible on the mantel.

Odd. Not the fingerprints, but the placement of the two sets. They were obviously four fingers of each hand, no thumbs. And they had been placed almost neatly in a row on either end of the mantel, along the edge about two feet apart, much like a pianist about to play his instrument. The fingerprint language was suddenly clear. Someone—most likely Jasper Coyne—had left these prints while raising the lid of the mantel.

One by one I removed the trophies from the mantel and set them on the kitchen table. Then I lifted the top of the mantel. Inside there was a ticket from the local courthouse, dated ten years earlier. The infraction: dumping ashes into the local lakes instead of the ocean.

Apparently Jasper Coyne had been doing illegal dumping for years.

I checked the date again. It matched the earliest dates of the ashes found in the warehouse. Jasper Coyne started storing his wares right after being fined. He must have figured he'd make more money hiding them instead of scattering them, so he quit distributing altogether—but kept collecting the paychecks from the mortuaries. Was it really that simple? I wondered.

And if Berkeley Mondshane had somehow found out about Jasper's scheme, maybe he was aka "Cash."

Sometimes, it's what you *don't* see that's important. Conspicuously absent among all Jasper's canceled checks was a single one ever paid to his brother Levi. I thought that was odd, considering they were once so close.

But there were two other odd receipts hidden in the mantel: a statement from a hospital and a bill from a car repair shop. The hospital bill was dated two months after Levi was paralyzed. And the repair bill for work on Jasper's truck was dated the day after the fight. I wondered why he kept these incriminating receipts—as a reminder of his responsibility?

I was certain the two receipts were tied together. I double-checked the amounts. The hospital bill was just under ten thousand dollars. Where would a fisherman/ash distributor get that kind of money without insurance? And the car repair bill was two thousand dollars.

It was time to return the key I had borrowed. Only this time I'd make a little more noise.

Levi was out front of the bed-and-breakfast, shooting baskets from his wheelchair. The hoop had been lowered in proportion to his seated height, but it still looked to be a challenge. I watched him make a few baskets before interrupting his game.

"You've got an arm," I said, and then regretted the implication.

He acknowledged me with a glance and returned to shooting hoops.

"I wondered if we could talk for a few minutes." I tried to look pleading. Must have worked. He tossed the ball into a corner of the yard, and wheeled his chair toward the front door, with a nod for me to follow.

While I took a seat in the parlor and contemplated the decor, Levi headed for the mini-bar, pulled out two colas, and poured them over ice. I hate cola, but I took it gracefully, and without making a face.

After a pretend sip, I set the drink down on a nearby end table and waited for Levi to finish gulping his.

"What do you want?"

I like a man who gets to the point. "I just had a few questions I hoped you might help me with."

"Like what?"

I paused for moment. This wasn't going to work if he didn't let down his guard.

"Are you angry with me, Levi?"

He looked at me, unblinking. "No. Why do you say that?"

"You seem to be upset with me, and I'm not sure why."

"I don't have a problem with you, Connor, despite your snooping around. I have a problem with your friend, Del Rey. I think she's really fucked things up. I don't know why you're trying to help her so much."

"Like you said, she's my friend. Wouldn't you try to help a friend?"

He glanced away, saying nothing.

"Levi, what really happened that night?"

"What night?"

"The night of the fight."

"I told you."

"Tell me again."

He took another gulp of soda. "Me and Jasper were drinking. That jerk, Chunker, started saying things. Jasper got mad and swung—I mean, Chunker swung at him—and all hell broke loose."

"And then?"

"And the next thing I remember, Jasper's carrying me like a baby to his truck."

"And then what happened?"

"What do you mean?"

"I mean, what happened on the drive home?"

Levi's hands gripped the sides of the wheelchair. "I don't know what you mean. I was unconscious during the ride home."

"You mean, you were conscious when you realized your brother was carrying you to the truck. And then you became unconscious again during the ride?"

"Yeah, I guess so."

"But you do remember him carrying you?"

"Sort of."

"Could you feel him carrying you?"

Levi didn't answer.

"Levi, I think your brother got in an accident that night, and wrecked the truck. We found a repair bill from around that date, for a very hefty amount."

To my surprise, Levi's eyes rimmed with tears. He blinked them back and took another swallow of his drink. "I . . . no, I don't remember. I was unconscious."

"Levi, why did you move off Jasper's boat after you were paralyzed?"

He sniffed. "I told you, because it wasn't accessible. It was too hard living there."

"You could have made it accessible. You're very talented at making accommodations. Was there another reason?"

"Look, I just didn't want to live with my brother anymore, okay? He was drinking more than ever, always trying to pick a fight with everyone. I got sick of it. Portia offered to let me stay with her, so I moved in."

"You and Portia became close, didn't you?"

He blinked rapidly a few more times, then stared at me. "What do you mean by that?"

"Well, you really took her death hard."

"She did a lot for me."

"More than just give you room and board?"

His face flushed like an opening rose in the sunlight. "No. She's way older than me . . . we were just good friends. She showed me I didn't have to be a cripple, sitting in this wheelchair, rotting away. She's the one who got me to believe in myself again."

"She did a great job. She must have really loved you."

"Maybe she did, like a sister. But that has nothing to do with anything. I overcame my disability, thanks to her, and now I can do anything an able-bodied person can do."

"I agree, you can do—"

"I built my own souped-up all-terrain wheelchair that's going to revolutionize the mobility of paraplegics. I added the attachments to Portia's truck so I could drive it without the use of my legs. I even fixed the motorcycle so I could control it fully with my hands, and balance it when the bike came to a stop."

"It's amazing what you've done—"

"And that's not all. I'm going to play professional sports again. No one is going to stop me from reaching my dream." He wheeled around and rolled his chair to a cupboard next to the mini-bar. Pulling out a stack of papers, he brought them to me and dropped them in my lap.

"What are these?"

"Letters. Copies of letters I've written to everyone from my local mayor to my congressman to the president of the United States."

"What do they say?"

"That I have rights, even though I'm disabled. I have the right to join a nondisabled team and play ball like anyone else. I don't want to be on one of those handicapped teams where everyone makes allowances for you. I want full equality."

"Did you get any responses?"

He shrugged. "Nothing yet. But things are going to change."

I realized he was going off on a tangent about his own personal agenda. This wasn't what I came for. Time to get back to the matter at hand.

"What else did Portia do for you?"

He looked out the window. Tears welled again. He pinched them back with his fingers.

"You loved her very much, didn't you?"

He dropped his head in hand.

"Levi, were you lovers?"

He kept his face covered, but I knew. And I wasn't all that surprised.

"Levi, do you have any idea what happened to her?" I asked gently.

He shook his head violently and looked up at me, smearing the tears with his gloved hand. "No, I don't. But when I find out who did this to her, I'm gonna kill him."

As I headed back to my office to pick up some work, I thought about Levi's reaction to Portia's death. He was quick to cry, and quick to anger. He was certainly emotionally involved in all this. Not surprising, since his brother and his lover had been murdered. Had someone killed them because of similar strong emotions?

Berkeley certainly wanted Del Rey's business, but did he want it enough to kill two people? It seemed to me there would be easier ways to ruin someone's reputation. I was sure he had some connection to Jasper's ash scam, but was there more to it than that? Chunker could have done the killing, out of revenge. Or even for Del Rey, out of some kind of misplaced need to protect her.

At the back of my mind was Andrew. He, too, could be carrying out some sort of personal justice, if he had somehow found out about his real father before now. Maybe it had been anger, instead of shock, that caused him to drop those beer bottles when he overheard Del Rey's admission about Jasper. Still, I didn't believe he had it in him to actually commit murder—twice. But where the hell was he?

Were there other people Jasper had hurt—like old Zack Samuels, whose wife was placed in storage instead of at sea? But he didn't know there was anything wrong until after Jasper died—or did he? He was old, but he was still able-bodied. There were probably many more like him who resented the fact that their loved ones were sitting in boxes.

The list was growing.

I couldn't keep my mind on work, although I made every effort the rest of the afternoon. Around four I gave it up and dropped by Dan's office to see if he might want to come for dinner later. Truthfully, I didn't want to be alone in that place, after all the knocks it had taken.

When Dan agreed, I picked up the makings for rigatoni bolognese at the Mom and Pop Market along with a bottle of Chianti. Dan promised to swing by the video store and rent a captioned video about paint ball games called *Kersplat!*, figuring we might learn some strategies for the next battle against the Whiskey Slide Wolves.

I had hosed the paint residue from the front of my diner, but the bullet holes remained. Until they were filled or covered up, I had a constant reminder of how easily my life could be placed in jeopardy. Just then, Dan's car pulled in behind me and I shivered as we entered my front door, hoping there were no further surprises. Fortunately, there was only Casper, who leaped at us as if we were her long-lost relatives.

As soon as we finished the pasta, we settled into the sofa bed with our wine for the video. Dan switched on the remote and pushed Play. In a matter of minutes, mostly guys in mostly camouflage gear were shooting one another from a bunch of bushes.

"This is strategy?" I asked, sipping the Chianti.

"It's guy strategy. You talk about your plans over a few beers, then you go out on the battlefield and try to kill everyone you see. Then you meet for beers again and rehash the whole game."

"Brilliant military tactics. If it were an all-girl team, we'd have some real strategies."

"Yeah, I can imagine. First you'd all go shopping for the right accessories for your brand-name camouflage outfits. Then you'd go out on the battlefield and politely ask if it's okay to shoot each other, and apologize when you did.

Then you'd all meet after the game and discuss who was sleeping with the referees."

I slapped his arm. It didn't seem to hurt. He nuzzled my chest. For some reason, Dan thought teasing me to the point of my having to slap him was foreplay.

"You're such a sexist."

"You know I was only kidding."

"Yeah, sure. Prove it."

"Prove it? Okay, how about you come to the shooting range with us guys tomorrow and learn how to manage a real gun. Think you can do that?"

Damn! He knew I hated guns. He'd tricked me.

"You know I have a love-hate relationship with guns. A gun is kind of like a penis. It's fascinating, but at the same time, I wouldn't want to touch one."

He laughed and made me prove myself wrong.

"Enough gunplay!" I said, about the same time the video ended. We'd both gotten a lot more exercise than the guys on the screen. We were sweating bullets.

Dan kissed a few drops of perspiration from my forehead. "I wasn't kidding about going to the firing range. I think you should find out what it's like to shoot a real gun."

"Why?"

"Because I was thinking of getting you a gun."

"I'd prefer diamonds. Or real estate. But that's sweet of you."

"It just might save your life if you know how to shoot one."

"But I don't want one. I love paint ball guns—they're fun. And basically harmless, when your office isn't being attacked. As a kid I was always playing war, terrorizing the neighborhood with my water pistols and rubber-tipped dart guns. But real guns—I don't think so. They terrify me."

"That's just it. If you learn how to handle one, it won't cause you so much anxiety. You're in control of the gun, it's not in control of you."

"You sound like a bumper sticker. 'Guns don't kill people. Idiots with guns kill people.' "

" 'Idiot' being the operative word."

I saw his point. And things *were* starting to get a little scary around here, what with real guns being used to shoot up my diner.

"Okay, I'll go. I'll try some target shooting."

Dan nuzzled my sweaty chest and licked a few more drops from the bumpy terrain. "I think you handled my gun fairly well."

Oh, God, I thought. *Here we go again.* And we did.

"Ready for some more gunplay?" Dan asked over our morning bagels and mochas.

I tried not to smile, but I couldn't help it. It had been an explosive evening and I didn't know if I could take much more—even as innuendo.

I dressed in what I decided would be my favorite shooting range outfit—jeans and a T-shirt that read "NYPD"—Dan's old cop shirt. On the ride over, I tried to picture what I was in for, and mentally practiced my quick draw, along with a few Robert De Niro and Clint Eastwood quotes. By the time we reached the place, I was starting to like the idea of being the first deaf Annie Oakley in these parts.

The shooting range in Whiskey Slide was nothing like what I had imagined. I had seen shooting ranges on TV, when I'd watched reruns of *Law & Order* and *Homicide: Life on the Street*. They made shooting ranges look exciting, with silhouetted bad guys sliding toward you with their guns raised. The good guys had about twenty seconds to unload their clips and take them down.

At least I knew the lingo.

But this place was more like an archery camp than a

shooting range. At the end of a stretch of dry grass were bales of hay stacked high, with standard bull's-eye targets pinned in the center. There were no divisions between the shooters, unlike on TV, where you get your own little compartment. The shooters just stood behind warped and weathered tables, side by side, discharging their guns. There was nothing to stop a guy from turning his gun on his fellow shooter and letting him have it. I'd read more than once that people had committed suicide at shooting ranges. I was starting to get nervous.

Dan set our equipment on the table we'd been assigned, and held his gun out for me to see. I reached for it. He pulled back.

"Hold on a second. We're going to start with some safety tips before I actually let you hold this thing."

I nodded and let him give me the spiel. The first thing he told me was to point the gun down toward the target at all times, and nowhere else. Guess he was afraid I might accidentally shoot someone. Like him.

"The safety's on. There's a clip of bullets there, maybe fourteen to fifteen rounds. After you load it, you'll get a feeling for the trigger pull and how much effort it takes to shoot. The first round is double-action, which means there's more resistance to the pull."

"Why?"

"For safety reasons. It's harder to shoot the first round. You have to really want to shoot it. The second round is easier, you'll see. By then you're serious about wanting to shoot the gun, so they make it less resistant."

"Cool."

Dan frowned at me, then went on. "Okay, when you hold the weapon, hold it straight out with both hands. Cup the gun in your left hand, since you're right-handed, and pull back slightly with your left arm, while you push forward with the right arm. Keep everything rigid."

He made me practice with an air gun—meaning it was invisible and I had to make believe. I went through the motions.

"Now, sight the picture."

"Huh?"

"Point the gun at the target with your finger. Then pull

the trigger gradually, nice and even. Don't anticipate the shot or you won't come close to the target."

"What do you mean, anticipate the shot? How can I not? I know it's coming."

"Try to let it surprise you. If you anticipate too much, you'll end up shooting the ground instead of the target. It's a big problem for beginners, who are afraid of the noise and the recoil."

"I'm not afraid of the noise."

He smiled. "Okay then, you're ahead of the game. Here's your weapon." Dan handed over a cold, heavy pistol that seemed to sparkle in my hand. My imagination?

"What kind is it?"

"A Glock. Nine millimeter, high-velocity, small-projectile. Here are your safety glasses and your ear protectors."

I gave him a look.

"I know, I know. I tried to tell the guy, but he says it's the law. Just pretend they're earmuffs and put them on."

I set the gun down on the table and donned the fashion accessories. Then I picked it up again, and Dan gave me a review lesson in how to hold, load, and discharge the weapon. His years at the New York Police Department were evident in the way he talked about and handled the weapon. After a few practice aims without the clip in, I was ready to shoot with real bullets.

"Hey, Connor, what are you doing here?" It was Deputy Marca Clemens, on her way to one of the tables. I almost didn't recognize her with the eye and ear wear. "Gonna join the department?"

I gave her a fake laugh. "Oh, no, just, you know, practicing. Dan thought it would be a good idea." I felt stupid. I looked stupid. I didn't belong here.

"Well, just be careful you don't shoot your toe off." She gave me a slap on the back and headed on to shoot up her own menacing bale of hay.

I stood between Dan and a guy wearing a Clampers uniform—red shirt, black vest and pants, black hat, and lots of pins symbolizing all kinds of accomplishments. He grinned when I took the place next to him. I could read that grin. "Girlie's got a gun! Isn't that cute!"

I grinned back and tried to look like the gun was part of my lifestyle.

Dan stood behind me, helping me aim and going through the motions of releasing the safety, cocking the gun, and firing. Then he dropped his arms and moved beside me so I could lip-read him.

"Stand with your feet spread the width of your shoulders, lean back slightly at the waist for balance, hold the gun with both hands, get your sight picture, then pull the trigger. That's all there is to it. Now wait until the range master blows the whistle."

"Why?"

"Fire control—just basic safety. Everyone has to shoot at once. That way no one goes to check their target and accidentally gets a bullet in the back. Everyone will line up, he'll say, 'Clear the line for fire; ready on the left; ready on the right; ready on the firing line.' Then he'll blow the whistle. He'll also blow the whistle to stop."

"But I won't hear it."

"That's why I've worked out a code. When he says, 'Clear the line for fire,' I'll touch your mid-back. When he says, 'Ready on the left,' then 'on the right,' I'll tap your left side, then your right, so you're prepared. When he says, 'Ready on the firing line,' I'll touch between your shoulders. And when he blows the whistle, I'll run my finger down your back. Okay?"

I nodded. I was ready to try it on my own—this time for real.

I stood there, staring at the bull's-eye, waiting for the signals on my back and willing the bullet to take the center hole, just to show these guys I could do it. Every muscle in my body was taut. I held the gun in both hands, just as Dan had taught me, and took aim.

I felt the series of taps, and finally the finger down my back.

I pulled the trigger.

The gun jumped. As prepared as I thought I was, the explosion surprised me.

"Whoa! Where'd it go?" I kept the gun aimed at the target as I spoke to Dan. He pointed into the dirt about three yards short of the target. I could see the guy next to me laughing. I thought about shooting him.

My arms ached. I lowered the gun and started rubbing my shoulder. Dan quickly slid his hand down my gun arm and raised it back up again, moving to the side so I could see his mouth.

"Your gun is still loaded. Remember that at all times." I glanced at the Clamper. He wasn't laughing anymore. In fact, he'd moved several steps away from me.

"Sorry," I said to him. He just shook his head like I was an idiot. I was, for being here and doing this. But Dan made me try again, and the second time I managed to hit the ground only two feet away from the target. On the third try I hit the target. The Clamper's target.

By the time I'd spent the clip, I had placed four bullets in my own target. Four out of twenty shots. That meant if twenty bad guys came after me, I might be able to take down four of them. It was enough for me.

We turned in our gear and headed out to the parking lot. My shoulders ached from the tension and my fingers felt gritty, almost greasy from the graphite powder. I had a blister on my palm.

The deputy stood at her patrol car, talking on a cell phone. She looked intent, but then, she always looked intent. It was part of her uniform, I suspected.

I shook out my arm and hand. My fingers were numb, and I thought I might never be able to shrug my right shoulder again, not to mention the left one, which had been injured in my bike fall.

But I had to admit, it was kind of neat, holding that gun. Something had come over me that I couldn't quite explain, except to say that it felt powerful and exciting. Kind of like sex.

"You did a good job today," Dan said, opening the car door for me.

"I sucked big time," I said, before slipping inside.

Dan moved around to the driver's side, which was next to Deputy Clemens's patrol car. I waited for him to get in, but it didn't happen. I could see him standing there, but couldn't see much of anything else. I stepped out of the car to see why.

"Goddamn kids." I caught the words on the deputy's lips before she snapped the phone shut. Dan had been eavesdropping on her side of the phone conversation.

"What's up? Has someone been shooting paint guns again?" I asked, thinking of my diner and my office.

"I wish it were just paint guns. Warren Pike's been shot. Stupid, stupid kids," said Marca.

Warren Pike. I knew that name—sort of. He was Jeff's younger brother. What was he—thirteen, fourteen years old?

"Is he . . . all right?" I asked.

"He's alive. They got him down at Mother Lode Hospital."

"What happened?"

"Got ahold of a gun somehow, and accidentally shot himself. At least, that's what he says. Sheriff's trying to find out where the gun came from. I gotta go over to the hospital and talk with the parents. Shit, I hate this part of the job."

Deputy Clemens climbed into her patrol car, backed up in a spray of gravel, and spun out a little before regaining control and hitting the highway, leaving us in her dust.

Dan and I got into the car. "What the hell is going on with these kids?"

"I don't know," said Dan, "but it's becoming an epidemic."

"Let's swing by the sheriff's office, see if he's learned anything," I said, as we headed back to Flat Skunk.

Dan fiddled with the radio dial, leaving me to think in peace. While he tapped his thumb on the steering wheel, I tried to make some sense of the recent spate of youth violence. But the thought that haunted me most was Andrew.

The sheriff wasn't in when we arrived. I told Dan I wanted to wait a while, that I'd see him back at the office. It took a little coaxing and a promise to join him that night for some paint ball—really—but I managed to get rid of him after a few minutes. I wanted to be alone—with Chunker Lansky.

The door to the jail area was locked, naturally. I returned to the main part of the sheriff's department and sidled up to Rebecca, who was studying a book on floral arranging. She had her dispatcher headphones on, waiting for that all-important emergency call.

"Rebecca, did you take that call about Warren Pike getting shot?" I asked, picking up a fake flower that might have been a rose, a pansy, or even a daisy—it was hard to tell.

"Oh, yeah. Gee, I hope that little kid is all right. His brother called, sounded frantic. I couldn't hardly understand him, he was screaming so. I finally figured out what was going on and sent an ambulance over there."

"What *did* happen?"

"Jeff kept saying, 'Warren shot himself. Warren shot himself.' Then he started screaming, 'It's all my fault. It's all my fault.' That's about all I could get from him before I called the ambulance. Probably got ahold of his dad's rifle or something."

I shook my head.

"Rebecca, could you do me a favor? Could you let me in to see Chunker Lansky? I need to ask him a few questions."

"Gee, I don't know, Connor." Rebecca put her book down and picked up a handful of wanna-be flowers. She tried sticking them into a pot filled with a Styrofoam block, but they wouldn't stay upright. "I don't think the sheriff would like it."

"I'm sure he wouldn't mind. I've already talked with Chunker a couple of times, and I just want to clarify a few things."

"Well, all right. But if the sheriff gets mad, you're taking full responsibility. I'll swear you strong-armed me, tied me up at gunpoint, and forced your way in."

"I have no doubt he'll believe you."

She came out from behind the counter wearing pink bunny slippers. But nothing surprised me anymore about Rebecca Matthews. I wanted to be just like her when I grew up . . . I mean, old.

Unlocking the door, she gave me a last warning to make it quick. Chunker was sitting up on his cot reading a magazine. He looked weary and depressed.

"Hi, Chunker."

"Hey, Ms. Westphal," he said without enthusiasm.

"How're you doing?"

He forced a smile. "Couldn't be better. How's Del Rey?" He pronounced Del Rey more like D'ray. It was a little tougher to read but I'd gotten used to the way he said her name.

"She's okay, Chunker. So are the kids."

"Good, that's good." He bobbed his head a few times, closed the magazine, and dropped it on the floor. "So why're you back?"

God, the man seemed so harmless. I had to remind myself he'd spent time in prison for attempted manslaughter and was now accused of murder.

"Chunker, tell me about the fight that night."

He stood up and lumbered over to the bars. "I already tol' you and tol' you, Ms. Westphal. We were all drunk. Jasper started saying rude things about Del Rey. It had been a long time since she'd been with either one of us, but he just wouldn't quit. Then he hit me . . ."

"He threw the first punch?"

"Yeah, then Levi joined in and everyone was swinging and it was just chaos in there . . ."

"Did you hit Levi over the head with a bottle?"

"No, ma'am, I did not."

"Then who did?"

"I honest-to-God don't know. The next thing I know, Levi was lying at the bottom of the stairs to the bathroom, thrashing around and groaning. The cops started coming in, and Jasper picked up Levi and carried him out of there."

"Did you say Levi was thrashing around on the floor?"

"Yes, ma'am."

"Why didn't someone call an ambulance?"

"I don't know. We were all too drunk to think about anything but getting out of there. Jasper doesn't like cops."

"Did you see Levi leave with his brother in the truck?"

"I don't remember."

"You hated him, didn't you?"

Chunker looked surprised, even angry. "I didn't hate Levi! What makes you say that?"

"No, I meant Jasper."

Chunker ran his fingers through his disheveled hair. "Look, I didn't hate Jasper. At least, not in the beginning.

He's the one that hated me, 'cause I went off with Del Rey. He wouldn't stop hassling me. Or her. Even after it was over between us."

"You hated him for sending you to prison."

Chunker shrugged.

"And you hated Levi for the same reason."

"I tol' you, I didn't hate Levi. But I think they were in cahoots. I think Jasper told Levi to say I hit him so I'd be sent to prison."

"What did he say in court?"

Chunker scratched the back of his neck. "Well, first Jasper got up on the stand and told everyone I started the fight. And then he said he saw me hit Levi over the head with the beer bottle. And then Levi fell down the stairs and Jasper carried him out. And Levi never walked again."

"Did Levi testify?"

"Yeah, but he wasn't too good on the stand, 'cause he couldn't remember much. He said he woke up the next day covered with bruises and cuts, and couldn't feel or move his legs. You shoulda seen the jury. They looked at me like I was the devil when Levi said the doctors told him he was paralyzed and would be confined to a wheelchair the rest of his life."

Chunker paused, blinking away the memory.

"Can you remember anything else?"

He thought a moment. "A bunch of stuff about how he'd never play football again and his promising career was over. And then the judge gave me five years for attempted manslaughter. Took the jury half an hour to convict me."

"Chunker, you've had a long time to plan your revenge. And I'll bet you're pretty angry about what they did to you."

"Yeah, I'm angry, and yeah, I had thoughts of revenge. That, and thinking about Del Rey, were the only things that kept me going. But when I saw Del Rey and Courtney, I just wanted to live the rest of my life in peace."

"When did you find out Courtney was your daughter?" I asked.

"Not until I saw her—just a few weeks ago. I knew right away. Now I just want to make up for all the time I've lost."

"And you're not bitter anymore about what Jasper did to you?"

"Oh, no. I'm bitter. And frankly, I'm glad Jasper Coyne is dead."

"But you didn't kill him?"

"Only in my dreams."

I'd hit a dead end. Time to do what I did at the newspaper when I was blocked. Go back to the beginning and start over.

Crystal Tannacito was hosing off the pavement between two rows of storage buildings when I drove up in my Chevy, Casper in tow. I thought it was time my dog had another outing. She needed to get out of the diner more. Especially when there were people around trying to shoot it.

Crystal squinted, baring her yellowed teeth, as she tried to make out who had arrived at her doorstep. She absently let the hose dangle, soaking the ground beneath her gold sandals. I could read her curse as she realized her shoes were wet. She shook off the water, then turned the nozzle off.

"Help you?" she said, shaking a cigarette from the pack she'd pulled out of her shorts pocket.

After freeing Casper, I approached Crystal so I could read her thin, red lips better.

"I'm Connor Westphal. We met the other day."

She scrunched her face, trying to stimulate her memory. It didn't seem to help.

"Huh?" she said.

"I publish the *Eureka!* I was here with the sheriffs after you called about the ashes."

She took a long drag. "Yeah, yeah, I remember. You were gonna do a story on me and my warehouse, right? Didja bring me a copy of the article?"

"I haven't finished it yet. That's why I'm here. To get a few more details, if you have a moment." I glanced around at the simplicity of her business and had a feeling she had lots of spare moments.

"Sure, sure. Come on in and I'll pour you a glass of lemonade. Unless you want something stronger." She winked.

"No, lemonade would be great."

"You sure? I got bourbon, whisky, piña colada mix. Even got some peppermint schnapps. That stuff's gooooood." She turned her head and kept on talking. I missed the rest, but I nodded every once in a while when she turned back to me, and that seemed to satisfy her.

She pushed open the screen door to her trailer and gestured into the multipurpose room—part living room, part dining room, and part kitchen. Bet it saved time being able to cook, eat, and entertain without having to take more than a step.

After a few amenities, I steered the conversation in the direction I wanted it to go.

"How did you feel when you found those ashes? I'll bet you weren't expecting anything like that."

"I was soooo shocked, I about had a heart attack. You never know what kinds of bizarre things people are storing in here, but I don't ask questions. It's none of my business. Still, when it comes to something like a bunch of dead people's remains, you gotta draw the line, don't you?"

"Did Jasper come here on a fairly regular basis?"

"I don't keep track exactly, but yeah, I'd seen him around a lot. Maybe once a week or so."

"Did you ever see anyone else around here who didn't belong? Someone you'd not seen before?"

She scrunched up her face again, took a drag on her cigarette, and blew the smoke sideways, as if that would keep it from going straight into my lungs. I stifled a cough.

"One guy, now that you mention it. Yep, this one guy came around a couple of times, asking about renting a warehouse. What was odd was, he came back twice, basically asked the same goddamn questions, but never rented. He wanted me to show him a few compartments, which I did, of course, but he said he wanted an end unit. I told him they were all filled, so he left. I didn't trust him, anyway."

"Why not?"

" 'Cause the second time he came by, he said he had a friend who rented a compartment here and his friend said he could have a look inside it. I told him that was against our policy, and that the friend would have to come and show him himself."

"Did he mention the friend's name?"

"Now that I think about it, it was Jasper Coyne. Ain't that a coincidence."

I doubt it, I thought, as my heart skipped a beat. I set my lemonade down and leaned in, not wanting to miss a word of what she was about to say. With that slit of a mouth, it was a challenge.

"Crystal, did you get the man's name?"

"Nope, no I didn't. Sorry."

I let out my breath and felt my shoulders sag.

"Any chance you can describe him?"

"He was tall, kind of skinny but he still had some muscle on him. Short hair, plain face. Regular shirt and slacks."

I shook my head. Too generic.

"Anything else you can remember about him? A scar, a limp, anything?"

"Naw, sorry. He looked like a regular guy. That's why it surprised me when he got into his car."

My breath caught. "Why did that surprise you?"

" 'Cause it was a limo. He didn't look like money until he got in that car."

Now who was likely to drive a limo in this area? Only a very rich person—and he'd have been driven. Or an undertaker. Like Berkeley Mondshane.

Berkeley wasn't in when I stopped by his mortuary fif-

teen minutes later. But his secretary was, busily typing at
her computer. I waited for a few moments to let her finish
her thought, then thrust out my hand in greeting.

Who would I be today? Ah, one of my favorite children's authors. I always wanted to be Eloise. This was the
next best thing. "Hi, I'm Kay Thompson. I'm interested in
having my great-aunt cremated next week and wondered if
you could help me?"

She blinked at me. "Next . . . next week? That's highly
unusual. We tend to wait until a client is deceased before we
make those kinds of plans . . ."

I should have rehearsed my lines. "Oh, I know! What I
meant was, her body is being shipped back home, and that
will take a few days, so we'd like to have it done when she
arrives next week. I just wanted to see what you have to offer so we'd be prepared."

The woman, middle-aged, overweight, with too much
makeup, nodded. "Yes, I see. Well, Mr. Mondshane, the
funeral director, isn't in right now. If you'd like to make an
appointment—"

"I'm kind of in a hurry and I just wanted to get some
information."

"But I thought . . . your great-aunt wouldn't be here until next week . . ."

"Yes, I know. *She's* not in a hurry, but I am. See . . . I
have to leave on a business trip for a few days, and I wanted
to get this taken care of now. Could you just answer a few
questions for me?"

"I suppose, if you're sure you can't wait for Mr.
Mondshane."

"Thanks so much." I pulled up a chair opposite her
and began asking her some of the basic details about their
cremation services. Then I mentioned the Memory Kingdom Mortuary, and that I was looking at their services to
compare.

"Oh, no. You don't want to go there. That place is involved in a big scandal."

I leaned in. "Really? What's going on? I was pretty impressed with the woman who runs the place."

The secretary pulled at the wattle under her chin.

"Well, I shouldn't say anything, but the mortician—it seems she and her ex-husband were running some kind of a scam."

"Like what?" I asked, conspiratorially.

"Well, they were cremating bodies, then instead of distributing the ashes at sea, they were storing them in a warehouse! Can you imagine?"

I shook my head and worked hard at looking horrified.

"Not only that. The sheriff just found out that she cremated the wrong body the other day!"

"Oh, my God!" I said, and slapped my chest. "How could such a thing happen?"

"I don't know. But Mr. Mondshane is very upset about all of it. Del Rey was a very dear friend of his. So was Jasper Coyne, her ex-husband, the man who was supposedly distributing the ashes."

"Mr. Mondshane was friends with him, too?"

The woman nodded. "Jasper used to come here at least once a week and see Mr. Mondshane, although I know Berkeley never did business with him. I keep the accounts, so I can verify that. I think Berkeley just felt sorry for the guy. He said Jasper kept coming over asking for work, but Berkeley didn't trust him enough to let him distribute any of his clients' ashes. Still, the man wouldn't give up, week after week."

That was interesting.

"Did Del Rey come around, too?"

"Oh, no, never. Like I said, Berkeley considered her a friend, but he doesn't have time for socializing. He's just devoted to his business."

I wanted to make one last stop before I headed back to the office. I checked the phone book at a pay phone in Flat Skunk, found the address I needed, and drove up into the hills past the cemetery until I located the Golden Years Retirement Village.

There were about a dozen golden people sitting on lounge chairs on the patio, talking, playing cards, snacking. A bulletin board posted at the entrance announced the upcoming recreation schedule. No shuffleboard, but plenty of nature walks, square dancing, gourmet cooking classes, and bridge tournaments were listed. Tai chi groups met in the morning, water aerobics in the afternoon, and karate lessons in the evening. This was no nursing home. There wasn't a nurse in sight.

I wondered briefly if Rebecca Matthews would be happy in a place like this, then decided it was too slow for her. She'd have the place turned into an amusement park within a week if she ever moved in.

I spotted Zack Samuels standing on a long stretch of immaculately tended lawn, hitting golf balls toward an automatic-return gizmo. Each time a ball hit the target, it was rolled back to the golfer. Zack was teeing up another ball when I arrived. Ignoring me, he pulled back, swung, and hit the golf ball with a gentleness that didn't match his crusty facade. I applauded when he hit his mark.

Startled, he looked up sharply. Not used to an audience, I figured, not way out here.

"What are you doing here?" he asked sharply. Apparently he'd recognized me from the encounter at Del Rey's.

"Hi, Mr. Samuels. You remember me?"

He nodded once. "Yeah, now what do you want?" He leaned over and set another golf ball on the tee.

"Well, as you probably know, I publish the *Eureka!* newspaper. I wondered if I could ask you a few questions?"

"About what?" He frowned, watching the ball and not me. I hoped he wasn't suddenly going to find another use for that golf club.

"About your wife's ashes. I'm doing a story on the tragedy and thought you might have a few words to add."

"I have a few words, all right. That guy, Jasper Whozitz, he deserved whatever he got. And that woman who runs the funeral home, I hope they give her seventy years. That's how old my wife was when she died." He swung, missed the ball, and hit the grass, sending chopped blades into the air. He had a mean grip and a vicious follow-through.

"What do you think happened to Jasper, Mr. Samuels?"

"Somebody murdered him, didn't they? Isn't that what I read in the paper? As a religious man, I don't condone murder, but that man was evil. And you can print that with my blessings."

"Mr. Samuels, when you were looking around for . . . disposition of your wife's body, did you ever visit the Mondshane Mortuary?"

He nodded without looking at me, and took another swing at the ball, sending a clod of dirt flying over the hill.

"Yeah, I checked them out. But they were too expensive. Now I wish I'd gone through them instead."

His eyes grew moist. Without another word, he dropped the club on the ground and headed for the clubhouse across the way. As I watched him go, I thought about what I'd gleaned from the encounter.

Zack Samuels might not be spry enough to pull it off, but there were definitely people out there who would kill to settle the score with Jasper Coyne. But had any of them known about the ashes before Crystal's phone call to the sheriff?

When I pushed open the secretary's door at Berkeley Mondshane's mortuary, the woman was still at the computer, typing away. She looked up and smiled when she saw me.

"Oh, hello! You've decided to go with Mondshane Mortuary. That's wonderful." She started to pull open her desk and remove some papers, when I stopped her.

"Actually, I had another question for you, before I make up my mind."

Her face fell. She shut the drawer and folded her hands on the desk. "Oh. Certainly. What do you need to know?"

Before I could answer, she looked past me and her face brightened. "Mr. Mondshane! I'm so glad you're back. This woman would like some information on our cremation services."

I'm sure my face brightened, too—bright red. Caught. I turned slowly and found Berkeley already in the middle of a sentence.

". . . hope you haven't said anything to her." To say he looked angry would be like saying his clients looked lifeless. He faced me and said, "What do you want?"

"Berkeley! This is one of our new clients. She was asking about—"

"I know what she was asking about, Barbara, and I hope you didn't tell her anything." He forced himself to resume a pleasant manner, but I could see it was an effort. "You know I like to handle these things."

"Oh yes, I know. But she . . . she was in a hurry to know . . . about cremating her great-aunt . . ." Barbara was obviously rattled. She appeared to have forgotten my nosy inquiries about Jasper and Del Rey.

"Ms. Westphal, if you'll step into my office, I'd like to ask you a few questions myself."

Berkeley opened the door to his office and I stepped in, but found myself alone when he pulled the door shut. I watched him through the glass, still talking with his secretary, but couldn't make out the words, only the body language. It looked like he was browbeating her, as she cowered behind her desk. There was a lot of finger pointing and head shaking on his part. Finally, she burst into tears, and pulled her purse from a side drawer.

Tightening his tie, Berkeley smoothed his sport jacket, then rubbed his hands as if they were cold. He entered his office looking as if he had just played ten rounds of tennis.

"What do you want, Ms. Westphal? I've had just about as much interference from you as I can take. If you trespass on this property one more time, I'm going to call—"

"How well did you know Jasper Coyne, Berkeley?"

It looked like he choked, but he may just have cleared his throat. It's tough to tell the difference when you can't hear the sound.

"I . . . knew of him, that's it. We all did, in this business. But I never worked with him, if that's what you mean."

"Then why did he come here every week?"

His eyes narrowed. It suddenly occurred to me that I might be alone in this mortuary with a killer. Wasn't a mortuary the perfect place to hide a body? Especially a fresh one. And he was blocking my exit.

"You're over the line, Westphal. I'm calling Sheriff Locke." He picked up the phone to dial. I let him make his call. I wanted the sheriff here, anyway, in case this guy flipped out on me. When he hung up, I'm sure he expected me to leave. Instead, I asked him another question.

"Why were you snooping around Jasper's storage compartment?"

"I wasn't—"

"Crystal Tannacito says you were. She saw you."

"As I was going to say, I wasn't snooping around. I was inquiring about a compartment for myself. There's nothing illegal about that."

"What did you plan to store?"

"I'm not going to answer any more questions. Sheriff Locke will be here soon, and I plan to have you arrested for trespassing."

"That's fine, because I'd like to talk to her about all the canceled checks I found at Jasper's boat, made out to Cash."

"That has nothing to do with me."

"Oh no? You weren't blackmailing him when you found out he was storing those ashes in the warehouse—instead of distributing them at sea?"

"Of course not. I knew nothing about that."

"And you don't have any idea why he was killed? It wasn't because he was going to tell someone that you knew about the ash scam? That you were trying to run Del Rey Montez out of business?"

His fists clenched, his face grew taut.

"You say the checks were all made out to Cash. There's nothing to tie me to his bogus business. And certainly nothing to tie me to his death, because I had nothing to do with it."

"I wonder what my newspaper readers will think when I write an editorial about your connections to Jasper Coyne. And how you stopped by the warehouse a couple of times. And the fact that you're doing so well, for such a small mortuary."

"If you write anything like that in your little newspaper, I'll sue you for everything you've got. Del Rey Montez won't be the only one whose business comes crashing down. Maybe the two of you can start up some kind of support group for women who talk too much."

Berkeley Mondshane moved to his desk, pulled open his desk drawer, and withdrew something from inside. I couldn't see it, but I had a good idea what it was. I stood still, hoping the sweat that had just broken out on my fore-head didn't show.

"Don't forget, the sheriff is on her way over. You don't want to do anything stupid."

He raised his hand from under the desk. He was holding a gun—a real one.

"Finally, I found something that will shut you up. For a deaf person, you sure make a lot of noise," Berkeley said, aiming the weapon in my direction. I took a step back, toward the door. Before I could think, he stepped around me and kicked the door shut.

"You must be the one who can't hear. I said, 'Sheriff Locke will be here any minute.' You won't have an easy time explaining this."

"What makes you think the sheriff is on her way?"

"Because . . . I saw you call her . . ."

He smiled. "I did? You must be mistaken. I dialed a wrong number. Didn't you know that? Oh, that's right! You're deaf. You can't hear a damn thing."

Uh-oh. No sheriff on her way to rescue me. Big gun pointed in my direction. No one in the building to hear my screams. I could feel the droplets of sweat trickle down my chest and back.

"Listen, Mondshane—"

"No, you listen, Westphal. Oh, I forgot again. You can't listen, can you? That's too bad."

"Look," I bluffed, "I'm not the only one who knows about your connections to Jasper and your visits to the warehouse. If you do something stupid now, you could be in even more trouble than you're in already."

"I'm not doing anything stupid. I'm protecting my private property. I warned you to stay off and you're back again. I have my secretary to back me up—she's certainly well aware of my feelings about trespassers, and about you. And she won't say anything about Coyne. Not with what I have on her." He smiled.

I decided to try another tack, in an effort to distract him. "Where'd you get the gun?"

He looked at it, holding it sideways. "What, this? Guns around here are a dime a dozen. Even a schoolkid can get a gun today. And in my business, you can't be too careful, what with all the body snatching going on lately."

Berkeley's eyes suddenly lit up. He dropped his hand behind the desk, hiding the gun.

The sheriff, I thought instantly. He *did* call her! I whirled around to greet her but found myself staring at a familiar face that didn't belong to the law.

It was the new apprentice from Del Rey's mortuary.

"What do you want, Keith?" Berkeley said sharply.

"Just came for my paycheck—whoops, looks like you're busy." Suddenly recognizing me, he glanced back at Berkeley, confused. "What's she doing here?"

"I was just leaving," I said quickly. I took that opportune moment to dash out the door, hoping Berkeley Mondshane wouldn't shoot me in front of a witness.

As I made haste down the driveway and out to the road, two thoughts fought for space in my mind:

Would Berkeley really have killed me if the guy hadn't walked in?

What was Del Rey's new assistant doing with Berkeley Mondshane?

In view of the circumstances, I wasn't in any mood to play the night version of paint ball Dan had suggested. In fact, I'd completely forgotten about it by the time Dan came by to pick me up. I had debated whether or not to call Sheriff Mercer about Berkeley pulling a gun on me, but it was my word against his—and I had been trespassing. It wasn't so much that I thought he wouldn't believe me as it was the fact that eventually Sheriff Mercer would force me to stop investigating if I kept getting myself in trouble.

"Ready to go?" Dan was dressed in jeans and a long-sleeved brown T-shirt with the letters "NYPD" on the front and back. He looked adorable in his battle fatigues.

"I forgot all about the game!" I said, ushering him into the diner. "Can I skip this one? I've had a rough day."

I thought about telling him the details of my encounter with Berkeley Mondshane, but I was afraid he'd become overprotective, too.

"You can't be serious! We're already short a man—Jake can't play cause he broke his arm in a motorcycle crash yesterday. We need you." I didn't want to let the team down so I downed the rest of the Sierra Nevada I held in my hand and conceded. Besides, I wasn't going to let anyone stop me from living my own life—threats or no threats. I went into the back room and searched for an outfit. I decided to wear the same thing I'd worn the first time—all black. The clothes had been washed but still sported faded stains from earlier paint shots. They'd never come out completely. Didn't matter. I kind of liked them. They felt like battle scars.

In ten minutes we were in Dan's truck, headed for the field.

"You'll enjoy a night game. It's completely different from playing in the daylight."

"But I won't be able to see anything. You hearies will have a distinct advantage."

"There are field lights. And we don't make any noise, so there's nothing to hear. Quit whining."

"I'm not whining."

We pulled into the parking lot, and I got out with my gear. Dan retrieved his stuff from the back and we headed for the check-in trailer. "I don't know. I'm just sick of guns, I guess."

"You really want to sit this one out?"

I shook my head. No wimping out for me. That was something I determined a long time ago.

We bought our bags of paint pellets, donned the goggles and masks, and huddled with our teammates for a last-minute strategy session. Sheriff Mercer, Sheriff Locke, Deputy Clemens, Miah, and two other guys from Flat Skunk made up tonight's version of the Stinkers.

And Andrew! It took me a minute to recognize him underneath the goggles.

"Where have you been?" I asked, surprised to see him.

He looked puzzled.

"You've been missing!"

He pulled off the goggles and nodded. "Yeah, I came back last night. I was staying with Miah for a while, so I could think things through."

I glared at Miah, who suddenly got busy retying his shoes.

"Well, don't do that again!" I sputtered. What could I say, really? He was old enough to do as he pleased. "We were worried about you."

He shrugged. "Sorry," he said simply. I shook my head and started for the field.

The Whiskey Slide Wolves had a few new players, in addition to regulars Berkeley Mondshane—in full military gear—and Levi Coyne, but there was no sign of the guy I'd seen in Berkeley's office, Keith Melton—the one who had inadvertently kept me alive. I shuddered when I saw Berkeley. I hoped he wouldn't try to shoot me with real bullets in public. Maybe he'd lose his cool again and get kicked out of the game.

Fifteen minutes into the first game, after everyone had scattered and hidden, the lights fizzled on and off, then went out completely.

Without a moon, we were left in total darkness.

I didn't know where any of my teammates were. I'd been too busy trying to take out Berkeley personally. A wave of panic moved over me. It was disorienting not to have any light at all, especially when I could have been shot with a paint ball at any minute.

I didn't know if anyone was calling time-out, or saying anything, for that matter. A second later, I felt something brush past my ear. Someone was shooting at me in the dark. Apparently there were no time-outs in paint ball.

I raised my paint gun, hoping to shoot the stalker, but I couldn't see anything. I blinked several times, hoping my eyes would become accustomed to the dark. The ref hadn't allowed night-vision goggles, so we had to try to make out our enemies in the shadows. In a few seconds I spotted a distant figure, moving toward me. My stalker.

Someone grabbed me from behind.

I whirled around and could just barely make out Dan's face. I reached up to feel his beard for confirmation, then breathed a sigh of relief.

"God, you startled me. What happened to the lights?"

I couldn't read his lips in the dark, although I knew he was saying something. I could see his jaw move.

"I can't understand you. It's too dark. Will you help me get off the field? I can't see a thing and I don't want to play if I can't see."

I assumed he said he would. He moved around in front of me, tucked my hands into the back of his pants, and starting bear-crawling toward what I hoped was the trailer. There were no lights there either.

Before we'd moved two steps, Dan stopped. I felt his body tense. Then suddenly it completely relaxed.

Dan dropped to the ground.

"Dan! What's wrong?" I felt around the front of his shirt, searching for proof that he'd been hit by a splotch of paint. Sure enough, the sticky liquid covered my fingertips.

But Dan didn't move.

"Dan? Dan!" I began to shake him, thinking the paint pellet must have knocked the wind out of him. Nothing. I touched the paint splatter again. It was warm and there was more of it than there had been a few seconds ago. I lifted my fingertips to my nose. A coppery smell.

This wasn't paint. This was blood.

I screamed, "Somebody help me! Dan's been shot! He's bleeding."

No one came. Another burst of air whizzed by my face.

Shit! Someone was still shooting at me. Really shooting. I had to get Dan out of here, not to mention myself. When were those damn lights going to come on? And how could the shooter see so well in the dark?

Night-vision goggles.

The screaming had probably not been a good idea. The shooter knew exactly where I was. I broke out in another sweat, as I tried to drag Dan toward a rock or tree, something to block him—and me—from another attack.

I had just reached a large pine when something struck my shoulder. A branch? It felt like it had snapped against my arm and scraped the skin off. I reached over and felt the wound reflexively, while keeping my other hand pressed on Dan's chest.

Blood! I'd been shot.

It was a toss-up—whether to scream for help in the hope that someone who wasn't trying to kill me was nearby, or whether to keep quiet so as not to help the gunman find me.

But then, he could find me at will. He'd just shot me. And I had a good idea who it was.

I screamed what I hoped was bloody murder.

"Sheriff! Anyone who can hear me! Dan's been shot. With a real gun. I've been shot, too! The gunman's over here somewhere. We need help."

I kept screaming the same thing over and over, until my throat felt raw. At the same time, I could feel Dan grip my hand as I tried to compress his chest wound. I had a feeling he was trying to reassure me while I screamed my lungs out.

Another hand grabbed me—fat, with sausagelike fingers. I screamed again; this time no words came out. Someone tried to cover my mouth. I bit the hand, hard. He grabbed my hand and slapped it to his face. It felt familiar. I smelled his mints.

Sheriff Mercer!

"Sheriff! Thank God!"

I couldn't see anything but a vague outline in the blackness. He let me hold his arm as he pulled out his cell phone, mainly cause I wouldn't let go. I could see a green glow against his face from the phone light—not enough to make out details or read his lips. But at least I knew he was calling for backup.

I turned my attention to Dan, lifting his head and cradling it in my lap while still pressing on his wound. In a few seconds I saw more shadows and felt more hands, as my teammates gathered around.

"Watch out," I said. "There's a sniper." I had a feeling they were all asking questions and trying to figure out exactly what happened, but I had no idea what was actually being said. All I knew was, Dan needed help—and fast.

In a matter of minutes, headlights appeared at the rim of the battlefield. EMTs and paramedics armed with heavy-duty flashlights came running, carrying stretchers, medical bags, and other emergency equipment.

Thank God I could see again!

Glancing around, I found my teammates forming a circle around Dan and me, all looking confused and upset.

"Andrew! Are you okay?" I wondered if the sniper had hit anyone else.

"I'm fine, Connor. Your shoulder—"

Before he could say more, the EMTs brushed him aside and took over my treatment of Dan. While two technicians worked on his wound and gave him oxygen, two others attended to my shoulder, covering it with strips of bandage.

Funny. The gunshot wound didn't really hurt. I couldn't move my shoulder, but the scratches I'd gotten while trying to drag Dan to safety stung a lot more.

"Everybody over here," I think the sheriff said, waving members of the Whiskey Slide Wolves toward him. "I want everyone accounted for before anybody leaves. Everyone."

I missed roll call. Before I could warn the sheriff about Berkeley Mondshane, the EMTs had set me on a gurney and were carrying me up the hill to the parking lot. I saw no sign of Dan. Apparently he'd already been whisked away.

As the EMTs rolled me into the ambulance, I tried to lift myself up. "Wait! Please!" I fell back down. "Please. I just want to know how Dan is."

The male EMT ignored me, too busy attaching tubes and

monitors. But the woman met my eyes and spoke slowly. "We won't know until we get to the hospital, but as soon as we arrive, I'll find out for you, okay?"

I nodded, tears stinging my eyes as I closed them. I tried to relax, but the bullet wound had begun to ache.

Mine turned out to be a "flesh wound," but by the time I reached the hospital, it hurt like hell. In the emergency room I was bandaged from my elbow to my neck for this little flesh wound. They forced me to sit half-naked on a tissue-paper-wrapped table until they finally got to me, then subjected me to a nurse who had missed her calling as a drill sergeant. The woman, who resembled a piano, gave me a couple of shots, took blood, and generally poked at me until the gunshot wound actually began to feel good in comparison to her treatment.

I was wheeled to a room for "overnight observation" against my will—I felt fine. Of course, it was probably the drugs talking. The paramedic who'd ridden with me to the hospital was as good as her word. I recognized her as soon as she entered my room. Her name tag read "Joan Kramer."

"How is he?" I said, pushing the button on the bed to sit up.

"Your friend is going to be fine."

I teared up immediately.

Joan Kramer approached and took my hand—the one not attached to the "flesh wound."

"He's out of surgery. They removed a bullet from under his rib cage. He was very lucky—no vital organs were punctured. He should be on his feet in a couple of days and out of the hospital in a week."

I tried to say, "Thank God," but the words bubbled on my lips, lips covered in salty tears. All I could do was nod.

"So how are you doing? I hear it was just a flesh wound."

I smiled when she said that. If I heard that term one more time, I was going to give somebody a flesh wound so they could see how it felt.

"Can I see him?"

"No, not until tomorrow. He needs to get some sleep, and so do you. That's why they're keeping you here overnight, isn't it?"

I nodded. "Where is he?"

"Second floor. Room two-fourteen. You can see him after you're released."

"Thank you," I whispered.

She smiled. I marveled at the woman, whose job dealt in life and death. I didn't know how she could stand it. But she obviously cared about her work. I thought about writing an article on her for the *Eureka!,* then wondered if she would want publicity. She seemed like the kind of person who helped people for her own reasons, not for the glory.

I pressed the bed button and lay back down as Joan slipped out of the room. A weight seemed to leave my body. Funny, I could hardly feel the pain in my shoulder anymore. Only a dull ache. Must be the drugs. In fact, the drugs are probably the best explanation for what I did next.

I left the hospital.

I know now that it was stupid. But at the time, it seemed like a great idea. Escaping from the minimum security Mother Lode Hospital wasn't difficult. Right after the drill sergeant came in to give me another dose of whatever it was they were giving me, I figured I could sneak away. She wouldn't be back for a while.

I slipped out of bed, allowing my left arm and shoulder to follow along. I pulled my black jeans out of the hospital bag and scanned them for wearability. The small amount of blood barely showed. It took me twice as long as usual to get into my pants with one hand, and I couldn't manage the zipper, but I buttoned the top button and figured the fashion risk wouldn't be a problem where I was going.

The black shirt was another matter. It was soaked in blood and crumpled into a sticky ball in the bag. Not wearable. It would attract too much attention as I made my escape.

Instead, I took off the hospital gown and reversed it, so the gaping hole was in the front. Then I tied the front corners together in a simple knot like I used to do to my shirts in the summer, and tucked the sleeve caps under until the top appeared sleeveless. I should have gone into fashion design, I thought, as I pirouetted in front of the small bathroom mirror.

The pirouette hurt my shoulder, so I stopped admiring myself and finished gathering my things—my backpack, my bag of bloody clothes, and the free sample of goodies the drill sergeant nurse had brought me. After all, I'd be paying for them.

After biting off the bracelet that carried my ID, I peeked around the door and waited until the coast was clear. Then I ducked into the elevator and took a ride to the second floor. Room 214.

Dan lay on the bed, asleep. He was heavily bandaged around the midsection and had monitors attached that flashed tiny green dots giving his vital signs every second.

I stepped over to him, laid a hand on his forehead, and brushed back his dark hair. He moved slightly, so I stopped, not wanting to disturb him. When I thought he'd returned to deep sleep again, I slipped my hand into his, pressed something into his palm, curled his fingers around it, and left the room. I wondered what he'd think when he woke up and found my plastic bracelet in his fingers.

From the downstairs lobby I asked a candy striper to call me a taxi. My car was still at the paint ball field, and it was too late to call Miah or Del Rey to come and get me. I figured this was the easiest way to make my escape.

I paced the floor for a good ten minutes, waiting to be discovered by the drill sergeant. When the cab finally arrived, I asked the driver to take me to the field where I could pick up my car. He obliged, wondering, I'm sure, why a heavily bandaged woman in a sexy hospital top that was cut to her navel wanted to go to a field in the middle of the night. He could wonder.

Police tape blocked the entrance to the parking lot, so I had the cab wait at the entrance until I'd made my way to my car. A few lights had come back on around the field, so I could sort of see. The driver watched until I was safely inside my Chevy, then I waved him off.

I sat in the eerie light, weighing whether or not to check out the field and see if I could find anything that might be a clue to the identity of the would-be assassin. Of course, I was pretty sure I knew who it was. But maybe he dropped something, like a gun with his initials engraved on it.

Yeah, sure.

But like I said, I was on drugs. Feel-good drugs. The kind that make you think you can do anything and that nothing bad is going to happen to you. These were great drugs. I wondered where I could get more, as I slipped out of the car and headed for the field.

This time I brought the flashlight that I kept in the car. Never know when complete darkness might strike. For a deaf person, it was essential to have light. Scanning the area for any sign of movement, I saw several pairs of eyes on the edge of the field. I started before I made out a family of deer.

Moving slowly, I ran the flashlight over the ground as I headed for the site of the shooting. The dirt was a collage of footprints and a couple of tire tracks that looked like they belonged to a bicycle.

I stepped carefully over to the spot where Dan and I had tried to hide. I knew the sheriff would be back in the morning to examine the area, but I had to see for myself. That's the kind of logic you get from these feel-good drugs.

Kneeling down, I ran my light over the dirt and saw blood that had pooled and dried. *Dan's or mine?* I wondered briefly. Shining the light around, my eyes caught a reflected glow in the dirt, about ten feet from the blood.

I moved to the spot, trying not to trample the crime scene. Squatting down, I picked up the shiny object that lay nearly obscured in the weeds. Nuts. It was only a paint ball gun. Must have been dropped during the chaos.

I picked up the gun at the corner of the butt with my fingertips, like I'd seen the sheriff do in the past, in case it had prints. It was loaded with pellets. I wondered whose gun was unaccounted for back at the trailer. And then I realized, this was not one of the rental guns. This belonged to one of the regular players.

Who was so gung-ho that he'd buy his own paint ball gun? There was only one person. The one who dressed in full military gear, complete with face paint and fake bushes.

The one who had a real gun in his desk.

Just as I was about to carry the paint ball gun back to my car, I saw something move out of the corner of my eye. In the bushes, near the parking lot, just beyond one of the field lights. This time I knew it wasn't a family of deer. I stuffed the gun in my pocket and made a run for it.

Lions and tigers and bears, oh shit."

I chanted my version of the *Wizard of Oz* line as I dashed for the car, fumbling in my backpack for my keys. Those feel-good drugs were wearing off, leaving me feeling not-so-good. In fact, I was becoming frantic, paranoid, and disoriented.

Lions and tigers and bears, oh fuck.

I found my keys about the same time I made it to the car. I hadn't looked back, since I was focused on my immediate task—getting the hell out of there. I jammed the key in the lock and twisted hard.

The key broke off in my hand.

I looked down at the door handle, stunned. Shit! What now? I glanced at my key ring and immediately realized what had happened. Wrong key! I had jammed my door key into my car and forced the lock.

Fumbling with the key ring again, I moved to the passenger's side and inserted the right key into the lock. It opened! I threw myself in, knocking my sore shoulder against the side of the door, and pulled the door shut with my good arm.

"Ow, ow, ow," I cried, sliding over to the driver's seat. I

stuck the key into the ignition and started the car on the third try. Slamming the gear into drive, I pressed the gas pedal to the floor. The car jerked along through the parking lot as if being held back by a giant, invisible hand.

Damn! Had he done something to my car?

I stomped on the pedal. The car jerked and died.

"Damn!" I slammed the steering wheel with my fist. "Ow!" The repercussion rippled through my sore shoulder. "Fuck!" I said, just because it suited my mood.

I rattled the gearshift a few times, trying to figure out what was wrong. The hand brake! I was always forgetting the hand brake. I reached under the dash and released it.

"Stupid!" I shouted. "Stupid, stupid, stupid!"

After restarting the engine, I pushed the gearshift into Drive, and spun wheelies out of the graveled lot.

I wasn't shaking too much by the time I arrived at Mondshane's Mortuary, a little after one in the morning. After repeated checks in my rearview mirror for suspicious headlights, I convinced myself no one was following me. I also had myself convinced I was about to do the right thing. After all, Berkeley didn't live in his mortuary, unlike Del Rey, so I was fairly certain I wouldn't get caught.

I pulled the Chevy into the dirt, behind a large bush, just in case. I got out on the passenger side, since the driver's side door still had a key stuck in it and wouldn't open. Making my way through the hedges, I took a detour to avoid the front door. The front of the place was lit up like a marquee, with "Mondshane's Mortuary" in bright white lights. I headed for the side entrance, where it was dark.

I pushed against the side door I'd used earlier in the day. It opened without resistance. I'd stuck a wadded-up corner of a Mondshane Mortuary brochure into the latch. Old deaf camp trick, for sneaking back into the cafeteria after hours.

Relief at being able to enter was quickly replaced with an overwhelming sense of dread. Of all places, why did I have to break into a mortuary? And where were those feel-good drugs when you really needed them?

Sneaking into places is one of those adrenaline rushes

some people live for. For me, it was like drinking five too
many mochas. It was scary but exciting at the same time. I
couldn't tell if I'd set off an alarm, since I couldn't hear anything. But I had a feeling Berkeley wasn't the type to add a
lot of security to the place. He probably felt he could handle
it himself, with all that war paraphernalia.

Visions of *Night of the Living Dead* loomed in my mind
as I moved through the side room and into the main
hallway toward Berkeley's office. His door was locked, but
the secretary's desk was right there in the open. I riffled
through her drawers and found a couple of keys at the back
of the center drawer. The second key I tried opened Berkeley's door.

I slipped in, holding my flashlight low, just so I could see
where I was going. I held my breath as I pulled open his top
drawer—the one where he'd kept his gun. But digging
through the papers and office supplies, I found nothing. His
gun was gone. I wasn't surprised. But if I couldn't prove it
had been here, I couldn't prove that its absence tonight was
suspicious.

I ran the light over the room and spotted a two-drawer
wooden filing cabinet, topped with a fake potted plant. I
pulled open the top drawer, ran my fingertips over the file
headings, and closed the drawer. Nothing but clients.

I pulled open the bottom drawer and found an interesting collection of Mondshane's hobbies. There was a bottle
of vodka, a couple of *Soldier of Fortune* magazines, and
some flyers inviting real men to join extremist groups.
Groups with names like Death Heads, Bash Brothers, and
Killer Instinct. This was also where he stored the camouflage battle fatigues that looked like they came from the
army-navy surplus store. Underneath the cammies, he'd
hidden a paint ball gun, this one called the Splatmaster. It
looked a lot like the one I'd found on the battlefield.

And buried under everything was a relatively recent
newspaper clipping. I moved the vodka, tempted to have a
snort, and lifted out the clipping.

It was a piece from the daily-except-weekends *Mother
Lode Monitor* about a boy who'd been shot the previous
day. The article said the minor, whose name was being

kept private, had received the gun from his older brother,
Jeff Pike.

The guy who ran paint ball war games in Angels Camp.

Pike, 21, said he found the gun lying on the
ground after a paint ball game. He kept it,
thinking whoever lost it would return. But the
owner never came forward. According to Sheriff
Locke, Pike thought he'd put the gun safely away.
He appeared devastated by his brother's shooting,
which the sheriff ruled accidental.

The story ended with the usual "pending further investigation" wrap-up. It needed better editing.

I wondered why Berkeley had saved that article. I decided to take one last look around, figuring I wouldn't get
another opportunity like this. After a tour of the back
rooms, including the embalming area, the chapel, and the
casket sales room, I tried to open a door marked "Closet."
The knob wouldn't turn.

It seemed odd for a closet door to be locked, if it contained the usual closet stuff, like brooms, sponges, uniforms. Unless it contained dangerous chemicals used for
making dead people look lifelike. Or something else?

I dug in my pocket and pulled out the other key—the
one that didn't open Mondshane's office. It fit in the closet
lock like a See's chocolate fits in my mouth. I turned the
knob and flashed my light inside the long, narrow room.

No brooms. No uniforms. No cleaning products, chemicals, or anything else I expected to see in there. Nothing but
shelves on both sides, four rows high, all lined with caskets,
with the exception of the top shelf. It held a row of urns. I
guessed this was the casket overflow room. Maybe Mondshane figured if he made the product seem limited by only
setting out a few, people were more likely to panic-buy.
Even caskets.

Curious, I tried to open one. It wouldn't budge. I examined it with my flashlight and found the reason. There was a
padlock on the casket. That was odd. Did they have to
lock the deceased in to make sure they didn't climb out at

inopportune moments? Or was it to prevent body snatching? There were no locks on the caskets at Del Rey's mortuary. I should know. I've been in one.

Damn, I wanted to see inside. Anyone who locks a casket must have a pretty good reason. And suddenly I had a hunch what it was.

But I'd run out of keys. I headed back down the hallway to search for a screwdriver, thinking I might be able to unscrew the hinges and open the casket from the back, when I spotted flashing lights outside the front windows.

The sheriff! Oh, shit! Berkeley must have had some kind of alarm hooked up to the sheriff's department after all! For the first time in my illegal trespassing career, I was about to be caught. I couldn't run out the side door—they'd see me for sure. I couldn't hide—they'd find me eventually.

I had a frantic, last-second idea, and ran back to the closet, digging in my backpack for a lipstick on the way. I scrawled a word on the first casket I reached. Then I switched on the light overhead, left the door open, and scrambled down the hall to find someplace to take cover.

The embalming room.

The smell was enough to kill you. It was a combination of seventh-grade-science formaldehyde, hospital antiseptic, and a splash of essence of institution.

I thought about lying on a gurney and covering up with a sheet, but how would I explain that if they found me? Too embarrassing. Besides, I didn't have a toe tag, and I wasn't going on display without accessorizing.

Instead, I climbed up on one of the stainless steel countertops, my arm aching with every movement, and pushed open the bottom half of the window. It took nearly every ounce of strength I had to wiggle out, and I skinned both ankles on the sill as I fell to the ground below. At this point, fresh pain was preferred over being caught inside by the sheriff.

The back of the building was deserted. Apparently the sheriff didn't have a SWAT team surrounding the place. I peeked around the side of the building and spotted two sheriff's cars out front, both with their doors open and lights still flashing. Sheriff Locke and Sheriff Mercer.

I hoped they hadn't seen my car tucked in the bushes on

their way in. I took a chance, stole over to the Chevy, opened the passenger door, then slammed it shut, as if I had just arrived on the scene. I headed inside the mortuary through the open front door.

"Sheriff Mercer? Are you in here?" I called down the hallway. He appeared instantly.

"C.W.! What in God's name are you doing here? Aren't you supposed to be in the hospital?"

I couldn't say I heard the police call over the scanner. I didn't have a scanner and I couldn't hear. Fortunately, another lie presented itself.

"They released me. Said it was just a flesh wound. I thought I'd stop by and return Berkeley's paint ball gun. I found it on the field—"

"At one-thirty in the morning—"

The sheriff jumped, and his face paled.

"What?" I asked, wondering if he'd had a heart attack or something.

"That was a gunshot—"

He raced down the hall toward the open closet. I was right behind him.

Sheriff Locke stood in the doorway, frowning, her gun in her hand. She didn't look particularly surprised to see me. Guess she was getting to know me.

"Elvis, I think you're going to want to see this." Sheriff Locke pointed to the casket I'd scrawled on in lipstick. The word written in L'Oreal's Matte Coffee Bean looked iridescent against the blond walnut casket:

"Help!"

She'd done just what I'd hoped. The casket stood open. The lock had been shot off with her revolver. She must have felt the unusual circumstances gave her grounds to open the casket without a warrant. Or maybe she really believed someone was alive in there. . . .

As Sheriff Locke stood aside, Sheriff Mercer and I peered inside. I held my breath, expecting to see Portia Bryson's body. Instead, I saw rifles. Dozens of rifles.

The three of us looked at each other in silence for several minutes. Then Sheriff Mercer picked up one of the urns from the top shelf and turned it upside down. The contents tumbled onto the floor. Handguns, covered with cremains.

"Smith and Wesson five-shot revolvers, aka Saturday night specials." He dumped out another urn. "Semiautomatics, Glocks, Ruger twenty-twos, Berettas." He glanced back in the casket. "Sawed-off shotguns, M-fourteens, sniper rifles, Colts. It's a regular arsenal in here."

"Looks like he's been smuggling guns in these coffins," Sheriff Locke said.

"And maybe selling them to the local kids?" I added.

I thought about the first time I met Berkeley Mondshane, all dressed in camouflage and no war to go to. He'd come off as a fanatic at the time, but when he'd put on that undertaker's suit, I'd forgotten how much he loved to battle—both on and off the battlefield.

"We can't open any more of these caskets without a warrant. You want to go wake Judge Obregar, Peyton? I'll call ATF."

Sheriff Locke stepped aside to talk on her cell phone.

"Do you think Jasper Coyne had anything to do with these guns?" I asked. I still had a feeling there was a connection, with all of Coyne's visits to Mondshane, but I couldn't quite figure out what it was.

"I suppose Berkeley could have been using Coyne and his fishing boat to pick up guns. They could have used the ashes as some kind of camouflage," Sheriff Mercer said.

Dan had mentioned those same suspicions—that ashes were involved in transporting some kind of contraband. Dan must have been a hell of a cop. I wondered if he'd ever considered private investigating? I'd have to ask him.

It was hard to imagine Berkeley as a gunrunner, but then again, what did a gunrunner look like? Your local neighborhood drug dealer? Or your local funeral director?

And where did all this leave Del Rey?

It hit me while driving home from Mondshane Mortuary at three in the morning. Figuratively first, then literally. I'd been trying to figure things out while coping with the pain in my shoulder, my legs—just about everywhere, it seemed.

The sheriff was no fool. It all came down to physical evidence. Sinister personalities meant nothing. Motives were nice, but anyone could have a motive. Opportunity? It was wide open. Physical evidence told the story. It was the body language of murder. And the victims were open books, if you just knew how to read them. Jasper was page one. Portia was page two. I was supposed to be page three.

That's when I got hit, the second time. My tire blew and I started fishtailing down the dark street. I remember thinking at the time how ironic to blow a tire when I'd finally figured it out. I had no idea I'd been shot at.

But it's hard to concentrate on clues when you're trying to control the body of a '57 Chevy as it zigzags out of control at forty-five miles per hour. At least the imminent crash kept me from thinking about my aches and pains for a few frightening seconds.

I slammed on the brakes and smelled rubber as I tried to keep two tons of steel from veering off the narrow country lane. Jerking me from side to side, the car spun around and stopped, sideways, blocking the road.

I caught my breath and checked my shoulder. It hurt like hell. I could see blood oozing underneath the bandages. I wasn't going to be much good at changing a tire with this bum wheel of an arm.

And then I felt the car jerk again. The front end sank to the ground. That was no accidental flat tire. Now I got it. Someone was shooting at my car.

I had already locked the passenger door—the driver's side was nonfunctional thanks to the stuck key—but I didn't know whether to stay put or make a run for it. I knew he was out there, somewhere, waiting to get a line on me. One way or another, he'd get his chance. If I ran, he could pick me off like a duck at a shooting gallery. If I stayed in the Chevy, he could sneak up on me and shoot me like a sitting duck.

This duck was fucked, either way you looked at it.

I shone the beam of my flashlight inside the glove compartment and found what I was looking for. The dropped paint ball gun. It was loaded—granted, only with paint. But it was all I had.

I wasn't going without a fight. A colorful one, at that.

Suddenly a shower of crystal droplets blew in on my face. The front window of the Chevy had shattered into a billion tiny pieces. The splash of glass rained down on me like a hailstorm.

Shaking the glass from my hair and shirt, I could feel the sting of tiny cuts on my exposed face and arms, as if I'd been attacked by a million killer bees. I tried wiping the glass from my arms and face, but that only made things worse, grinding the tiny chips into my skin.

I had to get out of the car.

Forgetting for a moment the driver's side was stuck, I tried the knob a few times, then remembered. I slid over to the passenger door, unlocked it, and pushed the heavy door open with my foot. I struggled to get out, caught a piece of clothing on the corner of the door, and nearly rolled onto the ground that was now littered with bits of broken glass. I scanned the road, looking up and down its length for whoever had shot at me. But it was so dark, I couldn't see much of anything.

I squatted and waddled behind the left back tire. Then I

waited, my paint gun cocked and ready to shoot. I didn't come to my senses for another few seconds, and when I did, I almost cried. What was I thinking? I was sitting in the middle of a dark road with a crazy killer after me, and all I had to protect myself was a frigging paint ball gun! What did I expect to do? Paint him to death?

Until other options occurred to me, I held the gun steady, and continued to wait.

Moments later, I caught a glimpse of movement down the road.

All I could make out was a small form, nearly camouflaged by the darkness, growing larger with every second. Whoever it was, was coming back.

I scrunched down lower and rolled under the car, barely making the squeeze. Turning over on my stomach, I propped myself up on one elbow. The other one hurt too much. I held the gun pointed into the darkness and waited for the form to get closer. And closer.

When he was nearly upon me, I blinked and aimed the gun the way Dan had taught me. It was an effort to hold it steady, with all the pain, but I forced my hand to remain as rigid as possible. And to keep my eyes open, not to anticipate the shot. I was determined to hit my target.

Who was nearly upon me. I kept my aim, squarely at his head.

I pulled the trigger.

And he disappeared!

I waited a few seconds, then slowly dragged myself out from under the car. Glancing around, I saw nothing but dark, motionless forms—trees, bushes, signs. I took a few steps forward in the general direction of the shot, puzzled by the vanishing act.

Another movement. This time it came from the ground only a few feet away. I saw the shooter push himself up to a sitting position and remove his helmet, which was covered in red paint. I'd managed to temporarily blind him with my shot!

I wondered how he'd managed to come up on me so quickly, then disappear. And then I knew. His motorcycle lay in a heap a short distance away. It had skidded across the road when he hit the ground.

As soon as he began to raise his gun again, I shot Levi Coyne three more times in the face.

Never underestimate the disabled, I thought, as I unraveled the dressing from around my shoulder. The paint in his eyes must have stung like acid—at least, he acted like it did. I couldn't hear the screaming, but someone did. A light went on at a house that I didn't even know was there in the dark, and a man came running with a shotgun in his hand. He held the gun on Levi and said something I couldn't make out, as I tied up Levi's hands with strips from the bottom of my hospital gown. There was no need to tie his feet.

I got to hold the gun next, while the man went back to his house and called the sheriff. He left me his flashlight, too, which I set on the ground, aimed at Levi Coyne's face, so I could read his lips in case he had anything to say.

I had a feeling he'd talk to me sooner or later. After all, not only did I have the rifle aimed at him, I had the paint ball gun in my other hand, aimed at his crotch. Moments ago, I'd remembered he said he still had feeling there, and sure enough, he wasn't lying about that. I'd shot a test pellet into his groin, just to make sure.

After the second shot, he cried, "Stop it, will you? You're killing me!"

"Okay, then, tell me what the hell has been going on and why you killed the two people in the world who loved you?"

He tried wiping his red-painted face again, using his shoulder, but couldn't do much except smear it, since his hands were tied in the back. It looked like war paint.

"They didn't love me. Jasper didn't love anyone but himself. That's why he didn't take me to the hospital that night, and drove me home instead, drunk as a skunk."

"He crashed his truck that night, didn't he? That's what really caused your paralysis, not the fight."

Levi said nothing.

"I don't think Chunker ever laid a hand on you. All these years you wanted to believe he did, because you couldn't accept the fact that your own brother caused your disability."

Tears formed around his paint-rimmed eyes.

"But why did you kill him, after all these years? Why didn't you do it back then, when it happened?"

"I didn't know the truth then. And when I found out, I didn't mean to kill him. It was kind of an accident."

"Kind of? How do you kind of murder someone?"

"You don't understand. You can't know what it's been like for me. Portia changed my life. I thought she did it all because she loved me. But she just felt sorry for me, like all the others. I thought, over time, she'd come around. But then I found out . . . she still had feelings for Jasper."

"So that's why you killed him?"

"No—I mean, that's not what I planned. Do you want to hear this or not? I really don't have to tell you anything."

I nodded. "Why are you telling me, then?"

"I don't know. I guess I thought of all people, you'd understand, being disabled yourself."

I nodded again. I didn't mean anything by it, except for him to continue.

"Okay, so when Portia heard Chunker was getting out of jail, she went to Jasper, hoping he wasn't planning on doing anything stupid. Jasper could really be stupid at times, and he never forgave Chunker for stealing Del Rey, even though he didn't want her anymore. When Portia came back from her visit, I could tell something had changed."

"She'd slept with him?"

"All of a sudden they started taking up again. I hardly ever saw her that week. She'd come home in the mornings, looking all sexed up. I knew what she'd been doing with him. And he was ruining my life all over again."

My God, I'd had no idea. "But why did you kill him? He was your brother."

"Listen, will you? Jesus! I got this idea that I thought would bring Portia back to me. When Chunker got out, I called him, trying to sound like my brother, and convinced him to go over to Jasper's boat for a talk about the fight. I told him I—Jasper—wanted to make up, that I wanted our friendship back. And, you know, in some ways I think Jasper did—he always kept a picture of the three of us: Chunker, Jasper, and me."

I knew the picture he was talking about only too well. I was quiet and he continued without any prompting.

"I planned to knock Chunker out after he got there, then make it look like Jasper did it so he'd go to jail for assault, leaving Portia behind for me to pick up where I left off."

"So what really happened?"

Levi spat out some red goo. I hoped it was paint. "I waited outside the boat for him, ready to knock him cold. When he showed up, I slammed one of my trophies down on his head. But it turned out it was Jasper. I thought he was passed out on the boat, but he must have gone out sometime after I checked, while I was waiting out of sight."

"You could have called an ambulance."

Levi shrugged. "I . . . I hit him a little too hard. Don't know my own upper body strength, I guess. Then I panicked. I didn't know what else to do, so I dumped his body over the side of the boat."

I shook my head. "Then what?"

"I had gotten rid of Jasper's body by the time Chunker arrived. I heard him coming and pushed my wheelchair behind the cabin of the houseboat. Chunker gave up waiting after a while, since Jasper never showed up to meet him. I realized I could still use Chunker—to keep the sheriff from suspecting me."

"But you didn't create any evidence that Chunker had been there."

"No, that was stupid. I wasn't thinking clearly at the time. But later I came up with a way to fix that. I told Portia I saw Chunker at the boat that night, and that he must have killed Jasper. But if I told the police, they probably wouldn't believe me, since they knew I hated Chunker and would love to see him go back to jail. She said she'd lie about seeing him there, to help get him put away again. She could see how upset I was and all. I think she felt sorry for me again. I figured she owed me, for the hell she'd put me through."

"Did you kill her too?"

He shrugged. "I loved her."

"But something happened, didn't it?"

He nodded, tears streaming in red rivulets down his cheeks. "She found out I was the one who killed Jasper."

"How?"

"She found the trophy. The one I hit Jasper with. I'd hidden it in my room. She asked me about it. I sort of stammered and suddenly she put it all together. She knew everything."

"So you drowned her too."

More tears. He tried to wipe his nose but couldn't reach it. "I had no choice. She wrote a postcard to Chunker, telling him to meet her at a bar, that she had something to tell him. I found it on her desk when she left to answer a phone call. She came back before I could grab it, but I knew she could just send another, and I knew what she was going to say. I couldn't let that happen."

"Why did you shoot up my diner? And my office? And send me those notes? Were you just trying to scare me off?"

He nodded. "You kept butting in. And then . . ." he paused.

"And then you had to kill me too."

Levi said nothing. He looked depleted.

I could see the sheriff's car off in the distance, the lights flashing red, white, and blue. Thank God. I didn't think I could take much more of Levi Coyne's pathetic excuses for murder.

In fact, I decided the man needed immediate punishment, not only for killing two people, but for all the times he tried to attack me.

So I shot him in the nuts one more time.

I had been blinded by my own bigotry, I thought, riding back to the Mother Lode Memorial Hospital in the ambulance. It had never occurred to me that a disabled person could have committed those murders.

And I'm the one who keeps saying disabled people are just like anyone else.

When we're not being treated as nearly invisible, we're being pitied or pampered or protected. We're not supposed to be capable of such things.

Like able-bodied people, Levi was neither good nor bad. He was a human being. He just happened to be in a wheelchair. And that wheelchair didn't stop him from doing nearly anything he wanted to do. Including killing his brother and ex-sister-in-law.

I shivered in the ambulance. The night had grown cold and the paramedics wouldn't give me a blanket. They were concerned about the lacerations in my skin, and didn't want to put any pressure on them, in case bits of glass were still embedded there.

Levi had been taken to the hospital in another ambulance, but after he was released, he'd be going to prison. I would be going home. With Dan.

I wondered how Dan was doing. Suddenly I ached for him. I knew he was going to be all right, but to see someone as sweet and strong and sexy as Dan, lying in a hospital bed with bandages and tubes and drugs—it was overwhelming.

Hurry, I silently told the ambulance driver. I couldn't wait much longer.

I spent two hours in the emergency room, while interns picked glass shards out of my face and arms. When they finished with the Betadine solution and bandages, it was around five in the morning and I looked like a clown with orange and pink measles. The road-kill hair didn't help the look, nor did the backless/buttless gown and the paper slippers.

Once again they were going to try to keep me overnight for observation. Since I hadn't really finished my first stint, I decided not to fight it this time. The night was practically over, but in a hospital, days and nights seem to blur together. The earlier drugs had worn off, but they gave me more, which made me sleepy and happy. After the nurse assisted me into my same old bed, and after a ten-minute lecture on how much trouble I'd caused the hospital, I fell asleep instantly.

That's why I cannot explain how I ended up in Dan's bed on the second floor. I swear.

The first thing I remember is someone shaking my hip. When I opened my eyes, I was staring into the open mouth of a male nurse, dressed in a print uniform top and pants to match. It had big blue waves and purple sharks and multi-colored fish all over it.

I thought for a moment I was drowning.

"What are you doing here?" I think he said. My eyes were still a little fuzzy, so it wasn't easy to lip-read him.

I pushed myself up on my good arm. I'd been lying on my side next to Dan, facing away from him because I couldn't lie down on my sore shoulder. I turned to see if he was awake. Sure enough. Big grin.

"I . . . must have sleepwalked here . . . I don't remember . . ."

The male nurse—his name tag read M. Barnard—shook his head and bit his lip. "You're in big trouble, girl, you know that. This is my patient, and I'm responsible for him.

And it doesn't say anywhere on his chart that he should have a woman lying in bed with him."

I sat up, rubbed my hair to give it some volume, if not style, and turned to Dan.

"Hi."

"Good morning, sleeping beauty."

I grinned. Dan's eyes moved to the nurse. I caught the man in midsentence.

". . . get on back to your own room before I call the anesthesiologist and have your body numbed from your neck to your knees."

I stood up on shaky legs.

"You need a wheelchair?" M. Barnard asked, reaching for me.

I shook my head, which made me even dizzier. "No thanks. No wheelchair for me."

"All right then, you get. I'll take care of the big boy here. We're going to do a little shaving, and a little bathing, and have him all spruced up for you when you come back for regular visiting hours."

The look on the nurse's face seemed to give Dan pause. He glanced at me, looking helpless and at the mercy of M. Barnard, who seemed to be extra attentive to his patient.

I winked at Dan. "I guess your nurse is going to take good care of you. I'll be back to check on you later." I turned to Nurse Barnard. "He's very ticklish. Be careful."

Dan looked horrified as his nurse giggled.

"Oh, I will, girl, I will. He's all mine for the next half hour."

I headed for the door, and turned to say good-bye to the two men. To Dan I said, "See you in thirty-one minutes." To M. Barnard I said, "He may be yours for the next half hour, but he's mine after that, you got it?"

The nurse frowned and nodded. Dan just shook his head.

As M. Barnard turned to begin work on Dan's hygiene, I let go of the back of my hospital gown. Would have loved to have seen Dan's face when he caught a glimpse of my exit.

I was sipping juice and trying to lip-read some talk show host from my hospital bed when Sheriff Mercer came in, carrying a box of See's chocolates and a bouquet of pink-dyed daisies I was sure were from the grocery store, not the flower mart.

"Sheriff! How sweet! You shouldn't have!"

He flushed. He hates being called sweet. "They're from Rebecca and Miah, too. I can't take all the credit."

I asked him to put the flowers in my juice glass, since the juice tasted like water anyway, and I buried the candy under my pillow, safe from the hungry nurses.

"How you doing?" He pulled up a chair and sat down.

"Fine. Just a few scratches. Some scrapes. Bruises here and there. A really sore shoulder. A little psoriasis—"

He held up his hand. "I get the picture."

"Nothing like Dan. Have you seen him yet?"

"Not this morning. Saw him last night for a few minutes. I'm going over there after I make sure you're chained to the bed until you're officially released."

"Hey, if it weren't for my escape from this place, Berkeley Mondshane would still be selling guns to kids, and Levi Coyne would still be getting away with murder."

He nodded. It was then that I saw it, tiny and pink, almost invisible.

"You got a hearing aid! That's great!"

He put his hand up to his ears. "Would you stop screaming? Jesus. You're hurting my ears."

"Sorry. I'm just so excited and proud of you. I know it will take some adjusting, but you'll get the hang of it. You can hardly see it."

"I might grow my hair a little. You women are lucky. You can wear hearing aids and nobody sees them 'cause of all that hair." He pulled at the tufts over his ears. There wasn't a chance in hell he'd be able to cover his aids with that hair.

I smiled. I knew getting hearing aids was big step for a man like Sheriff Mercer.

"Levi's in custody. Thought you'd want to know."

"He's out of the hospital already?"

"There was nothing really wrong with him. Except sore testicles. Can't do much about that. He's over at county, waiting for his arraignment. I feel for the poor guy."

There it was again. Pity for the disabled.

"Poor guy! He killed his brother. He killed Portia. He nearly got Del Rey arrested. And he tried to kill me. He was the one who shot up my diner. He was the one who set fire to the hillside. And he even tried to shoot me in my car. How about poor me? Or at least poor Jasper or poor Portia?"

"I just feel sorry for him, that's all. He's had a hard life. Being paralyzed can't be easy."

"Well, it's wheelchair-accessible where he's going, so that shouldn't be a problem. What about Berkeley Mondshane?"

"He's over in federal. ATF came and got him. Actually, Dan was onto something with his theory. Berkeley had Jasper meeting boats out on the bay and picking up guns for sale to the local residents. They'd hide the rifles in the caskets and the handguns in the urns, covered with ashes to mute the sound and keep them hidden. The weight of the ashes was comparable to the weight of the weapons."

"But why did he store them instead of dumping them?"

"My guess is, he couldn't dump them like he was supposed to because he had the guns in there, and he knew each trip was recorded by the Coast Guard, so he couldn't dump them later, because more frequent trips would be suspicious. And he had to do something with them. After he got caught for illegal dumping—his first plan—he decided to store them and save himself the hassle."

I nodded. "Makes sense. Then Mondshane took over?"

"Looks that way. Mondshane shipped the weapons across the country to all kinds of paramilitary groups. With this nationwide racket he had going, it's a wonder he had time to bury people."

"So that's where the kids were getting the guns?"

"Some of them. Some they just borrowed from their parents' collections. Most of the people around here have their own weapons. Been using guns for generations—and know how to handle them. But the kids today don't have the same reverence for guns as their parents do. They see all that violence on TV and think it's all a game. And now that guns are so easy to get, they want their own."

"How's Del Rey?"

"She's all right. Still a little shaken from everything, but relieved it's over. Says she plans to work hard building up her clientele again. She's waiting outside to see you."

"Good. Did you ever find out whose body was cremated, if it wasn't Portia's?"

"It was Portia after all. The guy who filled in at Del Rey's that day, Keith Melton, Berkeley paid him to put a bullet—one that had been shot and sent through his own crematory—into Portia's ashes after the cremation, to make it look like Del Rey had bungled things and cremated the wrong body. Berkeley finally confessed to his part in the gunrunning and the ash scam, in return for probation."

"Is Chunker out of jail?"

The sheriff nodded. "He's over at the mortuary. He'll be helping Del Rey put the business back in order. And getting acquainted with his daughter."

"So she knows. How's she doing?"

"She's fine. Decided to go back to school and get her degree in media arts. Wants to be an anchorwoman now. Go figure."

It made sense in a way. Courtney-Freedom probably just wanted attention. That's why she changed her name, got herself pierced and tattooed, and acted out. Maybe she was finished with all that and ready to join the real world. If you could call TV anchoring the real world.

"And Andrew?" I was still concerned about his involvement with the missing rifle.

"Andrew's fine. He told us where he got the gun—through Jeff Pike at the paint ball games. And Jeff got them from Berkeley. He was another one of Berkeley's middlemen. When Andrew found out Berkeley was at the root of all this, he was happy to tell us everything he knew. That's why he disappeared for awhile. He was doing a little investigating of his own."

"Where was the missing rifle?"

"Andrew hid it. He wasn't planning on using it. He just wanted to keep it as evidence, if he could figure out how the gun scheme worked."

"I wonder what he's going to do with his life now? He seemed at such loose ends. And then there's his dead father to deal with."

"According to Del Rey, Andrew's made some decisions,

too. He's going into the microbrewery/coffee bar business. Plans to open up a place called Beer and Beans downtown. Learning about his real father was a shock to him, but I guess Del Rey had a talk with both kids and explained that she had been trying to protect them. She wanted her third husband to be their father."

"Well, Beer and Beans should be a hit with the people around here," I said. "They don't know whether they want to stick to the old-fashioned brew or go with the caffeine wave. Now they'll have the best of both. I just hope he doesn't add meatloaf to the menu, or Mama Cody will kill him."

Sheriff Mercer nodded. "I better go check on Dan again. Last time I was there, some male nurse was giving him a massage."

Oh, great. How was I going to compete with that?

"One last question, Sheriff. I know Levi shot up my diner. But how did he shoot up my office?"

"You forget—Levi had tremendous upper body strength, in addition to fanatical determination. He could have pulled his body up the stairs and shot the place up fairly easily. And he'd do it knowing we'd never suspect he could get to the second floor using his chair."

"Sheriff?" I called out as he began to step out the door to my hospital room. He turned to face me. "You haven't forgotten my dinner invitation, have you? You and Sheriff Locke?"

I could tell by the rush of color to his round face that he hadn't. "When you're well, C.W. Then we'll talk about that."

After Sheriff Mercer left to visit Dan, I had a nonstop flow of visitors for the next hour, including Del Rey, who sneaked me in a beer, Andrew, who brought me a mocha to go, and Courtney, who offered me a free navel piercing any time I wanted it, until she returned to college. I'd been eager to see Del Rey. I wanted to find out how she was really doing after all that had happened.

"Cute outfit," Del Rey said, eyeing my hospital gown as she handed me a wrapped package.

"You don't think it's too much? Puke green isn't really my color. What's in here?" I held the gift box in my lap, not opening it. Courtney and Andrew stood back as their mother spoke.

"Your getting-out-of-the-hospital outfit. Thought you could use some blood-free clothes."

"That's very sweet of you, Del Rey."

We chatted a few minutes, then Andrew and Courtney excused themselves so Del Rey and I could have a few moments alone.

"Connor, I know we're friends and all, but why'd you do it? Why'd you do so much to help me with all this? I can never repay you for—"

I shook my head. "Stop, Del Rey. First of all, you're my friend. I . . . I haven't had a lot of friends in my life. I've always been reluctant to get close to people. Usually, when people find out I'm deaf, I'm a novelty to them. When they get bored, or they're tired of having to face me when they talk and take extra pains, they give up. You've been a great friend to me."

Del Rey nodded. "You've certainly been here for me. You went far beyond the call of duty on this."

"Well, I didn't want to print the article I would have had to write in the *Eureka!* Thank God I don't have a daily paper like the *Mother Lode Monitor*. They have to fill that space whether it's fleshed out or not. Since my newspaper doesn't come out until the weekend, I had the time to look into the ash scam in more detail. And I knew there was more to it."

"How did you know?"

"Because I know you. I could tell from your body language you had no idea what had really happened to Jasper."

Del Rey reached over and took my hand. "You're a dear friend, Connor. I'm grateful for all you did to help us."

I smiled, unable to say anything. The lump in my throat prevented any words from escaping.

"And I'm sorry I didn't tell you everything . . . about, you know, my exes."

"You're allowed to have secrets, Del Rey. Best friends don't have to tell each other everything. It's just being there when needed. I heard from the sheriff you had a talk with Andrew and Courtney about their real fathers?"

Del Rey nodded. "I tried to explain my motives to them. I think they understood. Chunker wants to get to know Courtney better. She seems open to it, but we'll see how it goes."

"You're doing the right thing, Del Rey. And they won't forget the man who raised them, don't worry."

Del Rey stood. "I better go. No doubt those kids of mine have found the cafeteria and run up a bill higher than the cost of that liposuction I've been saving for. I'll see you tomorrow."

"Wait! Del Rey, there's one more thing that's really bothering me. You know that pile of ash Berkeley dumped on your floor? Was that—?"

She shook her head. "Relax. It was fireplace ash. He was just trying to make a statement."

I nodded and sank back into the bed, feeling oddly relieved that someone's uncle Whozits wasn't sucked up by Del Rey's vacuum cleaner.

When everyone had gone and visiting hours were over, the doctor came by and released me, with a stern warning never to sneak out of hospitals again because it wasn't good for my health.

I put on the outfit Del Rey had bought me—a dress, for God's sake—packed up my flowers and candy and cards and gifts, stuffed what I could into my backpack, and left the hospital room legally.

On the way out, I swung by Dan's room. He was watching a rerun of *Law & Order* when I peeked in.

"Wow!" he said. At first I didn't know what he was talking about. Then I realized what he was staring at. The dress.

"What? It's just a dress. You act like you've never seen one before."

"Not on you, I haven't. You look . . . beautiful."

I glanced in the mirror tucked in the tiny bathroom—and shrieked.

"You liar! Look at me! My hair is sticking out like a cactus. I'm covered with Band-Aids and orange spots. I look like a sick leopard."

"I like cats."

I moved closer. "So how are you feeling? And when are you breaking out of here?"

"Oh, no. Michael told me all the details—sneaking out of the hospital and causing all kinds of havoc. You're damn lucky, Connor Westphal."

"Michael?"

"My nurse. I think he likes me."

"Where's my paint gun when I need it?"

Dan laughed.

"It's all your fault, you know," I snapped. "You got me into these war games. I was a nice, peace-abiding citizen until you gave me a weapon and turned me loose."

"What do you say we give up the paint ball games for a while? Stick to something not so violent, like checkers."

He must have noticed me suddenly turn serious. Something was still on my mind.

"What is it?" he asked gently.

"Boone. What are you going to do with his ashes?"

Dan took a deep breath before speaking. "Well, Sheriff Mercer said it's going to take some time to sort everything out. The ashes will all be returned to relatives, whenever possible. But that could take weeks or months. Once I have his ashes, I thought I'd scatter them up in the Sierra foothills. Then I'll know where they really are."

I nodded, still pensive. "Dan, can I say something?"

He nodded, looking wary.

"You found out a lot about Jasper, with your detective work. You're really good at investigating. I was wondering, have you thought about starting your own private investigation business? I know you don't want to be a cop anymore, but you still love the work."

Dan nodded. "I've been thinking about it. I just don't want to have to compete with you."

I smiled. "You can help me when I get stuck on a really tough investigative piece. It might happen."

"Did I ever tell you you remind me of Callie Shaw?"

"Frank Hardy's girlfriend, right?"

He reached out and gently took my Band-Aid–dotted hand. I tried to keep myself from wincing.

"Does it hurt?"

"Only when I sign."

"Well, shut up, then." He pulled me to him and kissed me. A long deep one.

As soon as I could breathe again, I whispered, "Does this door have a lock on it?"

Dan shook his head. "You don't want to make Michael jealous, do you?"

That did it. It wasn't easy with a bum shoulder, but I managed to roll Dan's wheeled bed against the hospital door, with the help of my back and a pair of good strong legs.

His next sponge bath with the smitten nurse could wait. It was my turn to play doctor.

ABOUT THE AUTHOR

PENNY WARNER has sold over thirty books, including four books in the Connor Westphal mystery series from Bantam: *Dead Body Language* (1997), *Sign of Foul Play* (1998), *Right to Remain Silent* (1998), and *A Quiet Undertaking* (2000). Warner has a Master's Degree in Special Education/Deaf, and teaches child development, sign language, special education, and mystery writing at the local colleges. She lives in Danville, CA, with her husband of thirty years and has two grown children.

PENNY WARNER

☠

DEAD BODY LANGUAGE

—57586-4 $5.50/$7.50

SIGN OF FOUL PLAY

—57587-2 $5.50/$7.50

RIGHT TO REMAIN SILENT

—57962-2 $5.50/$7.50

A QUIET UNDERTAKING

—579657 $5.50/$7.99

Ask for these books at your local bookstore or use this page to order.

Please send me the books I have checked above. I am enclosing $_____ (add $2.50 to cover postage and handling). Send check or money order, no cash or C.O.D.'s, please.

Name _____

Address _____

City/State/Zip _____

Send order to: Bantam Books, Dept. MC 20, 2451 S. Wolf Rd., Des Plaines, IL 60018
Allow four to six weeks for delivery.
Prices and availability subject to change without notice.   MC 20 1/00